Daphne du Maurier

FRENCHMAN'S CREEK

PENGUIN BOOKS

Penguin Books Ltd, Harmondsworth, Middlesex, England
Penguin Books Australia Ltd, Ringwood, Victoria, Australia

—

First published by Victor Gollancz 1941
Published in Penguin Books 1962
Reprinted 1964, 1965, 1967, 1969, 1970, 1972 (twice)

—

Copyright © Daphne du Maurier Browning, 1941

—

Made and printed in Great Britain
by C. Nicholls & Company Ltd
Set in Monotype Times

TO PADDY
AND CHRISTOPHER

Chapter 1

WHEN the east wind blows up Helford river the shining waters become troubled and disturbed, and the little waves beat angrily upon the sandy shores. The short seas break above the bar at ebb-tide, and the waders fly inland to the mud flats, their wings skimming the surface, and calling to one another as they go. Only the gulls remain, wheeling and crying above the foam, diving now and again in search of food, their grey feathers glistening with the salt spray.

The long rollers of the Channel, travelling from beyond Lizard point, follow hard upon the steep seas at the river mouth, and mingling with the surge and wash of deep sea water comes the brown tide, swollen with the last rains and brackish from the mud, bearing upon its face dead twigs and straws, and strange forgotten things, leaves too early fallen, young birds, and the buds of flowers.

The open roadstead is deserted, for an east wind makes uneasy anchorage, and but for the few houses scattered here and there above Helford passage, and the group of bungalows about Port Navas, the river would be the same as it was in a century now forgotten, in a time that has left few memories.

In those days the hills and the valleys were alone in splendour, there were no buildings to desecrate the rough fields and cliffs, no chimney pots to peer out of the tall woods. There were a few cottages in Helford hamlet, but they made no impression upon the river life itself, which belonged to the birds – curlew and red-shank, guillemot and puffin. No yachts rode to the tide then, as they do today, and that stretch of placid water where the river divides to Constantine and Gweek was calm and undisturbed.

The river was little known, save to a few mariners who had found shelter there when the south-west gales drove them in-shore from their course up-channel, and they found the place lonely and austere, a little frightening because of the silence, and when the wind was fair again were glad to weigh anchor and set sail.

Helford hamlet was no inducement to a sailor ashore, the few cottage folk dull-witted and uncommunicative, and the fellow who has been away from warmth and women over-long has little desire to wander in the woods or dabble with the waders in the mud at ebb-tide. So the winding river remained unvisited, the woods and the hills untrodden, and all the drowsy beauty of midsummer that gives Helford river a strange enchantment, was never seen and never known.

Today there are many voices to blunder in upon the silence. The pleasure steamers come and go, leaving a churning wake, and yachtsmen visit one another, and even the day-tripper, his dull eye surfeited with undigested beauty, ploughs in and out amongst the shallows, a prawning net in hand. Sometimes, in a little puffing car, he jerks his way along the uneven, muddy track that leads sharply to the right out of Helford village, and takes his tea with his fellow-trippers in the stone kitchen of the old farm building that once was Navron House. There is something of grandeur about it even now. Part of the original quadrangle still stands, enclosing the farm-yard of today, and the two pillars that once formed the entrance to the house, now over-grown with ivy and encrusted with lichen, serve as props to the modern barn and its corrugated roof.

The farm kitchen, where the tripper takes his tea, was part of Navron dining-hall, and the little half-stair, now terminating in a bricked-up wall, was the stair leading to the gallery. The rest of the house must have crumbled away, or been demolished, for the square farm-building, though handsome enough, bears little likeness to the Navron of the old prints, shaped like the letter E, and of the formal garden and the park there is no trace today.

The tripper eats his split and drinks his tea, smiling upon the landscape, knowing nothing of the woman who stood there once, long ago, in another summer, who caught the gleam of the river amidst the trees, as he does, and who lifted her head to the sky and felt the sun.

He hears the homely farm-yard noises, the clanking of pails, the lowing of cattle, the rough voices of the farmer and his son as they call to each other across the yard, but his ears are deaf to the echoes of that other time, when someone whistled softly

8

from the dark belt of trees, his hands cupped to his mouth, and was swiftly answered by the thin, stooping figure crouching beneath the walls of the silent house, while above them the casement opened, and Dona watched and listened, her hands playing a little nameless melody upon the sill, her ringlets falling forward over her face.

The river flows on, the trees rustle in the summer wind, and down on the mud flats the oyster-catchers stand at ebb-tide scanning the shallows for food, and the curlews cry, but the men and women of that other time are forgotten, their head-stones encrusted with lichen and moss, their names indecipherable.

Today the cattle stamp and churn the earth over the vanished porch of Navron House, where once a man stood as the clock struck midnight, his face smiling in the dim candle-light, his drawn sword in his hand.

In spring the farmer's children gather primroses and snowdrops in the banks above the creek, their muddy boots snapping the dead twigs and the fallen leaves of a spent summer, and the creek itself, swollen with the rains of a long winter, looks desolate and grey.

The trees still crowd thick and darkly to the water's edge, and the moss is succulent and green upon the little quay where Dona built her fire and looked across the flames and laughed at her lover, but today no ship lies at anchor in the pool, with rakish masts pointing to the skies, there is no rattle of chain through the hawse hole, no rich tobacco smell upon the air, no echo of voices coming across the water in a lilting foreign tongue.

The solitary yachtsman who leaves his yacht in the open roadstead of Helford, and goes exploring up-river in his dinghy on a night in midsummer, when the night-jars call, hesitates when he comes upon the mouth of the creek, for there is something of mystery about it even now, something of enchantment. Being a stranger, the yachtsman looks back over his shoulder to the safe yacht in the roadstead, and to the broad waters of the river, and he pauses, resting on his paddles, aware suddenly of the deep silence of the creek, of its narrow twisting channel, and he feels – for no reason known to him – that he is an interloper, a trespasser in time. He ventures a little way along the left bank of the creek, the sound of the blades upon the water seeming over-loud and echoing oddly among the trees on the farther bank, and as he creeps forward the creek narrows, the trees crowd yet more thickly to the water's edge, and he feels a spell upon him, fascinating, strange, a thing of queer excitement not fully understood.

He is alone, and yet – can that be a whisper, in the shallows, close to the bank, and does a figure stand there, the moonlight glinting upon his buckled shoes and the cutlass in his hand, and is that a woman by his side, a cloak around her shoulders, her dark ringlets drawn back behind her ears? He is wrong, of course, those are only the shadows of the trees, and the whispers are no more than the rustle of the leaves and the stir of a sleeping bird, but he is baffled suddenly, and a little scared, he feels he must go no farther, and that the head of the creek beyond the farther bank is barred to him and must remain unvisited. And so he turns to go, heading the dinghy's nose for the roadstead, and as he pulls away the sounds and the whispers become more insistent to his ears, there comes the patter of footsteps, a call, and a cry in the night, a far faint whistle, and a curious lilting song. He strains his eyes in the darkness, and the massed shadows before him loom hard and clear like the outline of a ship. A thing of grace and beauty, born in another time, a painted phantom ship. And now his heart begins to beat, and he strains at his paddles, and the little dinghy shoots swiftly over the dark water away from enchantment, for what he has seen is not of his world, and what he has heard is beyond his understanding.

Once more he reaches the security of his own ship, and looking back for the last time to the entrance of the creek, he sees the full moon white and shining in all its summer glory rise above the tall trees, bathing the creek in loveliness and light.

A night-jar churrs from the bracken on the hills, a fish breaks the surface of the water with a little plopping sound, and slowly his ship turns to meet the incoming tide, and the creek is hidden from him.

The yachtsman goes below to the snug security of his cabin, and browsing amongst his books he finds at last the thing for which he has been searching. It is a map of Cornwall, ill-drawn and inaccurate, picked up in an idle moment in a Truro book-

10

shop. The parchment is faded and yellow, the markings indistinct. The spelling belongs to another century. Helford river is traced fairly enough, and so are the hamlets of Constantine and Gweek. But the yachtsman looks away from them to the marking of a narrow inlet, branching from the parent river, its short, twisting course running westward into a valley. Someone has scratched the name in thin faded characters – Frenchman's Creek.

The yachtsman puzzles awhile over the name, then shrugs his shoulders and rolls away the map. Presently he sleeps. The anchorage is still. No wind blows upon the water, and the night-jars are silent. The yachtsman dreams – and as the tide surges gently about his ship and the moon shines on the quiet river, soft murmurs come to him, and the past becomes the present.

A forgotten century peers out of dust and cobwebs and he walks in another time. He hears the sound of hoof-beats galloping along the drive to Navron House, he sees the great door swing open and the white, startled face of the manservant stare upward at the cloaked horseman. He sees Dona come to the head of the stairs, dressed in her old gown, with a shawl about her head, while down in the silent hidden creek a man walks the deck of his ship, his hands behind his back, and on his lips a curious secret smile. The farm kitchen of Navron House is a dining-hall once more, and someone crouches on the stairs, a knife in his hand, while from above there rings suddenly the startled cry of a child, and down upon the crouching figure a shield crashes from the walls of the gallery, and two little King Charles spaniels, perfumed and curled, run yapping and screaming to the body on the floor.

On Midsummer Eve a wood fire burns on a deserted quay, and a man and a woman look at one another and smile and acknowledge their secret, and at dawn a ship sails with the tide, and the sun shines fiercely from a bright blue sky, and the sea-gulls cry.

All the whispers and echoes from a past that is gone teem into the sleeper's brain, and he is with them, and part of them; part of the sea, the ship, the walls of Navron House, part of a carriage that rumbles and lurches in the rough roads of Cornwall, part even of that lost forgotten London, artificial, painted, where link-boys carried flares, and tipsy gallants laughed at the corner of a cobbled mud-splashed street. He sees Harry in his satin coat, his spaniels at his heels, blundering into Dona's bedroom, as she places the rubies in her ears. He sees William with his button mouth, his small inscrutable face. And last he sees *La Mouette* at anchor in a narrow twisting stream, he sees the trees at the water's edge, he hears the heron and the curlew cry, and lying on his back asleep he breathes and lives the lovely folly of that lost midsummer which first made the creek a refuge, and a symbol of escape.

Chapter 2

THE church clock struck the half-hour just as the coach clattered into Launceston and drew up at the Inn. The driver grunted, and his companion swung himself to the ground and ran to the horses' heads. The driver put two fingers to his mouth and whistled. Presently an ostler came from the Inn on to the square, rubbing his sleepy eyes in astonishment.

'No time to linger. Bring water at once, and a feed for the horses,' said the driver, and he rose in his seat, and stretched himself, glancing sourly about him, while his companion stamped his numbed feet on the ground and grinned back at him in sympathy.

'Their backs are not yet broken, that's one blessing,' he called softly; 'perhaps they are worth all the guineas Sir Harry paid for them after all.' The driver shrugged his shoulders. He was too tired and too stiff to argue. The roads were damnation, and if the wheels were broken and the horses destroyed he would be to blame, not his companion. If they could have travelled quietly, taking a week over the journey, but this devilish break-neck speed, sparing neither man nor beast, all because of my lady's damned ill-humour. Anyway, thank God, she was asleep for the moment, and all was quiet within the coach. His wishes had misled him, however, for as the ostler returned, bearing a pail of water in either hand, and the horses began to drink greedily, the window of the coach was flung open and his mistress leant out, no trace of sleep about her, her eyes wide and clear, and that cool, imperious voice, which he had grown to dread during these last days, as commanding as ever.

'Why the devil this delay?' she said. 'Did you not stop to water the horses three hours ago?'

The driver muttered a prayer for patience, and climbing down from his seat he approached the open window of the coach.

'The horses are not accustomed to the pace, my lady,' he said; 'you forget that during the last two days we have covered nearly two hundred miles – besides, these roads are not fit for animals so highly bred as yours.'

'Nonsense,' came the reply, 'the higher the breeding the greater the endurance. In future you will halt the horses only when I give the command. Pay the fellow here what we owe him, and continue the journey.'

'Yes, my lady.' The man turned away, his mouth set in weary obstinate lines, and with a nod to his companion, and muttering under his breath, he climbed back again to his seat.

The pails of water were removed, the thick-headed ostler gaped without understanding, and once more the horses pawed at the ground and snorted, the steam rising from their hot flesh, and so away out of the cobbled square and the little sleepy town and out again on to the rough and jolting road.

Dona stared moodily out of the window, her chin cupped in her hands. The children were still asleep, that was one blessing, and even Prue, their nurse, her mouth open and her face flushed, had not stirred for two hours or more. Poor Henrietta had been sick for the fourth time, and now lay pale and wan, a tiny edition of Harry, her golden head against the nurse's shoulder. James never stirred; his was the true deep sleep of babyhood, he would not wake perhaps until they reached their destination. And then – what pitiful anti-climax awaited them! Damp beds no doubt, and closed shutters, the mouldy, stifling smell of unused rooms, the irritation of surprised, disgruntled servants. And all because of an impulse blindly obeyed, a sudden boiling up of resentment against the futility of her life, those endless suppers, dinners, card-parties, those foolish pranks worthy only of an apprentice boy on holiday, that stupid flirtation with Rockingham, and Harry himself, so lazy, so easy-going, fulfilling too well the part of perfect husband with his tolerance, his yawn before midnight, his placid and sleepy adoration. This sense of futility had been growing upon her for many months, nagging at her now and again like dormant toothache, but it had taken Friday night to arouse in her that full sense of self-loathing and exasperation, and because of Friday night she was jolting backwards and forwards now in this damnable coach, bound on a ridiculous journey to a house she had seen once in her life and knew nothing about, carrying

14

with her, in anger and irritation, the two surprised children and their reluctant nurse.

She was obeying an impulse, of course, as she always had done, from the beginning, throughout her life, following a whisper, a suggestion, that sprang into being from nowhere and mocked at her afterwards. She had married Harry on impulse, because of his laugh – its funny lazy quality had attracted her – and because she had thought that the expression in his blue eyes meant much more than it did – and now she realized that after all ... but then those were things one did not admit, not even to oneself, and what was the use, the thing was done, and here she was with her two great children, and next month anyway she would be thirty.

No, it was not poor Harry who was to blame, nor even the senseless life they led, nor the foolish escapades, nor their friends, nor the stifling atmosphere of a too early summer falling upon the caked mud and dust of London, nor the silly chatter in the playhouse, the froth, the frivolity, the bawdy nonsense Rockingham whispered in her ear. It was herself who was at fault.

She had played too long a part unworthy of her. She had consented to be the Dona her world had demanded – a superficial, lovely creature, who walked, and talked, and laughed, accepting praise and admiration with a shrug of the shoulder as natural homage to her beauty, careless, insolent, deliberately indifferent, and all the while another Dona, a strange, phantom Dona, peered at her from a dark mirror and was ashamed.

This other self knew that life need not be bitter, nor worthless, nor bounded by a narrow casement, but could be limitless, infinite – that it meant suffering, and love, and danger, and sweetness, and more than this even, much more. Yes, the full force of her self-loathing had come upon her that Friday evening, so that even now, sitting in the coach, with the soft country air bathing her face, she could conjure up once more the hot street smell that came up from the London gutters, a smell of exhaustion and decay, that had merged in some inexplicable way with the heavy, sultry sky, with Harry's yawn as he dusted the skirt of his coat, with Rockingham's pointed smile – as though they all typified a weary, dying world from which she must free herself and escape, before the sky fell in upon her and she was trapped. She

15

remembered the blind hawker at the corner, his ears pricked for the tinkle of a coin, and the apprentice boy from the Haymarket who ambled along with his tray on his head, shouting his wares in a shrill, disconsolate voice, and how he had fallen over some garbage in the gutter and spilled the contents on the dusty cobbled stones. And oh, heaven – the crowded playhouse, the stench of perfume upon heated bodies, the silly laughter and the clatter, the party in the Royal box – the King himself present – the impatient crowd in the cheap seats stamping and shouting for the play to begin while they threw orange peel on to the stage. Then Harry, laughing at nothing in particular as was his custom, became fuddled with the wit of the play, or possibly he had drunk too much before they had set out. Anyway he had started snoring in his seat, and Rockingham, seizing his chance to make a diversion, pressed against her with his foot and whispered in her ear. Damn his impudence, his air of possession, of familiarity, all because she had permitted him to kiss her once, in an idle moment, because the night was fine. And they had proceeded to supper at the Swan, which she had grown to detest, her amusement at its novelty having ceased – for it was no longer a stimulant to be the only wife amongst a crowd of mistresses.

Once it had held a certain attraction, it had sharpened her sense of fun to sup with Harry in these places where no other husband took his wife, to sit cheek by jowl with the ladies of the town and to see Harry's friends first scandalized, then fascinated, and finally whipped into a fever, like curious schoolboys who tread forbidden ground. And yet even then, even at the beginning, she had felt a little prick of shame, a curious sense of degradation, as though she had dressed up for a masquerade and the clothes had not fitted her well.

While Harry's lovable and slightly stupid laugh, his expression of half-shocked dismay: 'You've made yourself the talk of the town, you know, the fellows are gossiping about you in the taverns,' had not served as a rebuke but as an irritant. She had wished that he would be angry, would shout at her, insult her even – but he only laughed, shrugging his shoulders, and fondled her in heavy, clumsy fashion, so that she knew her folly had not touched him, that inwardly he was really quite pleased that men

16

were gossiping about his wife and admiring her, because it made him a person of importance in their eyes. The coach lurched over a deep rut in the road, and James stirred in his sleep. His little face puckered as though to cry, and Dona reached for the toy that had slipped from his grasp, and he cuddled it to his mouth, and so slept once more. He looked like Harry did when demanding a reassurance of her affection, and she wondered why it was that a quality so attractive and touching in James should seem to her, in Harry, more than a little absurd and a secret source of irritation.

Dressing that Friday night, placing the rubies in her ears to match the pendant round her throat, she had been reminded suddenly of James snatching the pendant, and stuffing it in his mouth, and she had smiled to herself, thinking of him, and Harry, standing beside her, dusting the lace at his wrists, had caught the smile and turned it into an invitation. 'Damn it, Dona,' he had said, 'why do you look at me like that? Don't let's go to the play, hang Rockingham, hang the world, why the devil don't we stay at home?' Poor Harry, how vain, how typical, provoked by a smile that was not for him into instant adoration. She had said: 'How ridiculous you are,' turning from him, so that he should not touch her bare shoulder with his clumsy hands, and at once his mouth set in that grumpy, obstinate line she knew so well, so that they set out to the play, as they had done to other plays and to other suppers, times without number, with moods ill-tuned and tempers frayed, putting an edge upon the evening before it had begun.

Then he had called to his spaniels, Duke and Duchess, and they had yapped up at him for sweetmeats, filling the room with their shrill barking, leaping and jumping at his hands.

'Hey, Duke, hey Duchess,' he had said, 'go seek, go find,' throwing a sweatmeat across the room and on to her bed, so that they clawed at the curtains, and tried to spring upon it, yapping horribly the while, and Dona, her fingers in her ears to thrust out the sound, swept from the room and downstairs to her waiting chair, white, and cold, and angry, to be met with the hot street smells and the breathless vapid sky.

Once more the coach shook and trembled in the deep ruts of the country road, and this time it was the nurse who stirred –

poor, wretched Prue, her foolish, honest face all heavy and mottled with fatigue, how she must grudge her mistress this sudden inexplicable journey – and Dona wondered whether she had left some young man forlorn in London who would prove false in all probability and marry somebody else and Prue's life would be blighted, all because of her, Dona, and her whims and fancies and savage ill-humour. What would poor Prue find to do at Navron House, but parade the children up and down the avenue and through the gardens, sighing for the streets of London hundreds of miles away. Were there gardens at Navron? She could not remember. It all seemed so long ago, that brief visit after she had married. There were trees surely, and a shining river, and great windows that peered from a long room, but more than this she had forgotten, because she had felt so ill during those days, with Henrietta on the way, and life one endless business of sofas, and sickness, and smelling-bottles. Suddenly Dona felt hungry, the coach had just rumbled past an orchard and the apple trees were in blossom, and she knew she must eat now, at once, without more ado, on the side of the road in the sunshine, they must all eat – so she thrust her head out of the window and called up to her coachman: 'We will halt here for a while, and eat. Come and help me spread the rugs beneath the hedge.'

The man stared down at her in bewilderment. 'But, my lady, the ground may be damp, you will take cold.'

'Nonsense, Thomas, I am hungry, we are all hungry, we must eat.'

He climbed down from his seat, his face red with embarrassment, and his companion turned away also, coughing behind his hand.

'There is a hostelry in Bodmin, my lady,' the coachman ventured, 'there you could eat in comfort, and rest perhaps; surely it would be more fitting. If anyone should pass this way, and see you by the side of the road. I hardly think Sir Harry would like . . .'

'Damn it, Thomas, can't you obey orders?' said his mistress, and she opened the door of the coach herself and stepped down into the muddy road, lifting her gown above her ankles in a most brazen way. Poor Sir Harry, thought the coachman, this was the

18

sort of thing he had to contend with every day, and in less than five minutes she had them all assembled on the grass by the side of the road, the nurse barely awake blinking her round eyes, and the children staring in astonishment. 'Let us all drink ale,' said Dona, 'we have some in the basket beneath the seat. I have a mad desire for ale. Yes, James, you shall have some.' And there she sat, her petticoats tucked beneath her and her hood falling away from her face, quaffing her ale like any beggaring gipsy, handing some on the tip of her finger for her baby son to taste, smiling the while at the coachman to show him that she bore no malice for his rough driving and his obstinacy. 'You must both drink, too, there is plenty for all,' she said, and the men were obliged to drink with her, avoiding the eye of the nurse. She thought the whole proceeding unseemly, as they did, and was wishing for a quiet parlour in a hostelry, and fresh warm water where she could bathe the children's hands and faces.

'Where are we going?' asked Henrietta for the twelfth time, looking about her in distaste, holding her dress close to her so that the mud should not stain it. 'Is the drive nearly finished, and shall we soon be home?'

'We are going to another home,' said Dona, 'a new home, a much nicer home. You will be able to run free in the woods and dirty your clothes, and Prue will not scold you because it will not matter.'

'I don't want to dirty my clothes. I want to go home,' said Henrietta, and her lip trembled; she looked up at Dona in reproach, and then, she was tired perhaps, it was all strange, this journey, this sitting by the roadside, she missed her monotonous routine, she began to cry, and James, placid and happy until then, opened his mouth wide and roared in sympathy. 'There, my pets, there my treasures, did they hate the nasty ditch and the prickly hedge,' said Prue, folding them both in her arms, a world of meaning in her voice for her mistress, the cause of all the upset, so that Dona, her conscience stung, rose to her feet, kicking at the remains of the feast. 'Come then, let us continue the journey by all means, but without tears, for pity's sake,' and she stood for a moment, while the nurse, and the food, and the children packed themselves in the coach. Yes, there was apple blossom on the air, and the scent of gorse as well, and the tang of moss and peat from the moors away in the distance, and surely somewhere, not too distant, over the farther hills, a wet sea smell.

Forget the children's tears, forget Prue's grievance, forget the pursed-up mouth of the coachman, forget Harry and his troubled distressed blue eyes when she announced her decision. 'But damn it, Dona, what have I done, what have I said, don't you know that I adore you?' Forget all these things, because this was freedom, to stand here for one minute with her face to the sun and the wind, this was living, to smile and to be alone.

She had tried to explain it to Harry on the Friday night, after that foolish idiotic escapade at Hampton Court; she had tried to tell him what she meant, how the ridiculous prank on the Countess was only a thwarted, bastard idea of fun, a betrayal of her real mood; that in reality it was escape she wanted, escape from her own self, from the life they led together; that she had reached a crisis in her particular span of time and existence, and must travel through that crisis, alone.

'Go to Navron by all means if you wish it,' he said sulkily. 'I will send word at once that preparation is made for you, that the house is opened up, the servants are ready. But I don't understand. Why suddenly, and why have you never expressed the desire before, and why do you not want me to come with you?'

'Because I would be alone, because my humour is such that if I am not alone I shall drive you mad, and myself as well,' she said.

'I don't understand,' he went on, his mouth set, his eyes sullen, and she, in despair, tried to paint a picture of her mood.

'Do you remember my father's aviary in Hampshire?' she said, 'and how the birds there were well fed, and could fly about their cage? And one day I set a linnet free, and it flew straight out of my hands towards the sun?'

'What of it?' he said, clasping his hands behind his back.

'Because I feel like that. Like the linnet before it flew,' she said, and then she turned away, smiling in spite of her sincerity, because he looked so puzzled, so hopelessly out of his depth, staring at her in his white nightshirt, and he shrugged his shoulders, poor dear, she could well understand it, he shrugged his shoulders, and climbed into bed, and turned his face to the wall away from her, and said: 'Oh hell and damnation, Dona, why must you be so confounded tricky?'

Chapter 3

SHE fumbled for a moment with the catch, it had jammed of course, through lack of use, probably it had not been touched for months, and then she flung the windows wide and let in the fresh air and the sun. 'Faugh! The room smells like a tomb,' she said, and as a shaft of sunlight struck the pane she caught the reflection of the manservant looking at her, she could have sworn he was smiling, but when she turned he was still and solemn as he had been from the first moment of their arrival, a thin, spare little man, with a button mouth and a curiously white face.

'I don't remember you,' she said, 'you were not here when we came before.'

'No, my lady,' he said.

'There was an old man – I forget his name – but he had rheumatism in all his joints, and could scarcely walk, where is he now?'

'In his grave, my lady.'

'I see.' She bit her lip, and turned again to the window. Was the fellow laughing at her or not?

'And you replaced him then?' she said, over her shoulder, looking out towards the trees.

'Yes, my lady.'

'And your name?'

'William, my lady.'

She had forgotten the Cornish people spoke in so strange a way, foreign almost, a curious accent, at least she supposed it was Cornish, and when she turned to look at him again he wore that same slow smile she had noticed in the reflected window.

'I fear we must have caused a good deal of trouble,' she said, 'our sudden arrival, the opening up of the house. The place has been closed far too long, of course. There is dust everywhere, I wonder you have not noticed it.'

'I had noticed it, my lady,' he said, 'but as your ladyship never came to Navron it scarcely seemed worth my while to see

22

that the rooms were cleaned. It is difficult to take pride in work that is neither seen nor appreciated.'

'In fact,' said Dona, stung to amusement, 'the idle mistress makes the idle servant?'

'Naturally, my lady,' he said gravely.

Dona paced up and down the long room, fingering the stuff of the chairs, which was dull and faded. She touched the carving on the mantel, and looked up at the portraits on the wall – Harry's father, painted by Van Dyck, what a tedious face he had – and surely this was Harry himself, this miniature in a case, taken the year they were married. She remembered it now; how youthful he looked and how pompous. She laid it aside, aware of the man-servant's eyes upon her – what an odd creature he was – and then she pulled herself together; no servant had ever got the better of her before.

'Will you please see that every room in the house is swept and dusted?' she said, 'that all the silver is cleaned, that flowers are placed in the rooms, that everything takes place, in short, as though the mistress of the house had not been idle, but had been in residence here for many years?'

'It will be my personal pleasure, my lady,' he said, and then he bowed, and left the room, and Dona, vexed, realized that he had laughed at her once again, not openly, not with familiarity, but as it were secretly, behind his eyes.

She stepped out of the window and on to the grass lawns in front of the house. The gardeners had done their work at least, the grass was fresh trimmed, and the formal hedges clipped, perhaps all in a rush yesterday, or the day before, when the word had come that their mistress was returning; poor devils, she understood their slackness, what a pest she must seem to them, upsetting the quiet tenor of their lives, breaking into their idle routine, intruding upon this queer fellow William – was it really Cornish, that accent of his? – and upsetting the slack disorder he had made for himself.

Somewhere, from an open window in another part of the house, she could hear Prue's scolding voice, demanding hot water for the children, and a lusty roar from James – poor sweet, why must he be washed, and bathed, and undressed, why not tossed, just as

23

he was, into a blanket in any dark corner and left to sleep – and then she walked across to the gap in the trees that she remembered from the last time, and yes – she had been right, it was the river down there, shining and still and soundless. The sun was still upon it, dappled green and gold, and a little breeze ruffled the surface, there should be a boat somewhere – she must remember to ask William if there was a boat – and she would embark on it, let it carry her to the sea. How absurd, what an adventure. James must come too, they would both dip their hands and faces in the water and become soaked with the spray, and fishes would jump out of the water and the sea-birds would scream at them. Oh, heaven, to have got away at last, to have escaped, to have broken free, it could not be possible, to know that she was at least three hundred miles away from St James's Street, and dressing for dinner, and the Swan, and the smells in the Haymarket, and Rockingham's odious meaning smile, and Harry's yawn, and his blue reproachful eyes. Hundreds of miles too from the Dona she despised, the Dona who from devilry or from boredom or from a spice of both, had played that idiotic prank on the Countess at Hampton Court, had dressed up in Rockingham's breeches and cloaked and masked herself, and ridden with him and the others, leaving Harry at the Swan (too fuddled with drink to know what was happening), and had played at foot-pads, surrounding the Countess's carriage and forcing her to step down into the high-road.

'Who are you, what do you want?' the poor little old woman had cried, trembling with fear, while Rockingham had been obliged to bury his face in his horse's neck, choking with silent laughter, and she, Dona, had played the leader, calling out in a clear cold voice:

'A hundred guineas or your honour.'

And the Countess, poor wretch, sixty if she were a day, with her husband some twenty years in the grave, fumbled and felt in her purse for sovereigns, terrified that this young rip from the town should throw her down in the ditch – and when she handed over the money and looked up into Dona's masked face, there was a pitiful tremor at the corner of her mouth, and she said:

'For God's sake spare me, I am very old, and very tired.'

So that Dona, swept in an instant by a wave of shame and degradation, had handed back the purse, and turned her horse's head, and ridden back to town, hot with self-loathing, blinded by tears of abasement, while Rockingham pursued her with shouts and cries of 'What the devil now, and what has happened?' and Harry, who had been told the adventure would be nothing but a ride to Hampton Court by moonlight, walked home to bed, not too certain of his direction, to be confronted by his wife on the doorstep dressed up in his best friend's breeches.

'I had forgotten – was there a masquerade – was the King present?' he said, staring at her stupidly, rubbing his eyes, and 'No, damn you,' said Dona, 'what masquerade there was is over and done with, finished now for ever more. I'm going away.'

And so upstairs, and that interminable argument in the bedroom, followed by a sleepless night, and more arguments in the morning, then Rockingham calling and Dona refusing him admittance, then someone riding to Navron to give warning, the preparations for the journey, the journey itself, and so here at last to silence, and solitude, and still unbelievable freedom.

Now the sun was setting behind the trees, leaving a dull red glow upon the river below, the rooks rose in the air and clustered above their nests, the smoke from the chimneys curled upwards in thin blue lines, and William was lighting the candles in the hall. She supped late, making her own time – early dinner, thank heaven, was now a thing of the past – and she ate with a new and guilty enjoyment, sitting all alone at the head of the long table, while William stood behind her chair and waited silently.

They made a strange contrast, he in his sober dark clothes, his small inscrutable face, his little eyes, his button mouth, and she in her white gown, the ruby pendant round her throat, her hair caught back behind her ears in the fashionable ringlets.

Tall candles stood on the table, and a draught from the open window caused a tremor in their flame, and the flame played a shadow on her features. Yes, thought the manservant, my mistress is beautiful, but petulant too, and a little sad. There is something of discontent about the mouth, and a faint trace of a line between the eyebrows. He filled her glass once more, comparing the reality before him to the likeness that hung on the wall in the bedroom upstairs. Was it only last week that he had stood there, with someone beside him, and the someone had said jokingly, glancing up at the likeness: 'Shall we ever see her, William, or will she remain forever a symbol of the unknown?' and looking closer, smiling a little, he had added: 'The eyes are large and very lovely, William, but they hold shadows too. There are smudges beneath the lids as though someone had touched them with a dirty finger.'

'Are there grapes?' said his mistress suddenly, breaking in upon the silence. 'I have a fancy for grapes, black and succulent, with the bloom on them, all dusty.' 'Yes, my lady,' said the servant, dragged back into the present, and he fetched her grapes, cutting a bunch with the silver scissors and putting them on her plate, his button mouth twisted as he thought of the news he would have to carry tomorrow, or the next day, when the spring tides were due again and the ship returned.

'William,' she said.

'My lady?'

'My nurse tells me that the servant girls upstairs are new to the house, that you sent for them when you heard I was arriving. She says one comes from Constantine, another from Gweek, even the cook himself is new, a fellow from Penzance.'

'That is perfectly true, my lady.'

'What was the reason, William? I understood always, and I think Sir Harry thought the same, that Navron was fully staffed?'

'It seemed to me, my lady, possibly wrongly, that is for you to say, that one idle servant was sufficient about the house. For the last year I have lived here entirely alone.'

She glanced at him over her shoulder, biting her bunch of grapes.

'I could dismiss you for that, William.'

'Yes, my lady.'

'I shall probably do so in the morning.'

'Yes, my lady.'

She went on eating her grapes, considering him as she did so, irritated and a little intrigued that a servant could be so baffling a person. Yet she knew she was not going to send him away.

'Supposing I do not dismiss you, William, what then?'

26

'I will serve you faithfully, my lady.'

'How can I be sure of that?'

'I have always served faithfully the people I love, my lady.'

And to this she could make no answer, for his small button mouth was as impassive as ever, and his eyes said nothing, but she felt in her heart that he was not laughing at her now, he was speaking the truth. 'Am I to take that as a compliment then, William?' she said at last, rising to her feet, as he pulled away her chair.

'It was intended as one, my lady,' he said, and she swept from the room without a word, knowing that in this odd little man with his funny half-courteous, half-familiar manner she had found an ally, a friend. She laughed secretly to herself, thinking of Harry and how he would stare without comprehension: 'What damned impertinence, the fellow needs whipping.'

It was all wrong of course, William had behaved disgracefully, he had no business to live alone in the house, and no wonder there was dust everywhere, and a graveyard smell. But she understood it for all that, because had she not come here to do the same thing herself? Perhaps William had a nagging wife, and an existence in another part of Cornwall too full of cares; perhaps he too had wished to escape? She wondered, as she rested in the salon, staring at the wood fire he had kindled, on her lap a book that she did not read, whether he had sat here amongst the sheets and coverlets before she came, and whether he begrudged her the use of the room now. Oh, the lovely luxury of stillness, to live alone like this, a cushion behind her head, a draught of air from the open window ruffling her hair, and to rest secure in the knowledge that no one would come blundering in upon her presence with a loud laugh, with a voice that grated – that all those things belonged to another world, a world of dusty cobbled stones, of street smells, of apprentice boys, of ugly music, of taverns, of false friendships, and futility. Poor Harry, he would be supping now with Rockingham probably, bemoaning his fate at the Swan, dozing over cards, drinking a little too much, saying: 'Damn it, she kept talking about a bird, saying she felt like a bird, what the devil did she mean?' And Rockingham, with his pointed, malicious smile and those narrow eyes that understood, or thought they understood, her baser qualities would murmer: 'I wonder – I very much wonder.'

Presently, when the fire had sunk, and the room cooled, she went upstairs to her bedroom, first passing through the children's rooms to see if all was well. Henrietta looked like a waxen doll, her fair curls framing her face, her mouth slightly pouted, while James in his cot frowned in his sleep, chubby and truculent, like a little pug-dog. She tucked his fist inside the cover, kissing it as she did so, and he opened one eye and smiled. She stole away, ashamed of her furtive tenderness for him – so primitive, so despicable, to be moved to folly simply because he was male. He would no doubt grow up to be fat, and gross, and unattractive, making some woman miserable.

Someone – William she supposed – had cut a sprig of lilac and placed it in her room, on the mantelshelf, beneath the portrait of herself. It filled the room with scent, heady and sweet. Thank God, she thought, as she undressed, there will be no pattering feet of spaniels, no scratching noises, no doggy smells, and the great deep bed is mine alone. Her own portrait looked down at her with interest. Have I that sulky mouth, she thought, that petulant frown? Did I look like that six, seven years ago? Do I look like it still?

She pulled on her nightgown, silken and white, and cool, and stretched her arms above her head, and leant from the casement. The branches stirred against the sky. Below the garden, away down in the valley, the river ran to meet the tide. She pictured the fresh water, bubbling with the spring rains, surging against the salt waves, and how the two would mingle and become one, and break upon the beaches. She pulled the curtains back, so that the light should flood the room, and she turned to her bed, placing her candlestick on the table at her side.

Then drowsing, half asleep, watching the moon play patterns on the floor, she wondered what other scent it was that mingled itself with the lilac, a stronger, harsher smell, something whose name eluded her. It stung her nostrils even now, as she turned her head on the pillow. It seemed to come from the drawer beneath the table, and stretching out her arm she opened the drawer, and looked inside. There was a book there, and a jar of tobacco. It was the tobacco she had smelt of course. She picked up the jar, the stuff was brown and strong and freshly cut. Surely William had not the audacity to sleep in her bed, to lie there, smoking, looking at her portrait? That was a little too much, that was really unforgivable. There was something so personal about this tobacco, so very unlike William, that surely she must be mistaken – and yet – if William had lived here at Navron, for a year, alone? She opened the book – was he then a reader as well? And now she was more baffled than before, for the book was a volume of poetry, French poetry, by the poet Ronsard, and on the flyleaf someone had scribbled the initials 'J.B.A. – Finistère' and underneath had drawn a tiny picture of a gull.

Chapter 4

WHEN she woke the next morning, her first thought was to send for William and, confronting him with the jar of tobacco and the volume of poetry, to inquire whether he had slept ill on his new mattress, and whether he had missed the comfort of her bed. She played with the idea, amusing herself at the picture of his small inscrutable face colouring up at last, and his button mouth dropping in dismay, and then, when the heavy-footed maid brought her breakfast, stumbling and blushing in her awkwardness, raw country girl that she was, she decided to bide her time, to wait a few days, for something seemed to warn her that any admission of her discovery would be premature, out of place.

So she left the tobacco-jar, and the poetry, in the table drawer beside her bed, and when she rose, and dressed, and went downstairs, she found the dining-hall and the salon had been swept and cleaned as she had commanded, there were fresh flowers in the rooms, the windows were opened wide, and William himself was polishing the tall candlesticks on the wall.

He inquired at once if she had slept well, and she answered, 'Yes,' thinking instantly that this would be the moment, and could not prevent herself from adding, 'And you too, I hope, were not fatigued by our arrival?' At which he permitted himself a smile, saying, 'You are very thoughtful, my lady. No, I slept well, as always. I heard Master James cry once in the night, but the nurse soothed him. It seemed strange to hear a child's cry in the house after the long silence.'

'You did not mind?' she said.

'No, my lady. The sound took me back to my own childhood. I was the eldest in a family of thirteen. There were always little ones arriving.'

'Is your home near here, William?'

'No, my lady.' And now there was a new quality in his voice, a note of finality. As though he said: 'A servant's life is his own. Do not intrude upon it,' and she had the insight to leave it, to question him no more. She glanced at his hands. They were clean and waxen white, no tobacco stains upon them, and there was an impersonal soapy texture about the whole of him, vastly different from that male tobacco smell, so harsh and brown, in the jar upstairs.

Perhaps she maligned him, perhaps the jar had stood there for three years – since Harry's last visit to the estate, when she had not accompanied him. And yet Harry did not smoke strong tobacco. She wandered to the shelves where great leather-bound volumes stood in rows, books that nobody ever read, and she made a pretext of taking a volume down and glancing through it, while the servant continued to polish the candlesticks.

'Are you a reader, William?' she said suddenly.

'You have gathered I am not, my lady,' he said, 'because the books in those shelves are coated with dust. No, I have never handled them. But I will do so tomorrow. I will take them all down and dust them well.'

'You have no hobby then?'

'Moths interest me, my lady. I have quite a fine collection in my room. The woods round Navron are excellent for moths.' And with that she left him. She wandered out into the garden, hearing the children's voices. Really the little man was an oddity, she could not fathom him out, and surely if it was he who read Ronsard in the night watches he would have browsed amongst these books, at least once or twice, out of curiosity.

The children called her with delight, Henrietta dancing like a fairy, and James, still very unsteady, rolling after her like a drunken sailor, and the three wandered into the woods to gather bluebells. The flowers were just appearing in the young green, short and stubby and blue; next week or the week after there would be a carpet for them to lie upon.

So the first day passed, and the next, and the one after, Dona exulting in her new-found freedom. Now she could live without a plan, without a decision, taking the days as they came, rising at noon if she had the mind or at six in the morning, it did not matter, eating when hunger came upon her, sleeping when she wished, in the day or at midnight. Her mood was one of lovely laziness. She would lie out in her garden hour after hour, her hands behind her head, watching the butterflies as they frolicked in the sun, and chased one another, and had their moment; listening to the birds intent upon domestic life among the branches, so busy, so ardent, like newly-wed couples proud of their first home polished as a pin. And all the while the bright sun shone down upon her, and little mackerel clouds scurried across the sky, and away in the valley beneath the woods there was the river, the river which she had not found yet, because she was too idle, because there was so much time; one day, quite soon, she would go down to it, early one morning, and stand in the shadows barefoot and let the water splash upon her, and smell the muddied river smell, pungent and sweet.

The days were glorious and long, the children were browning like little gypsies. Even Henrietta was losing her town ways, and consented to run with naked feet upon the grass, to play leapfrog, to roll on the ground as James did, like a puppy.

They were playing thus one afternoon, tumbling and falling upon Dona, who lay on her back with her gown anyhow and her ringlets in mad disorder (the disapproving Prue safely within the house) and as they pelted one another with daisy heads and honeysuckle, there came to Dona, warm and drugged, and foolish with the sun, the ominous sound of hoof-beats in the avenue, and presently a clatter into the court-yard before the house, and the jangle of the great bell. And horror upon horror there was William advancing towards her on the grass, and a stranger following him, a large, burly creature with a florid face and bulbous eyes, his wig over-curled, slashing at his boots as he walked with a gold-knobbed cane.

'Lord Godolphin to see you, my lady,' said William gravely, no whit abashed at her appearance, so tattered, so disgraceful. She rose to her feet at once, pulling at her gown, patting her ringlets: how infuriating, how embarrassing, and what a damnable intrusion. The creature stared at her in dismay, no wonder; well he must endure it, perhaps he would go the sooner. And then she curtsied, and said: 'I am enchanted to see you,' at which he bowed solemnly and made no reply. She led the way into the house, catching sight of herself in the mirror on the wall; there was honeysuckle behind her ear, she left it there obstinately, she did not care. And then they sat down on stiff chairs and stared at each other, while Lord Godolphin nibbled his gold-knobbed cane.

'I had heard you were in residence,' he said at length, 'and I considered it a duty, or rather a pleasure, to pay my respects as soon as possible. It is many years since you and your husband condescended to visit Navron. In fact, I may say you have become strangers. I knew Harry very well when he lived here as a boy.'

'Indeed,' said Dona, fascinated suddenly by the growth at the side of his nose; she had only just noticed it. How unfortunate, poor man. And then she glanced away quickly, for fear he should realize she was looking, and 'Yes,' he continued, 'I may say that I used to count Harry as among my dearest friends. But since his marriage we have seen so little of him, he spends his time in Town.'

A reproach to me, she thought, very natural of course, and 'I am sorry to say Harry is not with me,' she told him, 'I am here alone, with my children.'

'That is a great pity,' he said, and she answered nothing, for what was there to say?

'My wife would have accompanied me,' he continued, 'but she does not enjoy very good health at the moment. In short . . .' He paused, uncertain how to continue, and Dona smiled. 'I quite understand, I have two small children myself,' at which he looked a little abashed, and bowed. 'We hope for an heir,' he said, and 'Of course,' said Dona, fascinated once again by that growth at the end of his nose. How distressing for his wife, how did she endure it. But Godolphin was talking again, saying something about his wife being very glad to welcome her at any time, there were so few neighbours, and so on, and so forth. How boring and heavy he was, thought Dona, was there no middle course between this solemn pompous pretentiousness and the vicious frivolity of Rockingham? Would Harry become like this if he lived at Navron? A great turnip, with eyes that said nothing, and a mouth like a slit in a suet pudding. 'I was hoping', Godolphin was saying, 'that Harry would have given some assistance in the county. You have heard of our troubles, no doubt.'

'I have heard nothing,' said Dona.

'No? Perhaps you are too remote here for the news to reach

you, though the talk and chatter has been rife for miles around. We have been vexed and harried, almost at our wits' end, in fact, with acts of piracy. Goods of considerable value have been lost at Penryn, and along the coast. An estate of my neighbours' was sacked a week or so ago.'

'How distressing,' said Dona.

'It is more than distressing, it is a positive outrage!' declared Godolphin, his face reddening, his eyes more bulbous than ever, 'and no one knows how to deal with it. I have sent up complaints to London, and get no reply. They send us a handful of soldiers from the garrison at Bristol, but they are worse than useless. No, I can see that I and the rest of the land-owners in the county will have to band ourselves together and deal with the menace. It is very unfortunate that Harry is not at Navron, very unfortunate.'

'Can I do anything to help you?' asked Dona, digging her nails into her hands to stop herself from smiling: he looked so provoked, so highly indignant, almost as though he blamed her for the acts of piracy.

'My dear lady,' he said, 'there is nothing you can do, except ask your husband to come down, and rally round his friends, so that we can fight this damned Frenchman.'

'Frenchman?' she said.

'Why, yes, that's the plague of it,' he said, almost shouting in his anger; 'this fellow's a low sneaking foreigner, who for some reason or other seems to know our coast like the back of his hand, and slips away to the other side, to Brittany, before we can lay our hands on him. His craft is like quicksilver, none of our ships down here can catch him. He'll creep into our harbours by night, land silently like the stealthy rat he is, seize our goods, break open our stores and merchandise, and be away on the morning tide while our fellows are rubbing the sleep out of their eyes.'

'In fact, he is too clever for you,' said Dona.

'Why, yes, Madam – if you like to put it that way,' he answered haughtily, at once taking offence.

'I'm afraid Harry would never catch him, he is far too lazy,' she said.

'I do not for a moment suggest that he could,' said Godolphin, 'but we need heads in this business, the more the better. And we have to catch this fellow if it means spending all the time and money at our disposal. You perhaps do not realize how serious the matter is. Down here we are constantly robbed, our women-folk sleep in terror of their lives, and not only their lives.'

'Oh, he is that sort of pirate, then?' murmured Dona.

'No lives have been lost as yet, and none of our women have been taken,' said Godolphin stiffly, 'but as this fellow is a French-man we all realize that it is only a question of time before some-thing dastardly occurs.'

'Oh, quite,' said Dona, and seized with sudden laughter she rose to her feet and walked towards the window, for his gravity and pomposity were beyond bearing, she could stand it no longer, her laughter would win control. But, thank heaven, he took her rising as a gesture of dismissal, for he bowed solemnly, and kissed the hand she gave him.

'When you next send messages to your husband I trust you will remember me to him, and give him some account of our troubles,' he said, and 'Yes, of course,' answered Dona, deter-mined that whatever happened Harry should not come hot-foot down to Navron to deal with elusive pirates, breaking in upon her privacy and lovely freedom. When she had promised that she would call upon his wife, and he had uttered a few more formalities, she summoned William, and he withdrew, and she heard the steady trot of his horse as he vanished down the drive.

She hoped he would be the last visitor, for this sort of thing was not what she intended; this solemn sitting around on chairs exchanging small conversation with a turnip-head was one degree worse than supping at the Swan. William must be warned, in future she would not be at home to callers. He must make an excuse: she would be out walking, or asleep, or ill, or mad even – confined to her room in chains – anything, rather than face the Godolphins of the county, in all their grandeur and pomposity.

How dull-witted they must be, these local gentry, to be robbed in this way, their goods and merchandise seized in the night, and unable to prevent it, even with the help of soldiers. How slow they must be, how inefficient. Surely if they kept a watch, were constantly on the alert, it would be possible to lay some trap for the foreigner as he crept into their harbours. A ship was not a phantom thing, it depended on wind and tide, nor were men soundless, their feet must echo on the quays, their voices fall upon the air. That day she dined early, at six, and talked to William as he stood behind her chair, bidding him close the door to visitors in future.

'You see, William,' she said, 'I came to Navron to avoid people, to be alone. My mood is to play the hermit, while I am here.'

'Yes, my lady,' he said, 'I made a mistake about this afternoon. It shall not occur again. You shall enjoy your solitude, and make good your escape.'

'Escape?' she said.

'Yes, my lady,' he answered, 'I have rather gathered that is why you are here. You are a fugitive from your London self, and Navron is your sanctuary.'

She was silent a minute, astonished, a little dismayed, and then: 'You have uncanny intuition, William,' she said, 'where does it come from?'

'My late master talked to me long and often, my lady,' he said: 'many of my ideas and much of my philosophy are borrowed from him. I have made a practice of observing people, even as he does. And I rather think that he would term your ladyship's arrival here as an escape.'

'And why did you leave your master, William?'

'His life is such, at the moment, my lady, that my services are of little use to him. We decided I would do better elsewhere.'

'And so you came to Navron?'

'Yes, my lady.'

'And lived alone and hunted moths?'

'Your ladyship is correct."

'So that Navron is also, possibly, an escape for you as well?'

'Possibly, my lady.'

'And your late master, what does he do with himself?'

'He travels, my lady.'

'He makes voyages from place to place?'

'Exactly, my lady.'

'Then he also, William, is a fugitive. People who travel are always fugitives.'

'My master has often made the same observation, my lady. In fact I may say his life is one continual escape.'

'How pleasant for him,' said Dona, peeling her fruit; 'the rest of us can only run away from time to time, and however much we pretend to be free, we know it is only for a little while – our hands and our feet are tied.'

'Just so, my lady.'

'And your master – he has no ties at all?'

'None whatever, my lady.'

'I would like to meet your master, William.'

'I think you would have much in common, my lady.'

'Perhaps one day he will pass this way, on his travels?'

'Perhaps, my lady.'

'In fact, I will withdraw my command about visitors, William. Should your late master ever call, I will not feign illness or madness or any other disease, I will receive him.'

'Very good, my lady.'

And looking round, for she was standing now, and he had pulled away her chair, she saw that he was smiling, but instantly his smile was gone, when he met her eyes, and his mouth was pursed in its usual button. She wandered into the garden. The air was soft and languid and warm, and away to the west the sun flung great patterns across the sky. She could hear the voices of the children as Prue put them to bed. It was a time for going forth alone, a time for walking. And fetching a shawl and throwing it across her shoulders she went out of the garden and across the park-land to a stile, and a field, and a muddied lane, and the lane brought her to a cart-track, and the cart-track to a great stretch of rough wild grass, of uncultivated heath land, leading to the cliffs and the sea.

She had the urge within her to walk then to the sea, to the open sea itself, not the river even, and as the evening cooled and the sun sank in the sky, she came at length to a sloping headland where the gulls clamoured furiously at her approach, for it was the nesting season, and flinging herself down on the tussocky earth and the scrubby stones of the headland she looked out upon the sea. There was the river, away to the left, wide and shining as it met the sea, and the sea itself was still and very calm, while the setting sun dappled the water with copper and crimson. Down below, far and deep, the little waves splashed upon the rocks.

The setting sun behind her made a pathway on the sea, stretching to the far horizon, and as Dona lay and watched, her mind all drowsy and content, her heart at peace, she saw a smudge on the horizon, and presently the smudge took shape and form, and she saw the white sails of a ship. For a while it made no progress, for there was no breath upon the water, and it seemed to hang there, between sea and sky, like a painted toy. She could see the high poop-deck, and the fo'c'sle head, and the curious raking masts, and the men upon her must have had luck with their fishing for a crowd of gulls clustered around the ship, wheeling and crying, and diving to the water. Presently a little tremor of a breeze came off the headland where Dona lay, and she saw the breeze ruffle the waves below her, and travel out across the sea towards the waiting ship. Suddenly the sails caught the breeze and filled, they bellied out in the wind, lovely and white and free, the gulls rose in a mass, screaming above the masts, the setting sun caught the painted ship in a gleam of gold, and silently, stealthily, leaving a long dark ripple behind her, the ship stole in towards the land. And a feeling came upon Dona, as though a hand touched her heart, and a voice whispered in her brain, 'I shall remember this.' A premonition of wonder, of fear, of sudden strange elation. She turned swiftly, smiling to herself for no reason, humming a little tune, and strode back across the hills to Navron House skirting the mud and jumping the ditches like a child, while the sky darkened, and the moon rose, and the night wind whispered in the tall trees.

Chapter 5

SHE went to bed as soon as she returned, for the walk had tired her, and she fell asleep almost at once, in spite of the curtains drawn wide, and the shining moon. And then, just after midnight it must have been, for subconsciously she had heard the stable clock strike the hour, she was awake, aware of a footstep that had crunched the gravel beneath her window. She was instantly alert, the household should be sleeping at such an hour, she was suspicious of footsteps in the night. She rose from bed then, and went to the casement, and looked out into the garden. She could see nothing beneath her, the house was in shadow, and whoever had stood there, beneath the casement, must have passed on. She waited and watched, and suddenly, from the belt of trees beyond the lawn, a figure stole into a square patch of moonlight, and looked up towards the house. She saw him cup his hands to his mouth and give a soft low whistle. At once another figure crept out from the shadowed house, he must have been sheltering just inside the window of the salon, and this second figure ran swiftly across the lawn to the man by the belt of trees, his hand raised as though in warning, and she saw that the running figure was William. Dona leant forward, screened by the curtain, her ringlets falling over her face, and she breathed quicker than usual, and her heart beat fast, for there was excitement in what she saw, there was danger – her fingers beat a little nameless tune upon the sill. The two men stood together in the patch of moonlight, and Dona saw William gesticulate with his hands, and point towards the house, at which she drew back into the shadow for fear of being observed. The two continued talking, the strange man looking upward at the house also, and presently he shrugged his shoulders, spreading out his hands, as though the matter were beyond his powers of settlement, and then they both withdrew into the belt of trees, and disappeared. Dona waited and listened, but they did not return. Then she shivered, for the breeze was cool blowing upon her thin nightgown, and she returned to bed, but could not sleep, for this new departure of William's was a mystery that must be solved.

Had she seen him walk by moonlight into the trees, alone, she would have thought little of it, there might have been a woman in Helford hamlet by the river who was not unpleasing to him, or his silent expedition might have been more innocent still, a moth-hunt at midnight. But that stealthy tread, as though he waited for a signal, and that dark figure with his cupped hands and the soft whistle, William's run across the lawn with his warning hand, these were graver problems, giving cause for worry.

She wondered if she had been a very great fool in trusting William. Anyone but herself would have dismissed him that first evening, on learning of his stewardship, how he had lived there in the house alone, without orders to do so. And that manner of his, so unlike the usual servant, that manner which intrigued and amused her, would no doubt have caused offence to most mistresses, to a Lady Godolphin. Harry would have sent him away at once – except that no doubt his manner would have been different with Harry, she felt that instinctively. And then the tobacco jar, the volume of poetry – it was mystifying beyond her comprehension, but in the morning she must do something, take the matter in hand, and so without having decided anything, her mind in disorder, she fell asleep at length, just as the grey morning light broke into the room.

The day was hot and shining, like its predecessor, a high golden sun in a cloudless sky, and when Dona came down her first movement was towards the belt of trees where the stranger and William had talked, and disappeared, the night before. Yes it was as she had expected, their footsteps had made a little track through the bluebells, easy to follow, they led straight across the main pathway of the woods and down deep amongst the thickest trees. She continued for a while, the track leading downwards always, twisting, uneven, very hard to follow, and suddenly she realized that this way would lead her in time towards the river, or a branch of the river, because in the distance she caught the gleam of water that she had not suspected could be so close, for surely the river itself must be away behind her, to the left, and this thread of water she was coming to was something unknown, a discovery. She hesitated a moment, uncertain whether to continue, and then remembering the hour, and how the children would be looking for her, and William himself perhaps, for orders, she turned back, and climbed up through the woods once more, and so on to the lawns of Navron House. The matter must be postponed to a better time, later perhaps in the afternoon.

So she played with the children, and wrote a duty letter to Harry – the groom was riding back to London in a day or so, to bear him news. She sat in the salon by the wide open window, nibbling the end of her pen, for what was there to say except that she was happy in her freedom, absurdly happy, and that would be hurtful; poor Harry, he would never understand.

'That friend of your youth called upon me, one Godolphin,' she wrote, 'whom I found ill-favoured and pompous, and could not picture you together romping in the fields as little boys. But perhaps you did not romp, but sat upon gilt chairs and played cat's cradle. He has a growth on the end of his nose, and his wife is expecting a baby, at which I expressed sympathy. And he was in a great fuss and pother about pirates, or rather one pirate, a Frenchman, who comes by night and robs his house, and the houses of his neighbours, and all the soldiers of the west cannot catch him, which seems to me not very clever of them. So I propose setting forth myself, with a cutlass between my teeth, and when I have entrapped the rogue, who according to Godolphin is a very fierce fellow indeed, a slayer of men and a ravisher of women, I will bind him with strong cords and send him to you as a present.' She yawned, and tapped her teeth with her pen, it was easy to write this sort of letter, making a jest of everything, and she must be careful not to be tender, because Harry would take horse at once and ride to her, nor must she be too cold, for that would fret him, and would also bring him.

So 'Amuse yourself as you wish, and think of your figure when you take that fifth glass,' she wrote, 'and address yourself, if you should have the desire, to any lovely lady your sleepy eye should fall upon, I will not play the scold when I see you again.

'Your children are well and send their love, and I send you – whatever you would wish me to send.

Your affectionate wife
DONA'

She folded the letter, and sealed it. Now she was free once more, and began to think how she could rid herself of William for the afternoon, for she wished him well away before she started on her expedition. At one o'clock, over her cold meat, she knew how she would do it.

'William,' she said.

'My lady?'

She glanced up at him, and there was no night-hawk look about him, he was the same as always, attentive to her commands.

'William,' she said, 'I would like you to ride to my Lord Godolphin's manor this afternoon, bearing flowers for his lady who is unwell.'

Was that a flicker of annoyance in his eye, a momentary unwillingness, a hesitation?

'You wish me to take the flowers today, my lady?'

'If you please, William.'

'I believe the groom is doing nothing, my lady.'

'I wish the groom to take Miss Henrietta and Master James and the nurse for a picnic, in the carriage.'

'Very well, my lady.'

'You will tell the gardener to cut the flowers?'

'Yes, my lady.'

She said no more, and he too was silent, and she smiled to herself, for she guessed he did not want to go. Perhaps he had another assignation with his friend, down through the woods. Well, she would keep it for him.

'Tell one of the maids to turn back my bed and draw the curtains, I shall rest this afternoon,' she said, as she went from the room, and William bowed without reply.

This was a ruse to dull any fears he might have, but she was certain he was without suspicion. And so, playing her part, she went upstairs and lay down on her bed. Later she heard the carriage draw up in the courtyard, and the children's voices chattering excitedly at the sudden picnic, and then the carriage bowled away down the avenue. After a short while she heard a single horse clatter on the cobbled stones, and leaving her room, and going out on to the passage where the window looked out upon the yard, she saw William mount one of the horses, a great bunch of flowers before him on the saddle, and so ride away.

How successful the strategy, she thought, laughing to herself like a silly child on an adventure. She put on a faded gown which she would not mind tearing, and a silken handkerchief around her head, and slipped out of her own house like a thief.

She followed the track that she had found in the morning, but this time plunging down deep into the woods without hesitation. The birds were astir again, after their noonday silence, and the silent butterflies danced and fluttered, while drowsy bumble bees hummed in the warm air, winging their way to the topmost branches of the trees. Yes, there once again was the glimmer of water that had surprised her. The trees were thinning, she was coming to the bank – and there, suddenly before her for the first time, was the creek, still and soundless, shrouded by the trees, hidden from the eyes of men. She stared at it in wonder, for she had had no knowledge of its existence, this stealthy branch of the parent river creeping into her own property, so sheltered, so concealed by the woods themselves. The tide was ebbing, the water oozing away from the mud flats, and here, where she stood, was the head of the creek itself, for the stream ended in a trickle, and the trickle in a spring. The creek twisted round a belt of trees, and she began to walk along the bank, happy, fascinated, forgetting her mission, for this discovery was a pleasure quite unexpected, this creek was a source of enchantment, a new escape, better than Navron itself, a place to drowse and sleep, a lotus-land. There was a heron, standing in the shallows, solemn and grey, his head sunk in his hooded shoulders, and beyond him a little oyster-catcher pattered in the mud, and then, weird and lovely, a curlew called and, rising from the bank, flew away from her down the creek. Something, not herself, disturbed the birds, for the heron rose slowly, flapping his slow wings, and followed the curlew, and Dona paused a moment, for she too had heard a sound, a sound of tapping, of hammering.

She went on, coming to the corner where the creek turned, and then she paused, withdrawing instinctively to the cover of the trees, for there before her, where the creek suddenly widened, forming a pool, lay a ship at anchor – so close that she could have tossed a biscuit to the decks. She recognized it at once. This was the ship she had seen the night before, the painted ship on the horizon, red and golden in the setting sun. There were two men slung over the side, chipping at the paint, this was the sound of hammering she had heard. It must be deep water where the ship lay, a perfect anchorage, for on either side the mud banks rose steeply and the tide ran away, frothing and bubbling, while the creek itself twisted again and turned, running towards the parent river out of sight. A few yards from where she stood was a little quay. There was tackle there, and blocks, and ropes; they must be making repairs. A boat was tied alongside, but no one was in it.

But for the two men chipping at the side of the ship all was still, the drowsy stillness of a summer afternoon. No one would know, thought Dona, no one could tell, unless they had walked as she had done, down from Navron House, that a ship lay at anchor in this pool, shrouded as it was by the trees, and hidden from the open river.

Another man crossed the deck and leant over the bulwark, gazing down at his fellows. A little smiling man, like a monkey, and he carried a lute in his hands. He swung himself up on the bulwark, and sat cross-legged, and began to play the strings. The two men looked up at him, and laughed, as he strummed a careless, lilting air, and then he began to sing, softly at first, then a little louder, and Dona, straining to catch the words, realized with a sudden wave of understanding, and her heart thumping, that the man was singing in French.

Then she knew, then she understood – her hands went clammy, her mouth felt dry and parched, and she felt, for the first time in her life, a funny strange spasm of fear.

This was the Frenchman's hiding-place – that was his ship.

She must think rapidly, make a plan, make some use of her knowledge: how obvious it was now, this silent creek, this perfect hiding-place, no one would ever know, so remote, so silent, so still – something must be done, she would have to say something, tell someone.

Or need she? Could she go away now, pretend she had not seen the ship, forget about it, or pretend to forget it – anything so that she need not be involved, for that would mean a breaking up of her peace, a disturbance, soldiers tramping through the woods, people arriving, Harry from London – endless complications, and Navron no more a sanctuary. No, she would say nothing, she would creep away now, back to the woods and the house, clinging to her guilty knowledge, telling no one, letting the robberies continue – what did it matter – Godolphin and his turnip friends must put up with it, the country must suffer, she did not care.

And then, even as she turned to slip away amongst the trees, a figure stepped out from behind her, from the woods, and throwing his coat over her head blinded her, pinning her hands to her sides, so that she could not move, could not struggle, and she fell down at his feet, suffocated, helpless, knowing she was lost.

Chapter 6

HER first feeling was one of anger, of blind unreasoning anger. How dare anyone treat her thus, she thought, truss her up like a fowl, and carry her to the quay. She was thrown roughly on to the bottom boards of the boat, and the man who had knocked her down took the paddles and pushed out towards the ship. He gave a cry – a sea-gull's cry – and called something in a patois which she could not understand to his companions on the ship. She heard them laugh in reply, and the fellow with the lute struck up a merry little jig, as though in mockery.

She had freed herself now from the strangling coat, and looked up at the man who had struck her. He spoke to her in French and grinned. He had a merry twinkle in his eye, as though her capture were a game, an amusing jest of a summer's afternoon, and when she frowned at him haughtily, determined to be dignified, he pulled a solemn face, feigning fear, and pretended to tremble.

She wondered what would happen if she raised her voice and shouted for help – would anyone hear her, would it be useless?

Somehow she knew she could not do this, women like herself did not scream. They waited, they planned escape. She could swim, it would be possible later perhaps to get away from the ship, lower herself over the side, perhaps when it was dark. What a fool she had been, she thought, to linger there an instant, when she knew that the ship was the Frenchman. How deserving of capture she was, after all, and how infuriating to be placed in such a position – ridiculous, absurd – when a quiet withdrawal to the trees and back to Navron would have been so easy. They were passing now under the stern of the ship, beneath the high poop-deck and the scrolled windows, and there was the name written with a flourish, in gold letters, *La Mouette*. She wondered what it meant, she could not remember, her French was hazy suddenly, and now he was pointing to the ladder over the side of the ship, and the men on deck were crowding round, grinning, familiar – damn their eyes – to watch her mount. She managed the ladder well, determined to give them no cause for mockery, and shaking her head she swung herself down to the deck, refusing their offers of assistance.

They began to chatter to her in this patois she could not follow – it must be Breton, had not Godolphin said something about the ship slipping across to the opposite coast? – and they kept smiling and laughing at her in a familiar, idiotic way that she found infuriating, for it went ill with the heroic dignified part she wished to play. She folded her arms, and looked away from them, saying nothing. Then the first man appeared again – he had gone to warn their leader she supposed, the captain of this fantastic vessel – and beckoned her to follow him.

It was all different from what she had expected. These men were like children, enchanted with her appearance, smiling and whistling, and she had believed pirates to be desperate creatures, with rings in their ears and knives between their teeth.

The ship was clean – she had imagined a craft filthy and stained, and evil-smelling – there was no disorder about it, the paint was fresh and gay, the decks scrubbed like a man-o'-war, and from the forward part of the ship, where the men lived she supposed, came the good hunger-making smell of vegetable soup. And now the man was leading her through a swinging door and down some steps, and he knocked on a further door, and a quiet voice bade him enter. Dona stood on the threshold, blinking a little, for the sun was streaming through the windows in the stern, making water patterns on the light wood panelling. Once again she felt foolish, disconcerted, for the cabin was not the dark hole she had imagined, full of empty bottles and cutlasses, but a room – like a room in a house – with chairs, and a polished table, and little paintings of birds upon the bulkheads. There was something restful about it, restful yet austere, the room of someone who was sufficient to himself. The man who had taken her to the cabin withdrew, closing the door quietly, and the figure at the polished table continued with his writing, taking no notice of her entrance. She watched him furtively, aware of sudden shyness and hating herself for it, she, Dona, who was never shy, who cared for nothing and for no one. She wondered how long he would keep her standing there; it was unmannerly, churlish, and yet she knew

47

she could not be the first to speak. She thought of Godolphin suddenly, Godolphin with his bulbous eyes and the growth on the end of his nose, and his fears for his women-folk; what would he say if he could see her now, alone in the cabin with the terrible Frenchman?

And the Frenchman continued writing, and Dona went on standing by the door. She realized now what made him different from other men. He wore his own hair, as men used to do, instead of the ridiculous curled wigs that had become the fashion, and she saw at once how suited it was to him, how impossible it would be for him to wear it in any other way.

How remote he was, how detached, like some student in college studying for an examination; he had not even bothered to raise his head when she came into his presence, and what was he scribbling there anyway that was so important? She ventured to step forward closer to the table, so that she could see, and now she realized he was not writing at all, he was drawing, he was sketching, finely, with great care, a heron standing on the mudflats, as she had seen a heron stand, ten minutes before.

Then she was baffled, then she was at a loss for words, for thought even, for pirates were not like this, at least not the pirates of her imagination, and why could he not play the part she had assigned to him, become an evil, leering fellow, full of strange oaths, dirty, greasy-handed, not this grave figure seated at the polished table, holding her in contempt?

Then he spoke at last, only the very faintest trace of accent marking his voice, and still he did not look at her, but went on with his drawing of the heron.

'It seems you have been spying upon my ship,' he said.

Immediately she was stung to anger – she spying! Good God, what an accusation! 'On the contrary,' she said, speaking coldly, clearly, in the boyish voice she used to servants. 'On the contrary, it seems your men have been trespassing upon my land.'

He glanced up at once, and rose to his feet – he was tall, much taller than she had imagined – and into his dark eyes came a look surely of recognition, like a sudden flame, and he smiled slowly, as if in secret.

'My very humble apologies,' he said. 'I had not realized that the lady of the manor had come to visit me in person.'

He reached forward for a chair, and she sat down, without a word. He went on looking at her, that glance of recognition, of secret amusement in his eyes, and he leant back in his chair, crossing his legs, biting the end of his quill.

'Was it by your orders that I was seized and brought here?' she said, because surely something must be said, and he would do nothing but look her up and down in this singular fashion.

'My men are told to bind anyone who ventures to the creek,' he said. 'As a rule we have no trouble. You have been more bold than the inhabitants, and, alas, have suffered from that boldness. You are not hurt are you, or bruised?'

'No,' she said shortly.

'What are you complaining about then?'

'I am not used to being treated in such a manner,' she said, angry again, for he was making her look like a fool.

'No, of course not,' he said quietly, 'but it will do you no harm.'

God almighty, what insolence, what damned impertinence. Her anger only amused him though, for he went on tilting his chair and smiling, biting the end of his quill.

'What do you propose to do with me?' she said.

'Ah! there you have me,' he replied, putting down his pen. 'I must look up my book of rules.' And he opened a drawer in the table and took out a volume, the pages of which he proceeded to turn slowly, with great gravity.

'Prisoners – method of capture – questioning – detainment – their treatment – etc., etc.,' he read aloud, 'h'm, yes, it is all here, but unfortunately these notes relate to the capture and treatment of male prisoners. I have made no arrangements apparently to deal with females. It is really most remiss of me.'

She thought of Godolphin again, and his fears, and in spite of her annoyance she found herself smiling, remembering his words: 'As the fellow is a Frenchman it is only a matter of time.'

His voice broke in upon her thoughts. 'That is better,' he said. 'Anger does not become you, you know. Now you are beginning to look more like yourself.'

'What do you know of me?' she said.

He smiled again, tilting forward on his chair. 'The Lady St Columb,' he said, 'the spoilt darling of the Court. The Lady Dona who drinks in the London taverns with her husband's friends. You are quite a celebrity, you know.'

She found herself flushing scarlet, stung by the irony of his words, his quiet contempt.

'That's over,' she said, 'finished and done with.'

'For the time being, you mean.'

'No, for ever.'

He began whistling softly to himself, and reaching for his drawing continued to play with it, sketching in the background.

'When you have been at Navron a little while you will tire of it,' he said, 'and the smells and sounds of London will call to you again. You will remember this mood as a passing thing.'

'No,' she said.

But he did not answer, he went on with his drawing.

She watched him, stung with curiosity, for he drew well, and she began to forget that she was his prisoner and that they should be at enmity with one another.

'That heron was standing on the mud, by the head of the creek,' she said, 'I saw him, just now, before I came to the ship.'

'Yes,' he answered, 'he is always there, when the tide ebbs. It is one of his feeding grounds. He nests some distance away though, nearer to Gweek, up the main channel. What else did you see?'

'An oyster-catcher, and another bird, a curlew I think it was.'

'Oh, yes,' he said, 'they would be there too. I expect the hammering drove them away.'

'Yes,' she said.

He continued his little tuneless whistle, drawing the while, and she watched him, thinking how natural it was, how effortless and easy, to be sitting here, in this cabin, on this ship, side by side with the Frenchman, while the sun streamed in through the windows and the ebb-tide bubbled round the stern. It was funny, like a dream, like something she had always known would happen, as though this was a scene in a play, in which she must act a part,

and the curtain had now lifted, and someone had whispered:
'Here – this is where you go on.'

'The night-jars have started now, in the evenings,' he said,
'they crouch in the hillside, farther down the creek. They are so
wary though, it's almost impossible to get really close.'

'Yes,' she said.

'The creek is my refuge, you know,' he said, glancing up at
her, and then away again. 'I come here to do nothing. And
then, just before idleness gets the better of me, I have the strength
of mind to tear myself away, to set sail again.'

'And commit acts of piracy against my countrymen?' she said.

'And commit acts of piracy against your countrymen,' he
echoed.

He finished his drawing, and put it away, and then rose to his
feet, stretching his arms above his head.

'One day they will catch you,' she said.

'One day ... perhaps,' he said, and he wandered to the
window in the stern, and looked out, his back turned to her.

'Come and look,' he said, and she got up from her chair and
went and stood beside him, and they looked down to the water,
where there floated a great cluster of gulls, nosing for scraps.

'They come in dozens, always,' he told her; 'they seem to
know at once when we return, and they come in here from the
headlands. My men will feed them, I can't prevent them. And I
am as bad myself. I am always throwing crumbs to them, from
the windows here.' He laughed, and reaching for a crust of
bread, he tossed it to them, and the gulls leapt upon it, screaming
and fighting.

'Perhaps they have a fellow feeling for the ship,' he said; 'it is
my fault for naming her *La Mouette*.'

'*La Mouette* – the Sea-gull – why, of course,' she said, 'I had
forgotten what it meant,' and they went on watching the gulls,
leaning against the window.

'This is absurd,' Dona thought, 'why am I doing this, it is
not what I meant, not what I intended. By now surely I should
be bound with ropes and thrust into the dark hold of the ship,
gagged and bruised, and here we are throwing bread to the sea-
gulls, and I have forgotten to go on being angry.'

'Why are you a pirate?' she said at last, breaking the silence.

'Why do you ride horses that are too spirited?' he answered.

'Because of the danger, because of the speed, because I might fall,' she said.

'That is why I am a pirate,' he said.

'Yes, but...'

'There are no "buts". It is all very simple really. There are no dark problems about it. I have no grudge against society, no bitter hatred of my fellow-men. It just happens that the problems of piracy interest me, suit my particular bent of thought. It is not just a matter of brutality and bloodshed, you know. The organization takes many hours of many days, every detail of a landing has to be thought out, and prepared. I hate disorder, or any slipshod method of attack. The whole thing is very much like a geometrical problem, it is food for the brain. And then – well – then I have my fun, my spice of excitement, my beating of the other fellow. It is very satisfying, very absorbing.'

'Yes,' she said. 'Yes, I understand.'

'You are puzzled, aren't you,' he said, laughing down at her, 'because you expected to find me drunk here on the floor, surrounded by blood and knives and bottles and shrieking women.'

She smiled back at him; she did not answer.

Someone knocked at the door, and when the Frenchman called 'Enter' one of his men came in, bearing a great bowl of soup on a tray. It smelt rich and good. The hot steam rose in the air. The man proceeded to lay the table, spreading a white cloth on the farther end. He went to a locker in the bulkhead and brought out a bottle of wine. Dona watched. The smell of the soup was very tempting, and she was hungry. The wine looked cool, in its slim bottle. The man withdrew, and looking up she saw that the master of the ship was watching her, with laughter in his eyes.

'Will you have some?' he said.

She nodded, feeling foolish once again: why did he read her thoughts? And he fetched another plate and spoon, and another glass from the cupboard. Then he pulled up two chairs to the table. She saw that there was new bread too, freshly baked in the

French fashion, the crust dark and brown, and little pats of very yellow butter.

They ate their meal in silence, and then he poured out the wine. It was cold and clear, and not too sweet. And all the while she kept thinking how like a dream it was, a remembered dream that she had had once; a quiet, familiar thing, a dream she recognized.

'I have done this before,' she thought, 'this is not the first time.' Yet that was absurd, for of course it was the first time, and he was a stranger to her. She wondered what hour it was. The children would have returned from their picnic, Prue would be putting them to bed. They would run and knock upon her door and she would not answer. 'It does not matter,' she thought, 'I don't care,' and she went on drinking her wine, looking at the bird pictures on the bulkhead, and now and again stealing a glance at him when she knew that his head was turned from her.

Then he reached out an arm towards a tobacco-jar on a shelf, and began to shake the mixture into his hand. It was close cut, very dark and brown. And suddenly, the truth striking at her like a blow, she saw the tobacco-jar in her bedroom, and the volume of French poetry, with the drawing of a sea-gull on the title-page. She saw William running to the belt of trees – William – his master, his master who made voyages from place to place – whose life was one continual escape. She got up from her chair, staring at him.

'Good God!' she said.

He looked up. 'What is the matter?'

'It's you,' she said, 'you who left the tobacco-jar in my bed-room, and the volume of Ronsard. It's you have been sleeping in my bed.'

He smiled at her, amused at her choice of words, smiling too at her astonishment, her confusion and dismay.

'Did I leave them there?' he said. 'I had forgotten. How very remiss and careless of William not to have noticed.'

'It was for you that William stayed at Navron,' she said; 'it was for your sake that he sent the servants away. All these months, while we were in London, you have been at Navron.'

'No,' he said, 'not continually. From time to time, when it

suited my plans. And in the winter, you know, it can be damp here in the creek. It made a change, a luxurious change, to seek the comfort of your bedroom. Somehow, I always felt you would not mind.'

He went on looking at her, and always that glimmer of secret amusement in his eyes.

'I consulted your portrait, you know,' he said. 'I addressed myself to it several times. My lady, I said (for I was most subservient), would you grant a very weary Frenchman the courtesy of your bed? And it seemed to me that you bowed gracefully, and gave me permission. Sometimes you even smiled.'

'It was very wrong of you,' she said, 'very irregular.'

'I know,' he said.

'Besides being dangerous.'

'That was the fun of it.'

'And if I had known for one moment . . .'

'What would you have done?'

'I should have come down to Navron at once.'

'And then?'

'I should have barred the house. I should have dismissed William. I should have set a watch on the estate.'

'All that?'

'Yes.'

'I don't believe you.'

'Why not?'

'Because when I lay in your bed, looking up at your portrait on the wall, that was not how you behaved.'

'How did I behave?'

'Very differently.'

'What did I do?'

'Many things.'

'What sort of things?'

'You joined my ship's company, for one thing. You signed your name amongst the faithful. You were the first, and the last, woman to do so.'

And saying this, he rose from the table, and went to a drawer, and fetched out a book. This he opened, and on the page she saw the words *La Mouette*, followed by a string of names. Edmond

Vacquier . . . Jules Thomas . . . Pierre Blanc . . . Luc Dumont . . . and so on. And he reached then for his pen, and dipped it in the ink, and handed it to her.

'Well?' he said, 'what about it?'

She took it from him, balancing it in her hand a moment, as though weighing the question, and she did not know whether it was the thought of Harry in London, yawning over his cards, or Godolphin with his bulbous eyes, or the good soup she had taken and the wine she had drunk, making her drowsy and warm, and a little careless, like a butterfly in the sun, or whether it was because he was standing there beside her, but she looked up at him, laughing suddenly, and signed her name in the centre of the page, beneath the others, Dona St Columb.

'And now you must go back, your children will wonder what has happened to you,' he said.

'Yes,' she said.

He led the way out of his cabin, and on to the deck. He leant over the rail, and called down to the men amidships.

'First you must be introduced,' he said, and he called out an order, in the Breton patois she could not understand, and in a moment his company assembled themselves, glancing up at her in curiosity.

'I am going to tell them that from henceforth you come to the creek unchallenged,' he said; 'that you are free to come and go as you please. The creek is yours. The ship is yours. You are one of us.' He spoke to them briefly, and then one by one they came up to her, and bowed, and kissed her hand, and she laughed back at them, saying 'Thank you' – and there was a madness about, a frivolity, like a dream under the sun. Below, in the water, one of the men waited for her in the boat. She climbed the bulwark, and swung herself over the side on to the ladder. The Frenchman did not help her. He leant against the bulwark and watched her.

'And Navron House?' he said, 'is it barred and bolted, is William to be dismissed?'

'No,' she said.

'I must return your call, then,' he said, 'as a matter of courtesy.'

'Of course.'

'What is the correct hour? In the afternoon, I believe, between three and four, and you offer me a dish of tea?'

She looked at him, laughing, and shook her head.

'No,' she said, 'that is for Lord Godolphin and the gentry. Pirates do not call upon ladies in the afternoon. They come stealthily, by night, knocking upon a window – and the lady of the manor, fearful for her safety, gives him supper, by candle-light.'

'As you will,' he said, 'tomorrow then, at ten o'clock?'

'Yes,' she said.

'Good night.'

'Good night.'

He went on standing against the bulwark watching her, as she was pulled ashore in the little boat. The sun had gone behind the trees, and the creek was in shadow. The last of the ebb had run away from the flats, and the water was still. A curlew called once, out of sight, round the bend of the river. The ship, with its bold colouring, its raking masts, looked remote, unreal, a thing of fantasy. She turned, and sped through the trees towards the house, smiling guiltily to herself, like a child hugging a secret.

Chapter 7

WHEN she came to the house she saw that William was standing by the window of the salon, making a pretence of putting the room in order, but she knew at once he had been watching for her.

She did not tell him immediately, for the fun of teasing him, and coming into the room, casting her kerchief from her head, she said, 'I have been walking, William, my head is better.'

'So I observe, my lady,' he said, his eyes upon her.

'I walked by the river, where it is quiet and cool.'

'Indeed, my lady.'

'I had no knowledge of the creek before. It is enchanting, like a fairy-tale. A good hiding-place, William, for fugitives like myself.'

'Very probably, my lady.'

'And my Lord Godolphin, did you see him?'

'His lordship was not at home, my lady. I bade his servant give your flowers and the message to his lady.'

'Thank you, William.' She paused a moment, pretending to arrange the sprigs of lilac in their vase, and then, 'Oh, William, before I forget. I am giving a small supper party tomorrow night. The hour is rather late, ten o'clock.'

'Very well, my lady. How many will you be?'

'Only two, William. Myself and one other – a gentleman.'

'Yes, my lady.'

'The gentleman will be coming on foot, so there is no need for the groom to stay up and mind a horse.'

'No, my lady.'

'Can you cook, William?'

'I am not entirely ignorant of the art, my lady.'

'Then you shall send the servants to bed, and cook supper for the gentleman and myself, William.'

'Yes, my lady.'

'And you need not mention the visit to anyone in the house, William.'

'No, my lady.'

'In fact, William, I propose to behave outrageously.'

'So it would seem, my lady.'

'And you are dreadfully shocked, William?'

'No, my lady.'

'Why not, William?'

'Because nothing you or my master ever did could possibly shock me, my lady.'

And at this she burst out laughing, and clasped her hands together.

'Oh, William, my solemn William, then you guessed all the time! How did you know, how could you tell?'

'There was something about your walk, as you entered just now, my lady, that gave you away. And your eyes were – if I may say so without giving offence – very much alive. And coming as you did from the direction of the river I put two and two together, as it were, and said to myself: "It has happened. They have met at last."'

'Why "at last", William?'

'Because, my lady, I am a fatalist by nature, and I have always known that, sooner or later, the meeting was bound to come about.'

'Although I am a lady of the manor, married and respectable, with two children, and your master a lawless Frenchman, and a pirate?'

'In spite of all those things, my lady.'

'It is very wrong, William. I am acting against the interests of my country. I could be imprisoned for it.'

'Yes, my lady.'

But this time he hid his smile no longer, his small button mouth relaxed, and she knew he would no longer be inscrutable and silent, but was her friend, her ally, and she could trust him to the last.

'Do you approve of your master's profession, William?' she said.

'Approve and disapprove are two words that are not in my vocabulary, my lady. Piracy suits my master, and that is all there is to it. His ship is his kingdom, he comes and goes as he pleases, and no man can command him. He is a law unto himself.'

'Would it not be possible to be free, to do as he pleases, and yet not be a pirate?'

'My master thinks not, my lady. He has it that those who live a normal life, in this world of ours, are forced into habits, into customs, into a rule of life that eventually kills all initiative, all spontaneity. A man becomes a cog in the wheel, part of a system. But because a pirate is a rebel, and an outcast, he escapes from the world. He is without ties, without man-made principles.'

'He has the time, in fact, to be himself.'

'Yes, my lady.'

'And the idea that piracy is wrong, that does not worry him?'

'He robs those who can afford to be robbed, my lady. He gives away much of what he takes. The poorer people in Brittany benefit very often. No, the moral issue does not concern him.'

'He is not married, I suppose?'

'No, my lady. Marriage and piracy do not go together.'

'What if his wife should love the sea?'

'Women are apt to obey the laws of nature, my lady, and produce babies.'

'Ah, very true, William.'

'And women who produce babies have a liking for their own fireside, they no longer want to roam. So a man is faced at once with a choice. He must either stay at home and be bored, or go away and be miserable. He is lost in either case. No, to be really free, a man must sail alone.'

'That is your master's philosophy?'

'Yes, my lady.'

'I wish I were a man, William.'

'Why so, my lady?'

'Because I too would find my ship, and go forth, a law unto myself.'

As she spoke there came a loud cry from upstairs, followed by a wail, and the sound of Prue's scolding voice. Dona smiled, and shook her head. 'Your master is right, William,' she said, 'we are all cogs in a wheel, and mothers most especially. It is only the pirates who are free.' And she went upstairs to her children, to soothe them, and wipe away their tears. That night, as she lay in bed, she reached for the volume of Ronsard on the table by her side, and thought how strange it was that the Frenchman had lain there, his head upon her pillow, this same volume in his hands, his pipe of tobacco in his mouth. She pictured him laying aside the book when he had read enough, even as she did now, and blowing out the candle, and then turning on his side to sleep. She wondered if he slept now, in that cool, quiet cabin of his ship, with the water lapping against the side, the creek itself mysterious and hushed. Or whether he lay on his back as she did, eyes open in the darkness and sleep far distant, brooding on the future, his hands behind his head.

Next morning, when she leant from her bedroom window and felt the sun on her face, and saw the clear bright sky with a sharp gloss about it because of the east wind, her first thought was for the ship in the creek. Then she remembered how snug was the anchorage, tucked away in the valley, shrouded by the trees, and how they could scarce have knowledge there of the turbulent tide ripping up the parent river, the short waves curling, while the steep seas at the mouth of the estuary reared and broke themselves into spray.

She remembered the evening that was to come, and the supper party, and began to smile, with all the guilty excitement of a conspirator. The day itself seemed like a prelude, a foretaste of things to come, and she wandered out into the garden to cut flowers, although those in the house were not yet faded.

The cutting of flowers was a peaceful thing, soothing to her unquiet mind, and the very sensation of touching the petals, fingering the long green stalks, laying them in a basket, and later placing them one by one in the vases that William had filled for her, banished her first restlessness. William too was a conspirator. She had observed him in the dining-hall, cleaning the silver, and he had glanced up at her in understanding, for she knew why he worked with such ardour.

'Let us do full justice to Navron,' she said; 'bring out all the silver, William, and light every candle. And we will use that dinner service with the rose border that is shut away for banquets.' It was exciting, it was amusing – she fetched the dinner service herself and washed the plates, dusty with disuse, and she made a little decoration in the centre of the table with the young buds of fresh-cut roses. Then she and William descended together to the cellar, and peered by candle-light at the cobweb-covered bottles, and he brought forth a wine greatly prized by his master, which they had not known was there. They exchanged smiles, they whispered furtively, and Dona felt all the lovely wickedness of a child who does something wrong, something forbidden, and chokes with secret laughter behind his parent's back.

'What are we going to eat?' she said, and he shook his head, he would not tell. 'Rest easy, my lady,' he said, 'I will not disappoint you,' and she went out into the garden once more, singing, her heart absurdly gay. The hot noon passed, hazy with the high east wind, and the long hours of afternoon, and tea with the children under the mulberry tree, and so round to early evening once again, and their bed-time, and a ceasing of the wind, while the sun set, the sky glowed, and the first stars shone.

The house was silent once more, and the servants, believing her to be weary, to be retiring supperless to bed, congratulated themselves on the easiness of their mistress, and took themselves to their own quarters. Somewhere, alone in his room no doubt, William prepared the supper. Dona did not ask. It did not matter.

She went to her own room, and stood before her wardrobe, pondering which gown to wear. She chose one cream-coloured, which she had worn often, and which she knew became her well, and she placed in her ears the ruby ear-rings that had belonged to Harry's mother, and round her throat the ruby pendant.

'He will not notice,' she thought, 'he is not that sort of person, he does not care about women, or their clothes, or their jewels,' and yet she found herself dressing with great care, combing her ringlets round her fingers and setting them behind her ears. Suddenly she heard the stable clock strike ten, and in a panic she laid the comb aside, and went downstairs. The staircase led direct into the dining-hall, and she saw that William had lighted every candle, even as she had told him, and the bright silver shone on the long table. William himself was standing there, arranging dishes on the sideboard, and she went to see what it was he had prepared. Then she smiled. 'Oh, William, now I know why you went down to Helford this afternoon, returning with a basket.'

For there on the sideboard was crab, dressed and prepared in the French fashion, and there were small new potatoes too, cooked in their skins, and a fresh green salad sprinkled with garlic, and tiny scarlet radishes. He had found time too to make pastry. Thin, narrow wafers, interlaid with cream, while next to them, alone in a glass bowl, was a gathering of the first wild strawberries of the year.

'William, you are a genius,' she said, and he bowed, permitting himself a smile. 'I am pleased you are glad, my lady.'

'How do I look? Will your master approve?' she asked him, turning on her heels. 'He will make no comment, my lady,' replied the servant, 'but I do not think he will be entirely indifferent to your appearance.'

'Thank you, William,' she said gravely, and went out into the salon to await her guest. William had drawn the curtains for greater safety, but she pulled them back, letting in the summer night, and as she did so the Frenchman came towards her across the lawn, a tall, dark figure, walking silently.

She saw at once that he had fallen in with her mood, and knowing that she would play the lady of the manor he had dressed himself, even as she had done, as though for a party. The moonlight touched his white stockings, and glimmered on his silver-buckled shoes. His long coat was wine-coloured, and his sash the same, though in a deeper tone, and there was lace at his throat, and at his wrists. He still disdained the curled wigs of fashion, and wore his own hair, like a cavalier. Dona held out her hand to him, and this time he bent over it, as a guest should do, brushing it with his lips, and then stood on the threshold of the salon, by the long window, looking down upon her with a smile.

'Supper awaits you,' she said, shy suddenly, for no reason, and he did not answer, but followed her to the dining-hall, where William stood waiting behind her chair.

The guest stood a moment, looking about him at the blaze of candles, at the bright silver, at the shining plates with the rose border, and then he turned to the hostess, with that same slow mocking smile she had grown to expect: 'Is it wise of you, do you think, to put all this temptation before a pirate?'

'It is William's fault,' said Dona, 'it is all William's doing.'

'I don't believe you,' he said: 'William never made these preparations for me before, did you, William? You cooked me a chop and served it to me on a chipped plate, and you brushed away one of the covers of the chairs, and told me I must be content.'

'Yes, sir,' said William, his eyes glowing in his small round face, and Dona sat down, shy no longer, for the presence of William broke constraint between them.

He understood his role, playing the butt to perfection, laying himself open purposely to shafts of wit from his mistress, accepting with a smile and a shrug of the shoulder the mockeries of his master. And the crab was good, the salad excellent, the pastries light as air, the strawberries nectar, the wine perfection.

'I am a better cook than William, for all that,' pronounced his master, 'and one day you shall taste my spring chicken, roasted on a spit.'

'I will not believe it,' she said, 'chickens were never roasted in that cabin of yours, like a hermit's cell. Cooking and philosophy do not go together.'

'On the contrary, they go very well,' he said, 'but I will not roast your chicken in my cell. We will build a wood fire in the open, on the shores of the creek, and I will roast your chicken for you there. But you must eat it with your fingers. And there will be no candle-light, only the light of the fire.'

'And perhaps the night-jar you told me about will not be silent,' she said.

'Perhaps!'

He smiled at her across the table, and she had a sudden vision of the fire they would build, on the shore beside the water, and how the flames would hiss and crackle in the air, and how the good burnt smell of roasting chicken would come to their nostrils. The cooking would absorb him, even as his drawing of the heron absorbed him yesterday, and his planning of piracy would do tomorrow. She noticed, for the first time, that William had left them, and rising from the table she blew the candles, and led the way into the salon.

'Smoke, if you wish,' she said, and there, on the mantelpiece before him, he recognized his jar of tobacco.

'The perfect hostess,' he said.

She sat down, but he went on standing by the mantelpiece, filling his pipe, looking about the room as he did so.

'It is very different from the winter,' he said. 'When I came then, the covers shrouded the furniture, and there were no flowers. There was something austere about the room. You have changed all that.'

'All empty houses are like sepulchres,' she said.

'Ah, yes – but I don't mean that. Navron would have remained a sepulchre, had anyone else broken the silence.'

She did not answer. She was not sure what he meant.

For a while there was silence between them, and then he said, 'What brought you to Navron, in the end?'

She played with a tassel of the cushion behind her head.

'You told me yesterday that Lady St Columb was something of a celebrity,' she said, 'that you had heard gossip of her escapades. Perhaps I was tired of Lady St Columb, and wanted to become somebody else.'

'In other words – you wished to escape?'

'That is what William told me you would say.'

'William has experience. He has seen me do the same sort of thing. Once there was a man called Jean-Benoit Aubéry, who had estates in Brittany, money, friends, responsibilities, and William was his servant. And William's master became weary of Jean-Benoit Aubéry, and so he turned into a pirate, and built *La Mouette*.'

'And is it really possible to become somebody else?'

'I have found it so.'

'And are you happy?'

'I am content.'

'What is the difference?'

'Between happiness and contentment? Ah, there you have me. It is not easy to put into words. Contentment is a state of mind and body when the two work in harmony, and there is no friction. The mind is at peace, and the body also. The two are sufficient to themselves. Happiness is elusive – coming perhaps once in a life-time – approaching ecstasy.'

'Not a continuous thing, like contentment?'

'No, not a continuous thing. But there are, after all, degrees of happiness. I remember, for instance, one particular moment after I became a pirate, and I fought my first action, against one of your merchant ships. I was successful, and towed my prize into port. That was a good moment, exhilarating, happy. I had achieved the thing I had set myself to do, of which I had been uncertain.'

'Yes,' she said. 'Yes – I understand that.'

'And there have been other moments too. The pleasure felt after I have made a drawing, and I look at the drawing, and it has the shape and form of what I meant. That is another degree of happiness.'

'It is easier then, for a man,' she said, 'a man is a creator, his happiness comes in the things that he achieves. What he makes with his hands, with his brains, with his talents.'

'Possibly,' he said. 'But women are not idle. Women have babies. That is a greater achievement than the making of a drawing, or the planning of an action.'

'Do you think so?'

'Of course.'

'I never considered it before.'

'You have children, have you not?'

'Yes – two.'

'And when you handled them for the first time were you not conscious of achievement? Did you not say to yourself, "This is something I have done – myself." And was not that near to happiness?'

She thought for a moment, and then smiled at him.

'Perhaps,' she said.

He turned away from her, and began touching the things on the mantelpiece. 'You must not forget I am a pirate,' he said; 'here you are leaving your treasures about in careless fashion. This little casket, for instance, is worth several hundred pounds.'

'Ah, but then I trust you.'

'That is unwise.'

'I throw myself upon your mercy.'

'I am known to be merciless.'

He replaced the casket, and picked up the miniature of Harry. He considered it a moment, whistling softly.

'Your husband?' he said.

'Yes.'

He made no comment, but put the miniature back into its place, and the fashion in which he did so, saying nothing of Harry, of the likeness, of the miniature itself, gave to her a curious sense of embarrassment. She felt instinctively that he thought little of Harry, considered him a dolt, and she wished suddenly that the miniature had not been there, or that Harry was in some way different.

'It was taken many years ago,' she found herself saying, as though in defence; 'before we were married.'

'Oh, yes,' he said. There was a pause, and then –

'That portrait of you,' he said, 'upstairs in your room, was that done about the same time?'

'Yes,' she said, 'at least – it was done soon after I became betrothed to Harry.'

'And you have been married – how long?'

'Six years. Henrietta is five.'

'And what decided you upon marriage?'

She stared back at him, at a loss for a moment; his question was so unexpected. And then, because he spoke so quietly, with such composure, as though he were asking why she had chosen a certain dish for dinner, caring little about the answer, she told him the truth, not realizing that she had never admitted it before.

'Harry was amusing,' she said, 'and I liked his eyes.'

As she spoke it seemed to her that her voice sounded very far distant, as though it were not herself who spoke, but somebody else.

He did not answer. He had moved away from the mantelpiece, and had sat down on a chair, and was pulling out a piece of paper from the great pocket of his coat. She went on staring in front of her, brooding suddenly upon Harry, upon the past, thinking of their marriage in London, the vast assembly of people, and how poor Harry, very youthful, scared possibly at the responsibilities before him, and having little imagination, drank too much on their wedding-night, so as to appear bolder than he was, and only succeeded in seeming a very great sot and a fool. And they had journeyed about England, to meet his friends, for ever staying in other people's houses in an atmosphere strained and artificial, and she – starting Henrietta almost immediately – became irritable, fretful, entirely unlike herself, so unaccustomed to ill-health of any kind. The impossibility of riding, of walking, of doing all the things she wished to do, increased her irritation. It would have helped could she have talked to Harry, asked for his understanding, but understanding, to him, meant neither silence, nor tenderness, nor quiet, but a rather hearty boisterousness, a forced jollity, a making of noise in an endeavour to cheer her, and on top of it all great lavish caresses that helped her not at all.

She looked up suddenly, and saw that her guest was drawing her.

'Do you mind?' he said.

'No,' she said, 'of course not,' wondering what sort of drawing he would make, and she watched his hands, skilful and quick, but she could not see the paper, for it rested against his knee.

'How did William come to be your servant?' she asked.

'His mother was a Breton – you did not know that, I suppose?' he answered.

'No,' she said.

'His father was a mercenary, a soldier of fortune, who some-how or other found his way to France, and married. You must have noticed William's accent.'

'I thought it Cornish.'

'Cornishmen and Bretons are very much alike. Both are Celts. I discovered William first running bare-foot, with torn breeches, about the streets of Quimper. He was in some scrape or other, which I managed to save him from. From then he became one of the faithful. He learnt English, of course, from his father. I believe he lived in Paris for many years, before I fell in with him. I have never delved into William's life history. His past is his own.'

'And why did William decline to become a pirate?'

'Alas! For a reason most prosaic, and unromantic. William has an uneasy stomach. The channel that separates the coast of

Cornwall from the coast of Brittany is too much for him.'

'And so he finds his way to Navron, which makes a most excellent hiding-place for his master?'

'Precisely.'

'And Cornish men are robbed, and Cornish women go in fear of their lives, and more than their lives, so Lord Godolphin tells me?'

'The Cornish women flatter themselves.'

'That is what I wanted to tell Lord Godolphin.'

'And why did you not?'

'Because I had not the heart to shock him.'

'Frenchmen have a reputation for gallantry which is entirely without foundation. We are shyer than you give us credit for. Here – I have finished your portrait.'

He gave her the drawing, and leant back in his chair, his hands in the pockets of his coat. Dona stared at the drawing in silence. She saw that the face that looked up at her from the torn scrap of paper belonged to the other Dona – the Dona she would not admit, even to herself. The features were unchanged, the eyes, the texture of the hair, but the expression in the eyes was the one she had seen sometimes reflected in her mirror, when she was alone. Here was someone with illusions lost, someone who looked out upon the world from a too narrow casement, finding it other than she had hoped, bitter, and a little worthless.

'It is not very flattering,' she said, at length.

'That was not my intention,' he replied.

'You have made me appear older than I am.'

'Possibly.'

'And there is something petulant about the mouth.'

'I dare say.'

'And – and a curious frown between the brows.'

'Yes.'

'I don't think I like it very much.'

'No, I feared you would not. A pity. I might have turned from piracy to portraiture.'

She gave it back to him, and she saw he was smiling.

'Women do not like to hear the truth about themselves,' she said.

'Does anyone?' he asked.

She would not continue the discussion. 'I see now why you are a successful pirate,' she told him, 'you are thorough in your work. The same quality shows itself in your drawings. You go to the heart of your subject.'

'Perhaps I was unfair,' he said. 'I caught this particular subject unawares, when a mood was reflected in her face. Now if I drew you at another time, when you were playing with your children, for example, or simply when you were giving yourself up to the delight of having escaped – the drawing would be entirely differ-ent. Then you might accuse me of flattering you.'

'Am I really as changeable as that?'

'I did not say you were changeable. It just happens that you reflect upon your face what is passing through your mind, which is exactly what an artist desires.'

'How very unfeeling of the artist.'

'How so?'

'To make copy of emotion, at the expense of the sitter. To catch a mood, and place it on paper, and so shame the possessor of the mood.'

'Possibly. But on the other hand the owner of the mood might decide, on seeing herself reflected for the first time, to discard the mood altogether, as being unworthy, and a waste of time.' As he spoke he tore the drawing across, and then again into small pieces. 'There,' he said, 'we will forget about it. And anyway it was an unpardonable thing to do. You told me yesterday that I had been trespassing upon your land. It is a fault of mine, in more ways than one. Piracy leads one into evil habits.'

He stood up, and she saw that he had it in his mind to go.

'Forgive me,' she said, 'I must have seemed querulous, and rather spoilt. The truth is – when I looked upon your drawing – I was ashamed, because for the first time someone else had seen me as I too often see myself. It was as though I had some blemish on my body and you had drawn me naked.'

'Yes. But supposing the artist bears a similar blemish himself, only more disfiguring, need the sitter still feel ashamed?'

'You mean, there would be a bond between them?'

'Exactly.' Once more he smiled, and then he turned, and went towards the window. 'When the east wind starts blowing on this coast it continues for several days,' he said. 'My ship will be weather-bound and I can be idle, and make many drawings. Perhaps you will let me draw you again?'

'With a different expression?'

'That is for you to say. Do not forget you have signed your name in my book, and when the mood comes upon you to make your escape even more complete, the creek is accustomed to fugitives.'

'I shall not forget.'

'There are birds to watch, too, and fishes to catch, and streams to be explored. All these are methods of escape.'

'Which you have found successful?'

'Which I have found successful. Thank you for my supper. Good night.'

'Good night.'

This time the Frenchman did not touch her hand, but went out through the window, without looking back, and she watched him disappear amongst the trees, his hands thrust deep into the pockets of his coat.

Chapter 8

THE air was stifling inside the house, and because of his lady's condition Lord Godolphin had commanded that the windows should be shut, and the curtains drawn across them to screen her from the sun. The brightness of midsummer would fatigue her, the soft air might bring a greater pallor to her already languid cheeks. But lying on the sofa, backed with cushions, exchanging small civilities with her friends, the half darkened room humming with heavy chatter and the warm smell of humanity eating crumbling cake – that could tire nobody. It was both Lord Godolphin's and his lady's idea of relaxation.

'Never again,' thought Dona, 'never again will I be persuaded forth, whether for Harry's or for conscience's sake, to meet my neighbours,' and bending down, feigning an interest in a little lap-dog crouching at her gown, she gave him the damp chunk of cake forced upon her by Godolphin himself. Out of the tail of her eye she saw that her action had been observed, and horror upon horror, here was her host bearing down upon her once again, a fresh assortment in his hands, and she must smile her false, brilliant smile, and bow her thanks and place yet another dripping morsel between her reluctant lips.

'If you could only persuade Harry to forsake the pleasures of the Town,' observed Godolphin, 'we could have many of these small informal gatherings. With my wife in her present state, a large assembly would be prejudicial to her health, but a few friends, such as we have today, can do her nothing but good. I greatly regret that Harry is not here.' He looked about him, satisfied with his hospitality, and Dona, drooping upon her chair, counted once again the fifteen or sixteen persons in the room, who, weary of each other's company over too great a span of years, watched her with apathetic interest. The ladies observed her gown, the new long gloves she played with on her lap, and the hat with the sweeping feather that concealed her right cheek. The men stared dumbly, as though in the front seats at a playhouse, and one or two, with heavy jovial humour, questioned her about the life at Court, and the pleasures of the King, as though the very fact of her coming from London gave her full knowledge of his life and of his habits. She hated gossip for gossip's sake, and though she might have told them much, had she the mind, of the froth and frivolity from which she had escaped, the artificial London, the link-boys with their flares tip-toeing through the dusty cobbled streets, the swaggering gallants standing at the doors of the taverns laughing a little too loudly and singing over-much, that roystering, rather tipsy atmosphere presided over by someone with a brain he would not use, a dark roving eye, and a sardonic smile, she kept silent, saying instead how much she loved the country. 'It is a great pity that Navron is so isolated,' said someone, 'you must find it wretchedly lonely after town. If only we were all a little nearer to you, we could meet more often.'

'How kind of you,' said Dona, 'Harry would greatly appreciate the thought. But, alas, the road is exceedingly bad to Navron. I had great difficulty in coming here today. And then, you see, I am a most devoted mother. My children absorb nearly all my time.'

She smiled upon the company, her eyes large and very innocent, and even as she spoke there came a sudden vision to her mind of the boat that would be waiting for her at Gweek, the fishing lines coiled on the bottom boards, and the man who would be idling there, with coat thrown aside, and sleeves rolled up above the elbows.

'I consider you show remarkable courage', sighed her ladyship, 'in living there all alone, and your husband absent. I find I become uneasy if mine is away for a few hours in the day-time.'

'That is perhaps excusable, under the circumstances,' murmured Dona, quelling an insane desire to laugh, to say something monstrous, for the thought of Lady Godolphin languishing here upon her sofa, and aching for her lord, with that distressing growth upon his nose so wretchedly conspicuous, moved her to wickedness.

'You are, I trust, amply protected at Navron,' said Godolphin, turning to her, solemnly. 'There is much licence and lawlessness abroad these days. You have servants you can trust?'

72

'Implicitly.'

'It is as well. Had it been otherwise I should have presumed upon my old friendship with Harry, and sent you two or three of my own people.'

'I assure you it would be entirely unnecessary.'

'So you may think. Some of us believe differently.'

He looked across at his nearest neighbour, Thomas Eustick, who owned a large estate beyond Penryn – a thin-lipped man with narrow eyes – who had been watching Dona from the other side of the room. He now came forward, and with him also was Robert Penrose, from Tregony. 'Godolphin has told you, I think, how we are menaced from the sea,' he said abruptly.

'By an elusive Frenchman,' smiled Dona.

'Who may not remain elusive very much longer,' replied Eustick.

'Indeed? Have you summoned more soldiers from Bristol?'

He flushed, glancing at Godolphin in irritation.

'This time there will be no question of hired mercenaries,' he said. 'I was against that idea from the first, but as usual was overruled. No, we propose dealing with the foreigner ourselves, and I consider our methods will be effective.'

'Providing enough of us join together,' said Godolphin drily.

'And the most capable amongst us takes the lead,' said Penrose, of Tregony. There was a pause, the three men eyeing one another in suspicion. Had the atmosphere, for some reason or other, become a little strained?

'A house divided against itself will not stand,' murmured Dona.

'I beg your pardon?' said Thomas Eustick.

'Nothing. I was reminded suddenly of a line from the Scriptures. But you were talking about the pirate. One against so many. He will be caught, of course. And what is the plan of capture?'

'It is as yet in embryo, madam, and naturally enough cannot be unfolded. But I would warn you, and I rather think that is what Godolphin meant just now when he inquired about your servants, I would warn you that we suspect some of the country people in the district to be in the Frenchman's pay.'

'You astound me.'

'It is unpardonable, of course, and if our suspicions are verified they will all of them hang, as he will. The fact is we believe the Frenchman to have a hiding-place along the coast, and we believe one or two of the inhabitants must know of this, and are holding their tongues.'

'Have you not made a thorough search?'

'My dear Lady St Columb, we are forever combing the district. But, as you must have heard, the fellow is as slippery as an eel, like all Frenchmen, and he appears to know our coast better than we do ourselves. You have, I suppose, seen nothing of a suspicious nature around Navron?'

'Nothing whatever.'

'The manor commands a view of the river, does it not?'

'A most excellent view.'

'So that you would have seen any strange craft entering or leaving the estuary?'

'Most assuredly.'

'I have no wish to alarm you, but it is possible, you know, that the Frenchman has used Helford in the past, and may yet do so again.'

'You terrify me.'

'And I must warn you that he is the type of man who would have little respect for your person.'

'You mean – he is quite unscrupulous?'

'I fear so.'

'And his men are most desperate and savage?'

'They are pirates, madam, and Frenchmen at that.'

'Then I will take the greatest possible care of my household. Are they, do you think, cannibals also? My baby son is not yet two.'

Lady Godolphin gave a little shriek of horror, and began fanning herself rapidly. Her husband clicked his tongue in annoyance.

'Calm yourself, Lucy, Lady St Columb was jesting, of course. I would assure you, though,' he added, turning to Dona once again, 'that the matter is not a trifling one, nor to be treated with levity. I feel myself responsible for the safety of the people in the district around, and as Harry is not with you at Navron I must admit that I am concerned about you.'

Dona rose to her feet, holding out her hand. 'It is very good of you,' she said, treating him to her special smile, the one she reserved for difficult occasions. 'I shall not forget your kindness, but I assure you there is no need for anxiety. I can, if necessary, bar and bolt my house. And with neighbours such as yourselves' – she glanced from Godolphin to Eustick and to Penrose – 'I am aware that no harm can come to me. You are all three so reliable, so stalwart, so very – if I may say so – English, in your ways.'

The three men bowed over her hand in turn, and she smiled at each of them. 'Perhaps', she said, 'the Frenchman has left our coasts for good, and you need concern yourselves no more about him.'

'I wish we could think so,' said Eustick, 'but we flatter ourselves we are beginning to know the scoundrel. He is always most dangerous when he is most quiet. We shall hear of him again, and that before very long.'

'And', added Penrose, 'he will strike just where we least expect him, under our very noses. But it will be the last time.'

'It will be my very special pleasure', said Eustick slowly, 'to hang him from the tallest tree in Godolphin's park, just before sundown. And invite the company here present to attend the ceremony.'

'Sir, you are very bloodthirsty,' said Dona.

'So would you be, madam, if you had been robbed of your possessions. Pictures, silver, plate – all of considerable value.'

'But think what joy you will have replacing them.'

'I fear I consider the matter in a very different light.' He bowed and turned away, his cheek flushing once again in annoyance.

Godolphin accompanied Dona to her carriage. 'Your remark was somewhat unfortunate,' he said. 'Eustick is very near with his money.'

'I am notorious', said Dona, 'for making unfortunate remarks.'

'No doubt in London they are understood.'

'I think not. That was one of the reasons I came away from London.'

He stared at her without understanding, and handed her into her carriage. 'Your coachman is competent?' he asked, glancing up at William, who alone, and unattended by a footman, held the reins in his hands. 'Very competent,' said Dona. 'I would trust him with my life.'

'He has an obstinate face.'

'Yes – but so amusing, and I adore his mouth.'

Godolphin stiffened, and stepped away from the door of the carriage. 'I am sending letters to town within the week,' he said coldly, 'have you any message for Harry?'

'Only that I am well, and exceedingly happy.'

'I shall take it upon myself to tell him of my anxiety concerning you.'

'Please do not bother.'

'I consider it a duty. Also Harry's presence in the neighbourhood would be of enormous assistance.'

'I cannot believe it.'

'Eustick is apt to be obstructive, and Penrose dictatorial, I am constantly having to make the peace.'

'And you see Harry in the role of peacemaker?'

'I see Harry wasting his time in London, when he should be looking after his property in Cornwall.'

'The property has looked after itself for a number of years.'

'That is beside the point. The fact of the matter is we need all the help we can get. And when Harry knows that piracy is rampant on the coast. . . .'

'I have already mentioned it to him.'

'But not with sufficient force, I am persuaded. If Harry thought for one moment that Navron House itself might be menaced, his possessions stolen, his wife threatened – he would hardly stay in town. Were I in his shoes . . .'

'Yes, but you are not.'

'Were I in his shoes I would never have permitted you to travel west, alone. Women, without their husbands, have been known to lose their heads.'

'Only their heads?'

'I repeat, they have been known to lose their heads in a moment of crisis. You think yourself brave enough now, no doubt, but if

you came face to face with a pirate I dare swear you would shiver
and swoon, like the rest of your sex.'

'I would certainly shiver.'

'I could not say much in front of my wife, her nerves are very
bad at the moment, but one or two ugly rumours have come to
my ears, and Eustick's also.'

'What sort of rumours?'

'Women – er – distressed, and so on.'

'Distressed about what?'

'The country people are dumb, they give nothing away. But
it looks to us as if some of the women in the hamlets hereabouts
have suffered at the hands of these damned scoundrels.'

'Is it not rather unwise to probe into the matter?'

'Why so?'

'You may find they did not suffer at all but, on the contrary,
enjoyed themselves immensely. Drive on, will you, William?'
And bowing and smiling from her open carriage the Lady St
Columb waved her gloved hand to Lord Godolphin.

Down the long avenue they sped, past the peacocks on the
smooth lawns, and the deer in the park, and so out on to the
highway, and Dona, taking off her hat and fanning herself with
it, glanced up at William's stiff back and laughed silently.

'William, I have behaved very badly.'

'So I gathered, my lady.'

'It was exceedingly hot in Lord Godolphin's house, and his
lady had all the windows shut.'

'Very trying, my lady.'

'And I found none of the company particularly to my taste.'

'No, my lady.'

'And for two pins I would have said something perfectly
terrible.'

'Just as well you had no pins upon you, my lady.'

'There was a man called Eustick, and another called Penrose.'

'Yes, my lady.'

'I disliked both equally.'

'Yes, my lady.'

'The fact of the matter is, William, these people are beginning
to wake up. There was much talk of piracy.'

'I overheard his lordship just now, my lady.'

'Talks also of plans of capture, of banding themselves together, of hangings from the tallest tree. And they have their suspicions of the river.'

'I knew it was only a matter of time, my lady.'

'Do you think your master is aware of the danger?'

'I rather think so, my lady.'

'And yet he continues to anchor in the creek.'

'Yes, my lady.'

'He has been here nearly a month. Does he always stay as long as this?'

'No, my lady.'

'What is his usual visit?'

'Five or six days, my lady.'

'The time has gone very quickly. Possibly he does not realize he has been here so long.'

'Possibly not.'

'I am becoming quite knowledgeable about birds, William.'

'So I have noticed, my lady.'

'I am beginning to recognize the many differences in song, and the variations in flight, William.'

'Indeed, my lady.'

'Also I am quite an expert with rod and line.'

'That I have observed, my lady.'

'Your master is an excellent instructor.'

'So it would appear, my lady.'

'It is rather strange, is it not, William, that before I came to Navron I thought very little about birds, and even less of fishing?'

'It is rather strange, my lady.'

'I suppose that – that the desire to know about these things was always present, but lying dormant, if you understand what I mean.'

'I understand your meaning perfectly, my lady.'

'It is difficult for a woman to acquire knowledge of birds and of fishing alone, don't you think?'

'Almost impossible, my lady.'

'An instructor is really necessary.'

'Quite imperative, my lady.'

'But of course the instructor must be sympathetic.'

'That is important, my lady.'

'And fond of – imparting his knowledge to his pupil.'

'That goes without saying, my lady.'

'And possibly, through the pupil, the instructor's own knowledge becomes more perfect. He gains something he did not have before. In a sense, they learn from one another.'

'You have put the matter in a nutshell, my lady.'

Dear William, he was most companionable. He always understood. It was like having a confessor who never reproved or condemned.

'What story did you tell at Navron, William?'

'I said that you were staying to dine at his lordship's, and would be late, my lady.'

'And where will you stable the horses?'

'That is all arranged for. I have friends at Gweek, my lady.'

'To whom you have also spun a story?'

'Yes, my lady.'

'And where shall I change my gown?'

'I thought your ladyship would not be averse to changing behind a tree.'

'How very considerate of you, William. Have you chosen the tree?'

'I have gone so far as to mark one down, my lady.'

The road turned sharply to the left, and they were beside the river once again. The gleam of water shimmered between the trees. William pulled the horses to a standstill. He paused a moment, then put his hand to his mouth and gave a sea-gull's cry. It was echoed immediately from the river bank, just out of sight, and the servant turned to his mistress.

'He is waiting for you, my lady.'

Dona pulled out an old gown from behind the cushion in the carriage, and threw it over her arm. 'Which is the tree you mean, William?'

'The wide one, my lady, the oak with the spreading branches.'

'Do you think me mad, William?'

'Shall we say – not entirely sane, my lady?'

'It is rather a lovely feeling, William.'

'So I have always understood, my lady.'

'One is absurdly happy for no reason – rather like a butterfly.'

'Exactly, my lady.'

'What do you know of the habits of butterflies?'

Dona turned, and William's master stood before her, his hands busy with a line which he was knotting, and which he slipped through the eye of a hook, breaking the loose end between his teeth.

'You walk very silently,' she said.

'A habit of long practice.'

'I was merely making an observation to William.'

'About butterflies I gather. And what makes you so sure of their happiness?'

'One has only to look at them.'

'Their fashion of dancing in the sun you mean?'

'Yes.'

'And you feel like doing the same?'

'Yes.'

'You had better change your gown then. Ladies of the manor who drink tea with Lord Godolphin know nothing of butterflies. I will wait for you in the boat. The river is alive with fish.' He turned his back on her, and went off again to the river bank, and Dona, sheltered by the spreading oak, stripped herself of her silk gown, and put on the other, laughing to herself, while her ringlets escaped from the clasp that held them, and fell forward over her face. When she was ready she gave her silk gown to William, who was standing with his face averted by his horses' heads.

'We shall go down-river with the tide, William, and I will walk up to Navron from the creek.'

'Very good, my lady.'

'I shall be in the avenue shortly after ten o'clock, William.'

'Yes, my lady.'

'And you can drive me to the house as though we were just returning from Lord Godolphin's.'

'Yes, my lady.'

'What are you smiling at?'

'I was not aware, my lady, that my features were in any way relaxed.'

'You are a liar. Good-bye.'

'Good-bye, my lady.'

She lifted her old muslin gown above her ankles, tightening the sash at her waist to keep it in place, and then ran bare-foot through the trees to the boat that was waiting beneath the bank.

Chapter 9

THE Frenchman was fixing the worm on to the line, and looked up with a smile. 'You have not been long.'

'I had no mirror to delay me.'

'You understand now', he said, 'how simple life becomes when things like mirrors are forgotten.' She stepped down into the boat beside him.

'Let me fix the worm on the hook,' she said.

He gave her the line, and taking the long paddles he pushed down-stream, watching her as she sat in the bows of the boat. She frowned, concentrating on her task, and because the worm wriggled she jabbed her fingers with the hook. She swore under her breath and, glancing up, saw that he was laughing at her.

'I can't do it,' she said angrily, 'why must a woman be so useless at these things?'

'I will do it for you directly,' he said, 'when we are farther down-stream.'

'But that is beside the point,' she said. 'I wish to do it myself. I will not be beaten.'

He did not answer, but began whistling softly to himself, and because he took his eye from her, watching a bird flying overhead, saying nothing to her, she settled once again to her task, and presently cried out in triumph, 'I have done it, look, I have done it,' and held up her line for him to see.

'Very good,' he said, 'you are making progress,' and resting on the paddles he let the boat drift with the tide.

Presently, when they had gone some distance, he reached for a large stone under her feet, and fastening this to a long length of rope he threw it overboard, so that they came to anchor, and they sat there together, she in the bows of the boat and he on the centre thwart, each with a fishing-line.

There was a faint ripple on the water, and down with the ebbing tide came little wisps of grass, and a fallen leaf or two. It was very still. The thin wet line between Dona's fingers pulled gently with the tide, and now and again, from impatience, she pulled it in to examine the hook, but the worm remained untouched, save for a dark ribbon of seaweed that clung to the end of the line. 'You are letting it touch the bottom,' he said. She pulled in a length or so, watching him out of the tail of her eye, and when she saw that he did not criticize her method of fishing, or intrude upon her in any way, but continued with his own fishing, quietly content, she let the length of line slip once more between her fingers, and began to consider the line of his jaw, the set of his shoulders, the shape of his hands. He had been drawing as usual, while he waited for her, she supposed, for in the stern of the boat, under some fishing tackle, was a sheet of paper, bedraggled now and wet, and a rough sketch of a flight of sanderling rising from the mud.

She thought of the drawing he had made of her, a day or so ago, and how different it was from that first one he had done, the one he had torn in fragments, for the new drawing had caught her in a laughing mood, leaning over the rail of the ship and watching the comic Pierre Blanc sing one of his outrageous songs, and later he had nailed it up on the bulkhead of his cabin, over the fireplace, scrawling the date at the bottom of the paper.

'Why do you not tear it up, like you did the first?' she had asked.

'Because this is the mood I would capture and remember,' he had said.

'As being more fitting to a member of the crew of *La Mouette*?'

'Perhaps,' he answered, but he would say nothing more. And here he was now, forgetful of his drawing, intent only upon this business of fishing, while only a few miles away there were men who planned his capture, his death, and even at this moment possibly the servants of Eustick, and Penrose, and Godolphin were asking questions along the coast, and in the scattered hamlets of the countryside.

'What is the matter?' he said quietly, breaking in upon her thoughts. 'Do you not want to fish any more?'

'I was thinking about this afternoon,' she said.

'Yes, I know, I could see that by your face. Tell me about it.'

'You should not stay here any more. They are beginning to

suspect. They were all talking about it, gloating over the possibilities of your capture.'

'That does not worry me.'

'I believe them to be serious. Eustick had a hard, obstinate look about him. He is not a pompous dunderhead like Godolphin. He means to hang you from the tallest tree in Godolphin's park.'

'Which is something of a compliment after all.'

'Now you are laughing at me. You think that, like all women, I am afire with rumours and gossip.'

'Like all women you like to dramatize events.'

'And you to ignore them.'

'What would you have me do then?'

'First I would beg you to be cautious. Eustick said that the country people know you have a hiding-place.'

'Very possibly.'

'And one day someone will betray you, and the creek will be surrounded.'

'I am quite prepared for that.'

'How are you prepared?'

'Did Eustick and Godolphin tell you how they proposed to capture me?'

'No.'

'Neither shall I tell you how I propose to evade them.'

'Do you think for one moment I should . . .'

'I think nothing – but I believe you have a fish on your line.'

'You are being deliberately provoking.'

'Not at all. If you don't want to land the fish give the line to me.'

'I do want to land it.'

'Very well then. Haul in your line.'

She proceeded to do so, reluctantly, a little sulky, and then – feeling suddenly the tug and the pull upon the hook – she began to haul faster, the wet line falling upon her lap and down to her bare feet; and laughing at him over her shoulder she said, 'He's there, I can feel him, he's there, on the end of the hook.'

'Not quite so fast,' he said quietly, 'you may lose him. Gently now, bring him to the side of the boat.'

But she would not listen. She stood up in her excitement, letting the line slip for a moment, and then pulled harder than ever, and just as she caught the white gleam of the fish streaking to the surface it jerked upon the line, flashing sideways, and was gone.

Dona gave a cry of disappointment, turning to him with reproachful eyes. 'I have lost him,' she said, 'he has got away.'

He looked up at her, laughing, shaking the hair out of his eyes.

'You were too excited.'

'I can't help it. It was such a lovely feeling – that tug on the line. And I wanted to catch him so much.'

'Never mind. Perhaps you will catch another.'

'My line is all in a tangle.'

'Give it to me.'

'No – I can do it myself.'

He took up his own line once again, and she bent down in the boat, gathering the hopeless tangle of wet line into her lap. It had twisted itself into countless loops and knots, and as she strove to unwind it with her fingers it became more tangled than before. She glanced at him, frowning with vexation, and he stretched out his hand, without looking at her, and took the tangle from her. She thought he would mock her, but he said nothing, and she leant back in the bows of the boat and watched his hands as he unravelled the loops and turns of the long wet line.

The sun, away in the west, was flinging ribbons across the sky, and there were little pools of golden light upon the water. The tide was ebbing fast, gurgling past the bows of the boat.

Farther down the stream a solitary curlew paddled in the mud, and presently he rose in the air, and whistled softly, and was gone.

'When shall we build our fire?' said Dona.

'When we have caught our supper,' he answered.

'And supposing we catch no supper?'

'Then we cannot build a fire.'

She went on watching his hands, and miraculously, it seemed to her, the line became straight again, and loosely coiled, and he threw it once more over the side and gave her the end to hold.

'Thank you,' she said, her voice small, rather subdued, and looking across at him she saw that his eyes were smiling in the secret fashion she had grown to expect from him, and she knew, in some strange way, that the smile was connected with her although he said nothing, and she felt light-hearted suddenly, and curiously gay.

They continued with their fishing, while a single blackbird, hidden in the woods the other side of the river, sang his intermittent song, meditative and sweet.

It seemed to her, as they sat there side by side, without a word, that she had never known peace before, until this moment, that all the restless devils inside her who fought and struggled so often for release, were, because of this silence and his presence, now appeased. She felt, in a sense, like someone who had fallen under a spell, under some strange enchantment, because this sensation of quietude was foreign to her, who had lived hitherto in a turmoil of sound and movement. And yet at the same time the spell awoke echoes within her that she recognized, as though she had come to a place she had known always, and deeply desired, but had lost, through her own carelessness, or through circumstance, or the blunting of her own perception.

She knew that it was this peace that she had wanted when she came away from London, and had come to Navron to find, but she knew also that she had found only part of it alone, through the woods, and the sky, and the river; it became full and complete when she was with him, as at the moment, or when he stole into her thoughts.

She would be playing with the children at Navron, or wandering about the garden, filling the vases with flowers, and he away down in his ship in the creek, and because she had knowledge of him there her mind and her body became filled with life and warmth, a bewildering sensation she had never known before.

'It is because we are both fugitives,' she thought, 'there is a bond between us,' and she remembered what he had said that first evening, when he had supped at Navron, about bearing the same blemish. Suddenly she saw that he was pulling in his line, and she leaned forward in the boat, her shoulder touching his shoulder, and she called excitedly, 'Have you caught something?'

'Yes,' he said, 'do you want to pull it in?'

'It would not be fair,' she said longingly, 'he is your fish.' Laughing, he gave her the line, and she brought the struggling fish to the side of the boat, and landed it on the bottom boards, where it jumped and flapped, coiling itself in the twisted line. She knelt down and seized it between her hands, her dress all wet and muddied from the river, her ringlets falling over her face.

'He is not so big as the one I lost,' she said.

'They never are,' he answered.

'But I caught him, I brought him in all right, did I not?'

'Yes, you did very well.'

She was still kneeling, trying to take the hook out of the mouth of the fish. 'Oh, poor little thing, he is dying,' she said. 'I am hurting him, what shall I do?' She turned to him in great distress, and he came and knelt beside her, taking the fish from her hands and releasing the hook with a sudden jerk. Then he put his fingers in the mouth and bent back the head, so that the fish struggled an instant, and lay dead.

'You have killed him,' she said sadly.

'Yes,' he said, 'was that not what you wanted me to do?'

She did not answer, aware for the first time, now the excitement was over, how close he was to her, their shoulders touching, his hands beside her hands, and that he was smiling again in his silent secret way, and she was filled suddenly with a glow hitherto unknown to her, a brazen, shameless longing to be closer still, with his lips touching hers and his hands beneath her back. She looked away from him, out across the river, dumb and stricken with the new flame that had arisen within her, fearful that he might read the message in her eyes and so despise her, like Harry and Rockingham despised the women at the Swan, and she began to pat her ringlets into place again, and smooth her dress, silly little mechanical gestures she felt could not deceive him, but gave her some measure of protection from her own naked self.

When she was calm again, she threw a glance at him over her shoulder, and saw that he had wound in the lines, and was taking the paddles in his hands.

'Hungry?' he said.

'Yes,' she answered, her voice a little uncertain, not quite her own.

'Then we will build our fire and cook our supper,' he said. The sun had gone now, and the shadows were beginning to creep over the water. The tide was running fast, and he pushed the boat out into the channel so that the current helped to carry them downstream. She curled herself up in the bows and sat with her legs crossed beneath her, her chin cupped in her hands.

The golden lights had gone, and the sky was paler now, mysterious and soft, while the water itself seemed darker than before. There was a smell of moss about the air, and the young green from the woods, and the bitter tang of bluebells. Once, in midstream, he paused, and listened, and turning her head towards the shore she heard, for the first time, a curious churring sound, low and rather harsh, fascinating in its quiet monotony.

'Night-jar,' he said, looking at her an instant, and then away again, and she knew, at that moment, that he had read the message in her eyes a little while before, and he did not despise her for it, he knew and understood, because he felt as she did, the same flame, the same longing. But because she was a woman and he a man these things would never be admitted to one another; they were both bound by a strange reserve until their moment came, which might be tomorrow, or the day after, or never – the matter was not of their own choosing.

He pushed on down-stream without a word, and presently they came to the entrance of the creek, where the trees crowded to the water's edge, and edging up close inshore into the narrow channel they came to a little clearing in the woods where there had once been a quay, and he rested on his paddles and said, 'This?'

'Yes,' she answered, and he pushed the nose of the boat into the soft mud, and they climbed ashore.

He pulled the boat out of the tide, and then reached for his knife, and kneeling beside the water cleaned the fish, calling over his shoulder for Dona to build the fire.

She found some dry twigs, under the trees, and broke them across her knee, her dress torn now and hopelessly crumpled, and she thought, laughing to herself, of Lord Godolphin and his lady, and their stare of bewilderment could they see her now, no better than a travelling gypsy woman, with all a gypsy's primitive feelings too, and a traitor to her country into the bargain.

She built the sticks, one against the other. He came up from the water's edge, having cleaned the fish, and knelt beside the fire, with his flint and tinder, and slowly kindled the flame, which came

88

in a little flash at first, and then burnt brighter. Presently the long sticks crackled and flared, and they looked across the flames and laughed at one another.

'Have you ever cooked fish, in the open?' he asked.

She shook her head, and he cleared a little place in the ashes beneath the sticks, and laid a flat stone in the centre, and placed the fish upon it. He cleaned his knife on his breeches, and then, crouching beside the fire, he waited a few minutes until the fish began to brown, when he turned it with his knife, so that the heat came to it more easily. It was darker here in the creek than it had been in the open river, and the trees threw long shadows down to the quay. There was a radiance in the deepening sky belonging only to those nights of midsummer, brief and lovely, that whisper for a moment in time and go forever. Dona watched his hands, busy with the fish, and glanced up at his face, intent upon his cooking, the brows frowning a little in concentration, and his skin reddened by the glow of the fire. The good food smell came to her nostrils and to his at the same moment, and he looked at her and smiled, saying not a word, but turned the fish once again to the crackling flame.

Then when he had judged it brown enough, he lifted it with his knife on to a leaf, the fish all sizzling and bubbling with the heat, and slicing it down the middle he pushed one half of the fish on to the edge of the leaf, giving her the knife, and taking the other half between his fingers began to eat, laughing at her as he did so.

'It is a pity', said Dona, spearing her fish with the knife, 'that we have nothing to drink.' In answer he rose to his feet, and went down to the boat at the water's edge, coming back in a moment with a long slim bottle in his hands.

'I had forgotten', he said, 'that you were used to supping at the Swan.'

She did not reply at once, stung momentarily by his words, and then, as he poured the wine into the glass he had brought for her, she asked, 'What do you know of my suppers at the Swan?' He licked his fingers, sticky with the fish, and poured some wine into a second glass for himself.

'The Lady St Columb sups cheek by jowl with the ladies of the town,' he said, 'and later roysters about the streets and highways like a boy with his breeches down, returning home as the night-watchman seeks his bed.'

She held her glass between her hands, not drinking, staring down at the dark water, and into her mind suddenly came the thought that he believed her bawdy, promiscuous, like the women in the tavern, and considered that her behaviour now, sitting beside him in the open air at night, cross-legged, like a gypsy, was but another brief interlude in a series of escapades, that she had, in a similar fashion, behaved thus with countless others, with Rockingham, with all Harry's friends and acquaintances, that she was nothing but a spoilt whore, listing after new sensations, without even a whore's excuse of poverty. She wondered why the thought that he might believe this of her should cause her such intolerable pain, and it seemed to her that the light had gone out of the evening, and all the lovely pleasure was no more. She wished suddenly she was back at Navron, at home, in her own room, with James coming in to her, staggering on fat unsteady legs, so that she could pick him up in her arms, and hold him tight, and bury her face in his smooth fat cheek, and forget this new strange anguish that filled her heart, this feeling of sorrow, of lost bewilderment.

'Are you not thirsty after all?' he said, and she turned to him, her eyes tormented, 'No,' she said. 'No, I believe not,' and fell silent again, playing with the ends of her sash.

It seemed to her that the peace of their being together was broken, and a constraint had come between them. His words had hurt her, and he knew that they had hurt her, and as they stared into the fire without a word all the unspoken hidden things flamed in the air, creating a brittle atmosphere of unrest.

At last he broke the silence, his voice very low and quiet.

'In the winter,' he said, 'when I used to lie in your room at Navron, and look at your picture, I made my own pictures of you in my mind. I would see you fishing perhaps, as we did this afternoon, or watching the sea from the decks of *La Mouette*. And somehow, the pictures would not fit with the servants' gossip I had heard from time to time. The two were not in keeping.'

'How unwise of you', she said slowly, 'to make pictures of someone you had never seen.'

'Possibly,' he said, 'but it was unwise of you to leave your portrait in your bedroom, untended and alone, when pirates such as myself made landings on the English coast.'

'You might have turned it', she said, 'with its face to the wall – or even put another in its place, of the true Dona St Columb, roystering at the Swan, and dressing up in the breeches of her husband's friends, and riding at midnight with a mask on her face to frighten old solitary women.'

'Was that one of your pastimes?'

'It was the last one, before I became a fugitive. I wonder you did not hear it, with the rest of the servants' gossip.'

Suddenly he laughed, and reaching to the little pile of wood behind him, he threw fresh fuel on to the fire, and the flames crackled and leapt into the air.

'It is a pity you were not born a boy,' he said, 'you would have discovered then what danger meant. Like myself, you are an outlaw at heart, and dressing up in breeches and frightening old women was the nearest thing to piracy you could imagine.'

'Yes,' she said, 'but you – when you have captured your prize or made your landing – sail away with a sense of achievement, whereas I, in my pitiful little attempt at piracy, was filled with self-hatred, and a feeling of degradation.'

'You are a woman,' he said, 'and you do not care for killing fishes either.'

This time, looking across the fire, she saw that he was smiling at her in a mocking way, and it seemed as though the constraint between them vanished, they were themselves again, and she could lean back on her elbow and relax.

'When I was a lad,' he said, 'I used to play at soldiers, and fight for my king. And then, in a thunderstorm, when the lightning came and the thunder clapped, I would hide my head in my mother's lap and put my fingers in my ears. Also, to make my soldiering more realistic, I would paint my hands red and pretend to be wounded – but when I saw blood for the first time on a dog that was dying, I ran away and was sick.'

'That was like me,' she said, 'that was how I felt, after my masquerade.'

'Yes,' he said, 'that is why I told you.'

'And now,' she said, 'you don't mind blood any more, you are a pirate, and fighting is your life – robbing, and killing, and hurting. All the things you pretended to do and were afraid to do – now you don't mind them any longer.'

'On the contrary,' he said, 'I am often very frightened.'

'Yes,' she said, 'but not in the same way. Not frightened of yourself. Not frightened of being afraid.'

'No,' he said. 'No, that has gone for ever. That went when I became a pirate.'

The long twigs in the fire began to crumple and fall, and to break into fragments. The flames burnt low, and the ashes were white.

'Tomorrow', he said, 'I must begin to plan again.'

She glanced across at him, but the firelight no longer shone upon him, and his face was in shadow.

'You mean – you must go away?' she said.

'I have been idle too long,' he answered, 'the fault lies in the creek. I have allowed it to take a hold on me. No, your friends Eustick and Godolphin shall have a run for their money. I shall see if I can bring them into the open.'

'You are going to do something dangerous?'

'Of course.'

'Will you make another landing along the coast?'

'Very probably.'

'And risk capture, and possibly death?'

'Yes.'

'Why – and for what reason?'

'Because I want the satisfaction of proving to myself that my brain is better than theirs.'

'But that is a ridiculous reason.'

'It is my reason, nevertheless.'

'It is an egotistical thing to say. A sublime form of conceit.'

'I know that.'

'It would be wiser to sail back to Brittany.'

'Far wiser.'

'And you will be leading your men into something very desperate.'

'They will not mind.'

'And *La Mouette* may be wrecked, instead of lying peacefully at anchor in a port across the channel.'

'*La Mouette* was not built to lie peacefully in a port.'

They looked at each other across the ashes, and his eyes held hers for a long instant, with a light in them like the flame that had spent itself in the fire, and at last he stretched himself and yawned, and said: 'It is a pity indeed you are not a boy, you could have come with me.'

'Why must I be a boy to do that?'

'Because women who are afraid of killing fishes are too delicate and precious for pirate ships.'

She watched him a moment, biting the end of her finger, and then she said, 'Do you really believe that?'

'Naturally.'

'Will you let me come this once, to prove to you that you are wrong?'

'You would be sea-sick,' he said.

'No.'

'You would be cold, and uncomfortable, and frightened.'

'No.'

'You would beg me to put you ashore just as my plans were about to work successfully.'

'No.'

She stared at him, antagonistic, angry, and he rose to his feet suddenly, and laughed, kicking the last embers of the fire, so that the glow was gone, and the night became dark.

'How much', she said, 'will you wager that I am sick, and cold, and frightened?'

'It depends', he said, 'what we have to offer each other.'

'My ear-rings,' she said, 'you can have my ruby ear-rings. The ones I wore when you supped with me at Navron.'

'Yes,' he said, 'they would be a prize indeed. There would be little excuse for piracy if I possessed them. And what will you demand of me, should you win your wager?'

'Wait,' she said, 'let me think,' and standing silently a moment beside him, looking down into the water, she said, seized with amusement, with devilry: 'A lock from Godolphin's wig.'

'You shall have the wig itself,' he said.

'Very good,' she said, turning, and making her way down to the boat, 'then we need discuss the matter no further. It is all arranged. When do we sail?'

'When I have made my plans.'

'And you start work tomorrow?'

'I start work tomorrow.'

'I will take care not to disturb you. I too must lay my plans. I think I shall have to become indisposed, and take to my bed, and my malady will be of a feverish sort, so that the nurse and the children are denied my room. Only William will attend me. And each day dear faithful William will bear food and drink to the patient who – will not be there.'

'You have an ingenious mind.'

She stepped into the boat, and seizing the paddles he rowed silently up the creek, until the hull of the pirate ship loomed before them in the soft grey light. A voice hailed them from the ship, and he answered in Breton, and passing on brought the boat to the landing place at the head of the creek.

They walked up through the woods without a word, and as they came to the gardens of the house, the clock in the courtyard struck the half-hour. Down the avenue William would be waiting with the carriage, so that she could drive up to the house as she had planned.

'I trust you enjoyed your dinner with Lord Godolphin,' said the Frenchman.

'Very much so,' she answered.

'And the fish was not too indifferently cooked?'

'The fish was delicious.'

'You will lose your appetite when you go to sea.'

'On the contrary, the sea air will make me ravenous.'

'I shall have to sail with the wind and the tide, you realize that? It will mean leaving before dawn.'

'The best time of the day.'

'I may have to send for you suddenly – without warning.'

'I shall be ready.'

They walked on through the trees, and coming to the avenue, saw the carriage waiting, and William standing beside the horses.

'I shall leave you now,' he said, and then stood for a moment under the shadow of the trees, looking down at her.

'So you will really come?'

'Yes,' she said.

They smiled at one another, aware suddenly of a new intensity of feeling between them, a new excitement, as though the future, which was still unknown to them both, held a secret and a promise. Then the Frenchman turned, and went away through the woods, while Dona came out upon the avenue, under the tall beech trees that stood gaunt and naked in the summer night, the branches stirring softly, like a whisper of things to come.

Chapter 10

IT was William who awoke her, William shaking her arm and whispering in her ear 'Forgive me, my lady, but Monsieur has just sent word, the ship sails within the hour.' Dona sat up in bed at once, all wish for sleep vanishing with his words, and 'Thank you, William,' she said, 'I shall be ready in twenty minutes' time. What hour is it?'

'A quarter to four, my lady.'

He left the room, and Dona, pulling aside the curtains, saw that it was yet dark, the white dawn had not broken. She began to dress hurriedly, her heart beating with excitement and her hands unnaturally clumsy, feeling all the while like a naughty child proceeding to a forbidden venture. It was five days since she had supped with the Frenchman in the creek, and she had not seen him since. Instinct had told her that when he worked he would be alone, and she had let the days go by without walking through the woods to the river, without sending messages even by William, for she knew that when he had laid his plans he would send for her. The wager was not a momentary thing of folly, broached on a summer's night and forgotten before morning, it was a pact by which he would abide, a testing of her strength, a challenge to her courage. Sometimes she thought of Harry, continuing with his life in London, his riding, his gaming, the visits to the taverns, the play-houses, the card-parties with Rockingham, and the images she conjured seemed to her those of another world, a world which concerned her not at all. It belonged, in its strange fashion, to a past that was dead and gone, while Harry himself had become a kind of ghost, a phantom figure walking in another time.

The other Dona was dead too, and this woman who had taken her place was someone who lived with greater intensity, with greater depth, bringing to every thought and every action a new richness of feeling, and an appreciation, half sensuous in its quality, of all the little things that came to make her day.

The summer was a joy and a glory in itself, the bright mornings picking flowers with the children, and wandering with them in the fields and the woods, and the long afternoons, lazy and complete, when she would lie on her back under the trees, aware of the scent of whin, of broom, of bluebells. Even the simple things, the basic acts of eating, drinking, sleeping, had become, since she had been at Navron, a source of pleasure, of lazy still enjoyment.

No, the Dona of London had gone for ever, the wife who lay beside her husband in that great canopied bed in their house in St James's Street, with the two spaniels scratching in their baskets on the floor, the window opened to the stuffy laden air and the harsh street cries of chair-menders and apprentice boys – that Dona belonged to another existence.

The clock in the courtyard struck four, and the new Dona, in an old gown long laid aside to be bestowed upon a cottager, with a shawl about her shoulders, and a bundle in her hands, crept down the stairway to the dining-hall, where William awaited her, a taper in his hand.

'Pierre Blanc is outside, in the woods, my lady.'

'Yes, William.'

'I will supervise the house in your absence, my lady, and see that Prue does not neglect the children.'

'I have every confidence in you, William.'

'My intention is to announce to the household this morning that your ladyship is indisposed – a trifle feverish, and that for fear of infection you would prefer that the children did not come to your room, or the maid-servants, and that you have bidden me wait upon you myself.'

'Excellent, William. And your face, so solemn, will be exactly right for the occasion. You are, if I may say so, a born deceiver.'

'Women have occasionally informed me so, my lady.'

'I believe you to be heartless, William, after all. Are you sure I can trust you all alone amongst a pack of scatter-brained females?'

'I will be a father to them, my lady.'

'You may reprimand Prue if you wish, she is inclined to be idle.'

'I will do so.'

'And frown upon Miss Henrietta if she talks too much.'

'Yes, my lady.'

'And should Master James very much desire a second helping of strawberries –'

'I am to give them to him, my lady.'

'Yes, William. But not when Prue is looking ... afterwards, in the pantry, by yourself.'

'I understand the situation perfectly, my lady.'

'Now I must go. Do you wish you were coming with me?'

'Unfortunately, my lady, I possess an interior that does not take kindly to the motion of a ship upon the water. Your ladyship follows my meaning?'

'In other words, William, you are horribly sick.'

'Your ladyship has a happy turn of phrase. In fact, since we are discussing the matter I am taking the liberty to suggest, my lady, that you should take with you this little box of pills, which I have found invaluable in the past, and which may be of help to you should some unhappy sensation come upon you.'

'How very kind of you, William. Give them to me, and I will put them in my bundle. I have a wager with your master that I shall not succumb. Do you think I shall win?'

'It depends upon what your ladyship is alluding to.'

'That I shall not succumb to the motion of the ship, of course. What did you think I meant?'

'Forgive me, my lady. My mind, for the moment, had strayed to other things. Yes, I think you will win that wager.'

'It is the only wager we have, William.'

'Indeed, my lady.'

'You sound doubtful.'

'When two people make a voyage, my lady, and one of them a man like my master, and the other a woman like my mistress, the situation strikes me as being pregnant with possibilities.'

'William, you are very presumptuous.'

'I am sorry, my lady.'

'And – French in your ideas.'

'You must blame my mother, my lady.'

'You are forgetting that I have been married to Sir Harry for six years, and am the mother of two children, and that next month I shall be thirty.'

'On the contrary, my lady, it was these three things that I was most remembering.'

'Then I am inexpressibly shocked at you. Open the door at once, and let me into the garden.'

'Yes, my lady.'

He pulled back the shutters, and threw aside the long heavy curtains. Something fluttered against the window, seeking an outlet, and as William flung open the door, a butterfly, that had become imprisoned in the folds of the curtains, winged its way into the air.

'Another fugitive seeking escape, my lady.'

'Yes, William.' She smiled at him an instant, and standing upon the threshold sniffed the cool morning air, and looking up saw the first pale streak of the day creep into the sky. 'Good-bye, William.'

'Au revoir, my lady.'

She went across the grass, clutching her bundle, her shawl over her head, and looking back once saw the grey outline of the house, solid and safe and sleeping, with William standing sentinel by the window. Waving her hand to him in farewell she followed Pierre Blanc, with his merry eyes and his dark monkey face and his ear-rings, down through the woods to the pirate ship in the creek.

Somehow she had expected bustle and noise, the confusion of departure, but when they came alongside *La Mouette* there was the usual silence. It was only when she had climbed the ladder to the deck and looked about her that she realized that the ship was ready for sea, the decks were clear, the men standing at their appointed places.

One of the men came forward and bowed, bending his head low.

'Monsieur wishes you to go to the quarter-deck.'

She climbed the ladder to the high poop deck, and as she did so she heard the rattle of the cable in the hawser, the grind of the capstan, and the stamping of feet. Pierre Blanc, the song-maker, began his chant, and the voices of the men, low and soft, rose in the air, so that she turned, leaning over the rail to watch them. Their steady treading upon the deck, the creak of the capstan, and the monotony of their chant made a kind of poetry in the air, a lovely thing of rhythm, all seeming part of the fresh morning and part of the adventure.

Suddenly she heard an order called out behind her, clear and decisive, and for the first time she saw the Frenchman, standing beside the helmsman at the wheel, his face tense and alert, his hands behind his back. This was a different being from the companion of the river who had sat beside her in the little boat and mended her line, and later built a wood fire on the quay and cooked the fish, his sleeves rolled above his elbows, his hair falling into his eyes.

She felt an intruder, a silly woman amongst a lot of men who had work to do, and without a word she went and stood at a distance, against the rail, where she could not bother him, and he continued with his orders, glancing aloft, at the sky, at the water, at the banks of the river.

Slowly the ship gathered way, and the wind of the morning, coming across the hills, filled the great sails. She crept down the creek like a ghost upon the still water, now and again almost brushing the trees where the channel ran inshore, and all the while he stood beside the helmsman, giving the course, watching the curving banks of the creek. The wide parent river opened up before them, and now the wind came full and true from the west, sending a ripple on the surface, and as *La Mouette* met the strength of it she heeled slightly, her decks aslant, and a little whipping spray came over the bulwark. The dawn was breaking in the east, and the sky had a dull haze about it and a glow that promised fine weather. There was a salty tang in the air, a freshness that came from the open sea beyond the estuary, and as the ship entered the main channel of the river the sea-gulls rose in the air and followed them.

The men had ceased their chanting, and now stood, looking towards the sea, an air of expectancy about them, as though they were men who had idled and lazed too long and were suddenly thirsty, suddenly aflame. Once again the spray rose from the top of a high-crested sea, as the ship crossed the bar at the mouth of the estuary, and Dona, smiling, tasted it on her lips, and looking up, saw that the Frenchman had left the helmsman and was standing beside her, and the spray must have caught him too, for there was salt upon his lips and his hair was wet.

'Do you like it?' he said, and she nodded, laughing up at him, so that he smiled an instant, looking towards the sea. As he did so she was filled with a great triumph and a sudden ecstasy, for she knew then that he was hers, and she loved him, and that it was something she had known from the very beginning, from the first moment when she had walked into his cabin and found him sitting at the table drawing the heron. Or before that even, when she had seen the ship on the horizon stealing in towards the land, she had known then that this thing was to happen, that nothing could prevent it; she was part of his body and part of his mind, they belonged to each other, both wanderers, both fugitives, cast in the same mould.

Chapter 11

It was about seven o'clock in the evening, and Dona, coming up on deck, found that the ship had altered course again, and was now standing in once more towards the coast.

The land was a blur as yet upon the horizon, no clearer than a wisp of cloud. All day they had remained at sea, and in mid-channel, with never a sight of another vessel, while a spanking breeze had held for the full twelve hours, causing *La Mouette* to jump and dance like a live thing. Dona understood that the plan was to stay out of sight of land until dusk, and when evening came to creep inshore under cover of darkness. The day therefore had been little more than a filling up of time, with the added chance, of course, of meeting with some merchant vessel carrying a cargo up-channel, which might offer itself for plunder, but such a ship had not been encountered, and the crew, enlivened by the long day at sea, found their appetites whipped now for the adventure that lay before them, and the unknown hazard of the night. One and all seemed possessed by a sense of excitement, a spirit of devilry, they were like boys setting forth upon some foolhardy venture, and Dona, leaning over the rail of the poop deck to watch them, would hear them laugh and sing, cracking jokes with one another, and now and again glancing up in her direction, throwing her a look, a smile, all with a conscious air of gallantry, intensely aware of the presence on board of a woman, who had never sailed with them before.

Even the day was infectious, the hot sun, the fresh westerly breeze, the blue water, and Dona had a ridiculous longing to be a man amongst them, to handle ropes and blocks, to climb aloft to the tall raking spars and trim the sails, to handle the spokes of the great wheel. Now and again the spray broke on the deck, splashing her hands, soaking her gown, but she did not care, the sun would soon dry her clothes, and she found a little patch of dry deck to leeward of the wheel where she sat cross-legged like a gypsy, her shawl tucked into her sash, and the wind playing havoc with her hair. By noon, she was prodigiously hungry, and there came to her, from the bows of the ship, the smell of hot burnt bread and bitter black coffee, and presently she saw Pierre Blanc climb the ladder to the poop, bearing in his hands a tray.

She took it from him, almost ashamed of her eagerness, and he – winking at her with an absurd familiarity which made her laugh, rolled his eyes to heaven and rubbed his stomach.

'Monsieur will join you directly,' he said, smiling, like an accomplice, and she thought how like William they all were in their linking of the two together, and how they accepted it as natural, light-hearted, and lovely.

She fell upon the loaf of bread like a creature ravenous for food, cutting a chunk off the black crust, and there was butter, too, and cheese, and the heart of a lettuce. Presently she heard a step behind her and glancing up she saw the captain of *La Mouette* looking down upon her. He sat by her side and reached for the loaf of bread.

'The ship can take care of herself,' he said, 'and anyway this is her weather, she would keep to her course all day, with a finger to the wheel now and again. Give me some coffee.'

She poured out the steaming brew into two cups, and they drank greedily, watching each other over the rims.

'What do you think of my ship?' he asked.

'I think she is bewitched, and is not a ship at all, for I feel as though I had never been alive before.'

'That is the effect she first had upon me, when I turned to piracy. What is the cheese like?'

'The cheese is also enchanted.'

'And you do not feel sick?'

'I have not felt better in my life.'

'Eat all you can now, because tonight there will be little time for food. Do you want another crust of bread?'

'Please.'

'This wind will hold all day, but this evening it will fall light, and we shall have to creep along the coast, taking full advantage of the tide. Are you happy?'

'Yes. . . . Why do you ask?'

'Because I am happy too. Give me some more coffee.'

'The men are very gay today,' she said, reaching for the jug, 'is it because of tonight, or because they are at sea again?'

'A mixture of both. And they are gay, too, because of you.'

'Why should I make any difference?'

'You are an added stimulation. They will work all the better tonight because of you.'

'Why did you not have a woman on board before?'

He smiled, his mouth full of bread and cheese, but he did not answer.

'I forgot to tell you', she said, 'what Godolphin said the other day.'

'And what did he say?'

'He told me that there were ugly rumours about the countryside, because of the men belonging to your ship. He said that he had heard cases of women in distress.'

'In distress about what?'

'The very thing I asked him. And he replied, to my choking delight, that he feared some of the country-women had suffered at the hands of your damned scoundrels.'

'I doubt if they suffered.'

'So do I.'

He went on munching bread and cheese, glancing aloft now and again at the trim of the sails.

'My fellows never force their attentions upon your women,' he said, 'the trouble generally is that your women won't leave them alone. They creep out of their cottages, and stray upon the hills, if they think *La Mouette* is at anchor near their shores. Even our faithful William has trouble that way, I understand.'

'William is very – Gallic.'

'So am I, so are we all, but pursuit can sometimes be embarrassing.'

'You forget', she said, 'that the country-women find their husbands very dull.'

'They should teach their husbands better manners.'

'The English yokel is not at his best when he makes love.'

'So I have heard. But surely he can improve, upon instruction.'

'How can a woman instruct her husband in the things she does not know herself, in which she has had no tuition?'

'Surely she has instinct?'

'Instinct is not always enough.'

'Then I am very sorry for your country-women.'

He leant on his elbow, feeling in the pocket of his long coat for a pipe, and she watched him fill the bowl with the dark harsh tobacco that had lain once in the jar in her bedroom, and in a minute or two he began to smoke, holding the bowl in his hand.

'I told you once before', he observed, his eyes aloft at his spars, 'that Frenchmen have a reputation for gallantry that is not merited. We cannot all be brilliant our side of the channel, while the blunderers remain on yours.'

'Perhaps there is something in our English climate that is chilling to the imagination?'

'Climate has nothing to do with it, nor racial differences. A man, or a woman for that matter, is either born with a natural understanding of these things or he is not.'

'And supposing, in marriage for example, one partner has the understanding and the other has not?'

'Then the marriage is doubtless very monotonous, which I believe most marriages to be.' A wisp of smoke blew across her face, and looking up she saw that he was laughing at her.

'Why are you laughing?' she said.

'Because your face was so serious, as though you were considering writing a treatise on incompatibility.'

'Perhaps I may do so, in my old age.'

'The Lady St Columb must write with knowledge of her subject, that is essential to all treatises.'

'Possibly I have that knowledge.'

'Possibly you have. But to make the treatise complete you must add a final word on compatibility. It does happen, you know, from time to time, that a man finds a woman who is the answer to all his more searching dreams. And the two have understanding of each other, from the lightest moment to the darkest mood.'

'But it does not happen very often!'

'No, not very often!'

105

'Then my treatise will have to remain incomplete.'

'Which will be unfortunate for your readers, but even more unfortunate for yourself.'

'Ah, but instead of a word on – compatibility, as you phrase it, I could write a page or two on motherhood. I am an excellent mother.'

'Are you?'

'Yes. Ask William. He knows all about it.'

'If you are so excellent a mother what are you doing on the deck of *La Mouette* with your legs tucked up under you and your hair blowing about your face, discussing the intimacies of marriage with a pirate?'

This time it was Dona who laughed, and putting her hands to her hair she tried to arrange the disordered ringlets, tying them behind her ears with a ribbon from her bodice.

'Do you know what Lady St Columb is doing now?' she asked.

'I should love to know.'

'She is lying in bed with a feverish headache and a chill on the stomach, and she will receive no one in her room except William, her faithful servant, who now and again brings her grapes to soothe her fever.'

'I am sorry for her ladyship, especially if she browses on incompatibility as she lies there.'

'She does no such thing, she is far too level-headed.'

'If Lady St Columb is level-headed why did she masquerade as a highwayman in London, and dress herself in breeches?'

'Because she was angry.'

'Why was she angry?'

'Because she had not made a success of her life.'

'And finding she had not made a success, she tried to escape?'

'Yes.'

'And if Lady St Columb tosses on a bed of fever now, regretting her past, who is this woman sitting on the deck beside me?'

'She is a cabin-boy, the most insignificant member of your crew.'

'The cabin-boy has a monstrous appetite, he has eaten up all the cheese, and three-quarters of the loaf.'

'I am sorry. I thought you had finished.'

'So I have.'

He smiled at her, and she looked away, lest he should read her eyes and think her wanton, which she knew herself to be, and did not care. Then, emptying his pipe on the deck, he said: 'Would you like to sail the ship?'

She looked at him once again, her eyes dancing.

'May I? Will she not sink?'

He laughed and rose to his feet, pulling her up beside him, and they went together to the great wheel, where he said a word to the helmsman.

'What do I do?' asked Dona.

'You hold the spokes in your two hands – thus. You keep the ship steady on her course – thus. Do not let her come up too much, or you will catch the big foresail aback. Do you feel the wind on the back of your head?'

'Yes.'

'Keep it there then, and do not let it come forward of your right cheek.'

Dona stood by the wheel, with the spokes in her hands, and after a moment she felt the lifting of the ship, she sensed the movement of the lively hull, and the surge of the vessel as she swept forward over the long seas. The wind whistled in the rigging and the spars, and there was a sound of humming, too, in the narrow triangular sails above her head, while the great square foresail pulled and strained upon its ropes like a live thing.

Down in the waist of the ship the men had perceived the change of helmsman, and nudging one another, and pointing, they laughed up at her, calling to one another in the Breton patois she could not understand, while their captain stood beside her, his hands deep in the pockets of his long coat, his lips framed in a whistle, his eyes searching the seas ahead.

'So there is one thing', he said at last, 'that my cabin-boy can do by instinct.'

'What is it?' she asked, her hair blowing over her face.

'He can sail a ship.'

And laughing, he walked away, leaving her alone with *La Mouette*.

For an hour Dona stood her trick at the wheel, as happy, she thought to herself, as James would be with a new toy, and finally, her arms tiring, she looked over her shoulder to the helmsman she had relieved, who stood by the wheel watching her with a grin on his face, and coming forward he took the wheel from her again, and she went below to the master's cabin and lay down upon his bunk and slept.

Once, opening an eye, she saw him come in and lean over the charts on the table, jotting calculations on a piece of paper, and then she must have fallen asleep again for when she woke the cabin was empty, and rising and stretching herself she went on deck, aware, with a certain sense of shame, that she was hungry again.

It was seven then, and the ship was drawing near to the coast with the Frenchman himself at the wheel. She said nothing, but went and stood by him, watching the blur of the coast on the horizon.

Presently he called out an order to his men, and they began to climb the rigging, little lithe figures, hand over hand, like monkeys, and then Dona saw the great square topsail sag and fall into folds as they furled it upon the yard.

'When a ship comes in sight of land,' he said to her, 'the topsail is the first thing that shows to a landsman ashore. It is still two hours to dusk, and we do not wish to be seen.'

She looked towards the distant coast, her heart beating with a strange excitement, and she was seized, even as he and his men were seized, with the spirit of superb adventure.

'I believe you are going to do something very mad and very foolish,' she said.

'You told me you wanted Godolphin's wig,' he answered.

She watched him out of the tail of her eye, intrigued by his coolness, his quiet steady voice, just the same as it was when he went with her fishing on the river. 'What is going to happen?' she said. 'What are you going to do?'

He did not answer immediately. He called a fresh order to his men, and another sail was furled.

'Do you know Philip Rashleigh?' he said after a while.

'I have heard Harry speak of him.'

'He married Godolphin's sister – but that is by-the-way. Philip Rashleigh is expecting a ship from the Indies, a fact which came to my ears too late, otherwise I should have taken steps to meet her. As it is, I presume her to have arrived at her destination within the last two days. My intention is to seize her, as she lies at anchor, put a prize crew on board, and have them sail her to the opposite coast.'

'But supposing her men outnumbered yours?'

'That is one of the risks I take continuously. The essential thing is the element of surprise, which has never failed me yet.'

He looked down at her, amused by her frown of perplexity, and her shrug of the shoulder, as though she considered him crazy indeed.

'What do you suppose I do', he said, 'when I shut myself in my cabin and make my plans? Do I stake everything on a turn of luck? My men are not idle, you know, when I seek relaxation in the creek. Some of them move about the country, as Godolphin told you, but not with the intention of causing women to be distressed. The distress is a minor detail.'

'Do they speak English?'

'Of course. That is why I choose them for this particular work.'

'You are exceedingly thorough,' she said.

'I dislike inefficiency,' he countered.

Little by little the line of the coast became distinct, and they were entering a great sweeping bay. Away to the west she could see white stretches of sand, turning to shadowed grey now in the gathering dusk. The ship was heading north, sailing towards a dark headland, and as yet there seemed to be no creek or inlet where a vessel could lie at anchor.

'You don't know where we are going?' he asked.

'No,' she answered.

He smiled, saying nothing, and began to whistle softly under his breath, watching her as he did so, so that at last she looked away, knowing that her eyes betrayed her, and his also; they were speaking to each other without words. She looked out over the smooth sea towards the land, the smell of it came to her with the evening breeze, warm cliff grass, and moss, and trees, hot sand where the sun had shone all day, and she knew that this was happiness, this was living as she had always wished to live. Soon there would be danger, and excitement, and the reality perhaps of fighting, and through it all and afterwards they would be together, making their own world where nothing mattered but the things they could give to one another, the loveliness, the silence, and the peace. And then, stretching her arms above her head and smiling, and glancing back at him over her shoulder she said to him, 'Where are we bound then?'

'We are bound for Fowey Haven,' he told her.

Chapter 12

THE night was dark, and very still. What breeze there was came from the north, but here, under the lee of the headland, there was none of it. Only a sudden whistle in the rigging now and again and a ripple across the face of the black water told that a mile or two offshore the breeze still held. *La Mouette* lay at anchor on the fringe of a little bay, and close at hand – so close that you could toss a pebble on to the rocks – rose the great cliffs, shadowy and indistinct in the darkness. The ship had come stealthily to her appointed place, no voices were raised, no commands given as she bore up into the wind to drop anchor, and the cable that dropped through the padded hawser gave a hollow muffled sound. For a moment or so the colony of gulls, nesting in hundreds in the cliffs above, became restive and disturbed, and their uneasy cries echoed against the cliff face and travelled across the water, and then, because there was no further movement, they settled again, and the silence was unbroken. Dona stood against the rail on the poop deck watching the headland, and it seemed to her that there was something eerie in the stillness, something strange, as though they had come unwittingly to a land asleep, whose dwellers lay under a spell, and these gulls that had risen at their approach were sentinels, placed there to give warning. She remembered then that this country and these cliffs, which were another part of her own coast, must be for her, this night at any rate, a hostile place. She had come to enemy territory, and the townsfolk of Fowey Haven, who at this moment were sleeping in their beds, were alien too.

The crew of *La Mouette* were gathered in the waist of the ship, she could see them standing shoulder to shoulder, motionless and silent, and for the first time since she had started on the adventure she was aware of a tiny prick of misgiving, a feminine chill of fear. She was Dona St Columb, wife of an English landowner and baronet, and because of impulsive madness she had thrown in her lot with a pack of Bretons, of whom she knew nothing but that they were pirates and outlaws, unscrupulous and dangerous, led by a man who had never told her anything of himself, whom she loved ridiculously without rhyme or reason, a thing which – if she stayed to consider it in cold blood – would make her hot with shame. It might be that the plan would fail, that he and his men would be captured, and she with them, and the whole band of them would be brought ignominiously to justice, and then it would not be long before her identity would be established, Harry brought hot-foot from London. She could see in a flash the whole story blazed over the country, the horror and the scandal it would cause. A sordid tarnished air would cling upon it, there would be smutty laughter in London amongst Harry's friends, and Harry himself would probably blow his brains out, and the children be orphaned, forbidden to speak her name, their mother who had run away after a French pirate like a kitchen-maid after a groom. The thoughts chased themselves round her head, as she gazed down at the silent crew of *La Mouette*, seeing, in her mind, her comfortable bed at Navron, the peaceful garden, the safety and normality of life with the children. And then, looking up, she saw that the Frenchman was standing beside her, and she wondered how much he could read in her face.

'Come below,' he said quietly, and she followed him, feeling subdued suddenly like a pupil who was to receive chastisement from his master, and she wondered how she would answer him should he chide her for her fear. It was dark in the cabin, two candles gave a feeble glow, and he sat down on the edge of the table considering her, while she stood in front of him, her hands behind her back.

'You have remembered that you are Dona St Columb,' he said.

'Yes,' she answered.

'And you have been wishing, up there on the deck, that you were safe home again, and had never set eyes on *La Mouette*.'

There was no reply to this, the first part of his sentence might be true, but the last could never be. There was silence between them for a moment, and she wondered if all women, when in love, were torn between two impulses, a longing to throw modesty and reserve to the winds and confess everything, and an equal determination to conceal the love forever, to be cool, aloof, utterly detached, to die rather than admit a thing so personal, so intimate.

She wished she were somewhere else, whistling carelessly, hands stuck into breeches pockets, discussing with the captain of the ship the schemes and possibilities of the coming night, or that he was different, another personality, someone for whom she felt no concern, instead of being the one man in the world she loved and wanted.

And there was a flame of anger in her suddenly, that she, who had laughed at love and scorned the sentimental, should be brought, in so few weeks, to such shaming degradation, to such despicable weakness. He got up from the table and opened the locker in the bulkhead, and brought out a bottle and two glasses.

'It is always unwise', he said, 'to set forth upon an adventure with a cold heart and an empty stomach, that is, if one is untrained to adventure.' He poured the wine into a glass, leaving the other empty, and gave the full one to her.

'I shall drink afterwards,' he said, 'when we return.'

She noticed, for the first time, that there was a tray on the sideboard by the door, covered with a napkin, and he went now and brought it to the table. There was cold meat, and bread upon it, and a slice of cheese. 'This is for you,' he said, 'eat it quickly, for time is getting short.' He turned his back on her, busying himself with a chart on the side table, and she began to eat and drink, despising herself already for the reluctance that had come upon her on the deck, and when she had eaten some of the meat, and cut herself a slice of bread and cheese, and had finished the glass of wine he had poured for her, she felt that the doubts and fears would not return, they had been, after all, the outcome of chilled feet and an empty stomach, and he had realized this from the beginning, understanding her mood in his strange incalculable way.

She pushed back her chair, and he turned, hearing the sound, and he was smiling at her, and she laughed at him in return, flushing guiltily, like a spoilt child.

'That is better, is it not?' he said.

'Yes,' she answered, 'how did you know?'

113

'Because the master of the ship makes it his business to know these things,' he said, 'and a cabin-boy must be broken in to piracy rather more gently than the rest of my crew. And now to business.' He picked up the chart he had been studying and she saw that it was a plan of Fowey Haven, and he placed it before her on the table.

'The main anchorage is there, in deep water, opposite the town,' he said, putting his finger on the plan, 'and Rashleigh's vessel will be lying about here, where his vessels always lie, moored to a buoy at the entrance of this creek.'

There was a cross in red upon the plan to indicate the buoy.

'I am leaving part of the crew on board *La Mouette*,' he said, 'and if you wish to, you know, you can stay here with them.'

'No,' she said, 'a quarter of an hour ago I should have said yes, but not now, not any more.'

'Are you certain about that?'

'I have never been more certain about anything in my life.'

He looked down at her in the flickering candle-light, and she felt gay suddenly, and absurdly light-hearted, as though nothing mattered, nothing at all, and even if they were caught and brought to justice and both hanged from the tallest tree in Godolphin's park, it would be worth it, for first there would be this adventure they would have together.

'So Lady St Columb has returned to her sick-bed?' he said.

'Yes,' said Dona, and she looked away from him, down to the plan of Fowey Haven.

'You will remark', he said, 'there is a fort at the entrance of the haven, which is manned, and there are two castles, one on either side of the channel, but these will not be guarded. In spite of the dark night it would be unwise to attempt the passage by boat. Although I have a fair knowledge of your Cornishman by now, and he is a great fellow for sleeping, I cannot guarantee that every man within the fort will have his eyes shut for my benefit. So there is nothing for it but to go overland.'

He paused, and fell to whistling under his breath, considering the plan as he did so. 'This is where we are lying', he said, pointing to a small bay a mile or so to the eastward of the haven, 'and I propose going ashore here, on this beach. There is a rough

114

path up the cliffs, and then we strike inshore and come to a creek – something similar to the creek we have left at Helford but possibly less enchanting – and at the entrance to the creek, in face of the town of Fowey, we shall find Rashleigh's ship.'

'You are very sure of yourself,' she said.

'I could not be a pirate if I were not. Can you climb cliffs?' he said.

'If you would lend me a pair of your breeches I could climb better,' she said.

'That is what I thought', he told her, 'there is a pair belonging to Pierre Blanc on the bunk there, he keeps them for Saints' days and confession, so they should be clean enough. You can try them on directly. He can lend you a shirt too and stockings and shoes. You will not need a jacket, the night is too warm.'

'Shall I cut off my hair with a pair of scissors?' she said.

'You would look more like a cabin-boy perhaps, but I would rather risk capture than have you do it,' he answered.

She said nothing for a moment, for he was looking at her, and then,

'When we reach the shores of the creek, how do we get to the ship?' she asked.

'We will get to the creek first and then I will tell you,' he said.

He reached down for the plan, and folded it up, throwing it back in the locker, and she saw he was smiling to himself in his secret way.

'How long will it take you to change your clothes?' he asked.

'Five minutes or longer,' she said.

'I will leave you then. Come up on deck when you are ready. You will want something to tie up those ringlets.' He opened a locker drawer, and ruffling there a moment, drew out the crimson sash he had worn round his waist the night he had supped with her at Navron. 'Lady St Columb becomes a highwayman and a mountebank for the second time in her life', he said, 'but this time there won't be any old lady for you to frighten.'

Then he went out of the cabin, shutting the door behind him. When she joined him, some ten minutes later, he was standing by the ladder that had been thrown over the ship's side. The first party had already gone ashore, while the rest were now assembled in the boat below. She went towards him a little nervously, feeling small and rather lost in Pierre Blanc's breeches, while his shoes cut her heels, a secret she must keep to herself. He ran his eye over her and then nodded briefly. 'You will do', he said, 'but you would not pass in moonlight,' and she laughed up at him, and climbed down into the boat with the rest of the men. Pierre Blanc himself was crouching in the bows of the boat like a monkey, and when he saw her he closed one eye, and put one hand over his heart. There was a ripple of laughter in the boat, and one and all they smiled at her with a mingled admiration and familiarity that could not offend, and she smiled back at them, leaning back in the stern thwart and clasping her knees with a lovely freedom, no longer hampered by petticoats and ribbons.

The captain of *La Mouette* descended last, and he took his seat beside her, holding the tiller, and the men bent to their oars and the boat sped across the little bay to the shingle beach beyond. Dona trailed her hand a moment in the water, which was warm, with a velvet softness about it, the phosphorescence gleaming like a shower of stars, and she thought, smiling to herself in the darkness, that at last she was playing the part of a boy, which as a child she had so often longed to be, watching her brothers ride off with her father, and she gazing after them with resentful eyes, a doll thrown aside on the floor in disgust. The bows of the boat touched the shingle, and the first group of men, waiting there on the beach, laid their hands on either side of the gunwale and pulled the boat out of the wash. They had disturbed the gulls again, and two or three pairs rose with a wailing cry and a flapping of wings.

Dona felt the shingle crunch under her heavy shoes, and she could smell the turf on the cliffs above. Then the men turned to the narrow path that skirted the cliff face like a snake, and they began to climb. Dona set her teeth, for the climb would be a hard one in these shoes that did not fit, and then she saw the Frenchman beside her, and he took her hand, and they climbed the cliff together, she holding on to him for all the world like a small boy clasping his parent. Once they paused for breath, and looking back over her shoulder, she could see the dim outline of *La Mouette* anchored in the bay, and the sound of muffled oars as the boat that had put them ashore crept back across the water. The gulls had settled again, and now there was no sound but the small scraping noises of the men's feet as they climbed the path ahead, and away below the wash of the sea as it broke upon the shore.

'Can you go on again now?' the Frenchman said, and she nodded, and his grasp on her hand tightened; so she felt little strain on her back or her shoulders, and she thought to herself, happily, brazenly, that this was the first time he had touched her, and the strength of his hand was good to feel. When the cliff was scaled there was still much climbing to be done, for the going was rough, and the young bracken already knee-high, and he continued to lead her after him, while his men spread themselves fan-wise across country, so that she could no longer count their numbers. He had studied his map carefully, of course, and they too, she supposed, for there was no faltering in their steps or his, and no pause to reconnoitre, and all the while her clumsy shoes rubbed the sides of her feet, and she knew there was a blister on her right heel the size of a gold piece.

Now they were descending again, having crossed a cart track that no doubt served as a road, and at last he dropped her hand, and struck off a little in front, she following close behind like a shadow. Once, away to the left, she fancied she caught a glimpse of a river, but soon it was lost again, they were walking under cover of a hedge, and then down once more, through bracken and undergrowth and gorse – the smell of it warm in the air like honey – and so at last to thick stunted trees crouching by the water's edge, and there was a narrow strip of beach, and a creek in front of them, opening out into a harbour with a little town beyond.

They sat down under cover of the trees, and waited; and presently, one by one, came the ship's company, silent figures slipping towards them out of the darkness.

The captain of *La Mouette* called their names softly, and when they had answered, each one in turn, and he knew they were all together, he began to speak to them in the Breton that Dona could not understand. Once he looked out across the creek and pointed, and Dona saw the dim outline of a ship at anchor; she was swinging now, the bows pointing up-stream towards them as the first of the ebb-tide bubbled down the channel.

There was a riding-light high in the rigging, but otherwise no sign of life, and now and again there came a hollow creaking sound across the water as the ship swerved at the buoy to which she was moored. There was something desolate in this sound, something mournful, as though the ship had been abandoned and was a lost thing, and then with the sound came a little ripple of wind down the creek from the harbour, and the Frenchman, raising his head sharply and looking west towards the little town, frowned a moment, and turned his cheek to the breeze.

'What is it?' whispered Dona, for she felt instinctively that suddenly, for some reason, all was not well, and he waited a second or two before replying, still sniffing the air like an animal for scent, and then, 'The wind has backed to the south-west,' he said briefly.

Dona turned her cheek in the direction of the wind, and she, too, saw that the breeze that had blown off the land for the past twenty-four hours was now coming from the sea, and there was a tang about it that was different, a wet salt smell, and it came in gusts. She thought of *La Mouette* lying at anchor in the little bay, and she thought too of this other ship, moored here in the creek, and how the tide now was their only ally, for the wind had changed sides and had become a hostile force.

'What are you going to do?' she asked, but he did not answer, he had risen to his feet, and was making his way down over the slippery rocks and the dank sea-weed to the strip of beach beside the creek, and the men followed him without a word, each in turn looking upwards at the sky, and to the south-west where the wind blew.

They all stood there on the beach, looking out across the creek to the silent vessel, and now there was a strong ripple upon the water, for the wind was blowing against the ebb-tide, and the sound of the hollow cable straining against the buoy became louder than before. Then the captain of *La Mouette* walked a little way apart, and he beckoned to Pierre Blanc, who went to him, and stood listening to his master, his monkey-head nodding now and again in understanding. When they had finished, the Frenchman came to Dona, and stood beside her, and he said, 'I have just told Pierre Blanc to take you back to *La Mouette*.'

She felt her heart beat suddenly in her breast, and a chill feeling come over her, and 'Why?' she said, 'why do you want me to go?' Once more he looked up at the sky, and this time a spot of rain fell on to his cheek.

'The weather is going to play us false,' he said. '*La Mouette* is now on a lee-shore, and the men I left on board will be making ready to beat out of the bay. You and Pierre Blanc will have time to return and hail her before they get sail on her.'

'I understand', she said, 'about the weather. It is going to be difficult for you to get the ship away. Not *La Mouette* I mean, but this ship. You no longer have the wind and the tide with you. That is why you want me to go back to *La Mouette*, is it not? In case there is trouble.'

'Yes,' he said.

'I am not going,' she said.

He did not answer, and she could not see the expression on his face for he was looking out once more towards the harbour.

'Why do you want to stay?' he said at last, and there was something in his voice that made her heart beat afresh, but for another reason, and she remembered the evening they had gone fishing on the river and he had said the word 'Night-jar' to her, in the same voice, with the same softness.

A wave of recklessness came upon her, and 'What does it matter?' she thought, 'why do we go on pretending, we may both die tonight, or tomorrow, and there will be so much that we shall not have had together.' And digging her nails in her hands and looking out with him across the harbour she said with sudden passion: 'Oh, death and damnation, you know why I want to stay.'

She felt him turn and look at her, and away again, and then he said, 'I wanted you to go, for the same reason.'

Once more there was silence between them, each one searching for words, and if they had been alone there would have been no need for speaking, for the shyness that had been a barrier between them had dissolved suddenly, as though it had never been, and he laughed, and reached for her hand, and kissed the palm of it, saying, 'Stay then, and we will make a fight for it, and hang together from the same tree, you and I.'

Once more he left her, and beckoned again to Pierre Blanc, who grinned all over his face because the orders were changed. But now the spots of rain increased, the clouds had gathered in the sky, and the south-west wind was blowing in gusts down the creek from the harbour.

'Dona', he called, using her name for the first time, but carelessly, easily, as though he had always done so, and 'Yes', she answered, 'what is it, what do you want me to do?'

'There is no time to lose', he said, 'we must get the ship under way before the wind strengthens. But first we must have the owner on board.'

She stared at him as though he was crazy.

'What do you mean?' she said.

'When the wind was off the land', he told her briefly, 'we could have sailed her out of Fowey Haven before the lazy fellows ashore had rubbed the sleep out of their eyes. Now we shall have to beat out, or even warp her through the narrow channel between the castles. Philip Rashleigh will be safer on board his own vessel than raising the devil ashore, and sending a cannonball across our bows as we pass the fort.'

'Are those not rather desperate measures?' she said.

'No more desperate than the undertaking itself,' he answered.

He was smiling down at her, as though nothing mattered, and he did not care. 'Would you like to do something with a spice of danger in it?' he asked.

'Yes,' she said, 'tell me what to do.'

'I want you to go with Pierre Blanc and find a boat,' he said. 'If you walk a little way along the shores of the creek here, towards the harbour entrance, you will come to some cottages, on the hill-side, and a quay. There will be boats moored there by the quay. I want you and Pierre Blanc to take the nearest boat you find and cross over to Fowey town, and go ashore, and call on Philip Rashleigh.'

'Yes,' she said.

'You won't mistake his house,' he said, 'it is hard by the

120

church, facing the quay. You can see the quayside from here. There is a light upon it now.'

'Yes,' she said.

'I want you to tell him that his presence is urgently required on board his ship. Make up any story you like, play any part you have a fancy for. But keep in the shadow. You are a passable enough cabin-boy in darkness, but a woman under the light.'

'Suppose he refuses to come?'

'He will not refuse, not if you are clever.'

'And if he suspects me, and keeps me there?'

'I shall deal with him then.'

He walked to the water's edge, and the men followed him. Suddenly she knew why they none of them wore jackets, why one and all were hatless, and why they now kicked off their shoes, tying them round their necks with a cord through the buckle. She looked out towards the ship, straining at her moorings there in the creek, the riding-light swaying to the freshening wind, while the men on board her slept soundly; and she thought of those silent trespassers who would come upon her out of the darkness. No creaking of oars in the night, no shadows of boats, but a wet hand stretching from the water upon the chain, and a wet foot-mark upon the fo'c'sle head, and lithe dripping figures dropping down upon her decks, a whisper, and a whistle, and a strangled smothered cry.

She shivered for no reason, except that she was a woman, and turning to her from the water he smiled at her and said, 'Go now, turn your back on us, and go,' and she obeyed him, stumbling once more across the rocks and the seaweed, with little Pierre Blanc trotting at her heels like a dog. Not once did she look back over her shoulder to the river, but she knew that they were all swimming now to the ship, that the wind was blowing stronger every moment, and the tide was running swiftly. She lifted her face, and then the rain began to fall, hard and fast, from the south-west.

Chapter 13

DONA crouched in the stern of the little boat, the rain beating on her shoulders, and Pierre Blanc fumbled in the darkness for the paddles. Already there was a run in the pool where the boats were anchored, and a white wash was breaking against the steps of the quay. There was no sign of life from the cottages on the side of the hill, and they had taken the first boat to hand without difficulty. Pierre Blanc pulled out into mid-channel, and as soon as they opened up the harbour entrance they met the full force of the rising wind, which, with the strong ebb-tide, set up a short cross-sea that splashed over the low gunwale of the small boat. The rain came fiercely, blotting out the hills, and Dona, shivering in her thin shirt, felt something of hopelessness in her heart, and she wondered if perhaps it was all her fault, she had broken the luck, and this was to be the last adventure of *La Mouette*, which had never before sailed with a woman on board.

She looked at Pierre Blanc as he strained at the paddles, and now he was no longer smiling, he kept glancing across his shoulder at the harbour mouth. They were coming closer to the town of Fowey, she could see a group of cottages by the side of the quay, and above them rose the tower of a church.

The whole adventure had become suddenly like an evil dream from which there could be no waking, and little Pierre Blanc with his monkey face was the partner of it.

She leant forward to him, and he rested a moment on his paddles, the boat rocking in the trough of a short sea.

'I shall find the house alone,' she said, 'and you must wait for me in the boat, by the side of the quay.'

He glanced at her doubtfully, but she spoke with urgency, laying her hand on his knee. 'It is the only way,' she said, 'and then if I do not return in half-an-hour, you must go at once to the ship.'

He seemed to turn her words over in his mind, and then he nodded, but still he did not smile, poor Pierre Blanc who had never been serious before, and she guessed that he too sensed the hopelessness of the adventure. They drew close to the quay, and the sickly lantern light shone down upon their faces. The water surged round the ladder, and Dona stood up in the stern of the boat, and seized the rungs in her hand. 'Do not forget, Pierre Blanc,' she said, 'you are not to wait for me. Give me a half-hour only,' and she turned swiftly, so that she should not see his anxious troubled face. She went past the few cottages towards the church, and came to the one house standing in the street, by the side of the hill.

There was a light in the lower casement, she could see the glow of it through the drawn curtains, but the street itself was deserted. She stood beneath the casement uncertainly, blowing on her cold fingers, and it seemed to her, not for the first time, that this scheme of summoning Philip Rashleigh was the most foolhardy of the whole enterprise, for surely he would soon be abed and asleep and therefore would give them no trouble. The rain beat down upon her, and she had never felt more lonely, never more helpless and more lost to action.

Suddenly she heard the casement above her head open, and in panic she flattened herself against the wall. She could hear someone lean his elbows on the sill, and the sound of heavy breathing, and then there was a scattering of ashes from a pipe, they fell upon her shoulder, and a yawn and a sigh. There was a scraping of a chair in the room within, and whoever had moved the chair asked a question and he by the window made reply in a voice that was startlingly familiar. 'There is a gale of wind blowing up from the south-west,' said Godolphin, 'it is a pity now that you did not moor the ship up the river after all. They may have trouble with her in the morning if this weather holds.'

There was silence, and Dona could feel her heart thumping in her side. She had forgotten Godolphin, and that he was brother-in-law to Philip Rashleigh. Godolphin, in whose house she had taken tea less than a week before. And here he was, within three feet of her, dropping the ash from his pipe on to her shoulder.

The foolish wager of the wig came to her mind, and she realized then that the Frenchman must have known that Godolphin would be staying with Philip Rashleigh in Fowey that night, and that side by side with the capture of the ship he had planned the seizing of Godolphin's wig.

In spite of her fear and her anxiety she smiled to herself, for surely this was sublime folly if anything was, that a man could so risk his life for the sake of a crazy wager. The thought of it made her love him the more, that besides those qualities of silence and understanding that had drawn her to him in the beginning, he should have this total indifference to the values of the world, this irrepressible madness.

Godolphin was still leaning at the open casement, she could hear his heavy breathing and his yawns, and the words he had just spoken lingered in her mind, his reference to the ship, and the moving of her up-river. An idea began to shape in her brain, whereby the summoning of the owner on board would seem legitimate; then the other voice spoke abruptly from the room inside, and the casement was suddenly closed. Dona thought rapidly, reckless now of capture, the whole crazy folly of the night rousing in her the old choking sensation of delight she had known months ago when superbly indifferent to gossip and more than a little drunk she had roystered in the streets of London.

Only this time the adventure was real, and not a practical joke trumped up to alleviate the boredom of the small hours when the London air was stifling, and Harry too insistent in his claims. She turned away from the window, and went to the door, and without hesitation jangled the great bell that hung outside.

The sound was greeted by the immediate barking of dogs, and then footsteps, and the drawing of bolts, and to her consternation Godolphin himself stood there, a taper in his hand, his great bulk filling the doorway. 'What do you want?' he said angrily, 'don't you know the hour, it's close on midnight, and everyone abed.'

Dona crouched back out of the light, as though timid at the reception he gave her. 'Mr Rashleigh is wanted,' she said, 'they sent me for him. The master is anxious to move the ship now, before the gale worsens.'

'Who is it?' called Philip Rashleigh from within, and all the while the dogs were barking and scratching at her legs, and Godolphin was kicking them back. 'Down, Ranger, you devil, get back, Tancred,' and then, 'Come inside, boy, can't you?'

'No, sir, I'm wet through to the skin, if you would please tell Mr Rashleigh they have sent for him, from the ship,' and already she began to edge away, for he was staring down at her, his brows drawn together in perplexity, as though there was something about her appearance that he did not understand, that was irregular. Once more Philip Rashleigh called out in irritation from the room within: 'Who the devil is it then, is it Dan Thomas's boy, from Polruan, is it young Jim?'

'Not so fast, then,' called Godolphin, laying a hand upon Dona's shoulder. 'Mr Rashleigh would talk to you, is your name Jim Thomas?'

'Yes, sir,' said Dona, snatching insanely at the straw he offered her, 'and the matter is urgent, the master says would Mr Rashleigh go on board at once, there is no time to lose, the ship is in danger. Let me go, sir, I have another message to deliver, my mother is desperately ill, I must run now for the physician.'

But still Godolphin kept his hand on her shoulder, and now he brought the taper close to her face. 'What have you round your head?' he said. 'Are you ill, also, as well as your mother?'

'What is all this nonsense?' shouted Rashleigh, coming into the hall, 'Jim Thomas's mother has been in her grave these ten years. Who is it? what is wrong with the ship?' and now Dona shook herself clear from the hand that held her, and calling to them over her shoulder to make haste, the gale was freshening all the while, she ran across the square and down to the quay, hysterical laughter rising in her throat, with one of Rashleigh's dogs barking at her heels.

She pulled up sharply just short of the quay, taking refuge in the doorway of a cottage, for there was someone standing there by the ladder who had not been before, and he was staring out across the harbour towards the entrance of the creek. He carried a lantern in his hand, and she guessed that he must be the night-watchman of the town, making his rounds, and now, through very cussedness it seemed to her, had taken up a position on the quay. She dared not venture forward until he had gone, and anyway Pierre Blanc would have taken the boat some little distance away, at sight of the night-watchman.

She sheltered there in the doorway, watching the man, and

biting at her finger-nails in anxiety, and still he stared out across the harbour towards the creek, as though there was something there which engaged his attention, some movement. A little sick feeling stole over her, for perhaps after all the boarding of the ship had not gone according to plan, and even now the crew of *La Mouette* were struggling in the water, and their leader with them, or the resistance had been stronger than they had expected, and they were fighting now on the decks of Rashleigh's ship, and it was these sounds that the night-watchman could hear, straining his eyes across the water. She could do nothing to help them; as it was she had probably drawn suspicion upon herself, and even as she stood there helpless in the doorway she heard the sound of voices, and footsteps, and round the corner of the street came Rashleigh himself and Godolphin, clad in great-coats against the weather, and Rashleigh with a lantern in his hand.

'Ho, there,' he called, and the night-watchman turned at his voice and hurried to meet him.

'Have you seen a lad run this way?' said Rashleigh, but the watchman shook his head. 'I have seen no one,' he said, 'but there is something amiss yonder, sir, it looks as though your vessel has broken from the buoy.'

'What's that?' said Rashleigh, making towards the quay, and Godolphin, following him, said, 'Then the lad did not lie after all.' Dona crouched back in the doorway. They were past her now, and on to the quay, never once looking in the direction of the cottage. She watched them from the cover of the door, and they were standing with their backs to her, staring across the harbour as the watchman had done, and Godolphin's cape was billowing in the gusty wind, while the rain streamed down upon their heads.

'Look, sir,' called the watchman, 'they are getting sail on her, the master must be going to take her up-river.'

'The fellow is crazy,' shouted Rashleigh, 'there are not a dozen men on board, three-quarters of the fellows are sleeping ashore, they'll have her aground before they've finished. Go rouse some of 'em, Joe, we must get all hands on to her. Blast that incompetent fool Dan Thomas, what in the name of the Almighty does he think he is doing?'

He put his hands to his mouth and bellowed across the harbour.

'Ahoy, there! *Merry Fortune*, Ahoy!' and the night-watchman sped across the quay, and seized the rope of a ship's bell that was hanging there beside the lantern, and the sound of it clanged in the air, loud and insistent, compelling enough to waken every sleeping soul in Fowey. Almost at once a window was thrust open in a cottage up the street, and a head looked out and said, 'What ails you, Joe, is anything wrong?' and Rashleigh, stamping up and down in a blind fury shouted back, 'Put your breeches on, damn you, and get your brother too, the *Merry Fortune* is adrift there in the harbour.'

A figure came out from a doorway in another cottage, struggling into a coat as he emerged, and another man came running down the street, and all the while the ship's bell clanged, and Rashleigh shouted, and the rain and the wind tore at his cloak and the swaying lantern he carried in his hand.

Lights appeared now in the windows of the cottages beneath the church and voices shouted, and voices called, and men appeared from nowhere, running on to the quay. 'Get me a boat, can't you?' yelled Rashleigh, 'put me aboard, one of you, put me aboard.'

Someone was astir in the cottage where Dona had been hiding, she heard the patter of footsteps on the stairs, and she left the doorway and came out upon the quay. In the darkness and confusion, in the whistling wind and the streaming rain, she was only another figure mixing with the rest, staring out towards the ship that with sails hoisted on her yards was bearing down now towards the centre of the channel, her bows pointing to the harbour mouth.

'Look, she's helpless,' cried a voice, 'the tide is taking her to the rocks, they must be mad aboard, or dead drunk, all of them.'

'Why doesn't he wear ship and get up, out of it,' shouted another, and 'Look, the tide has her,' came the answer, and someone else, shrieking in Dona's ear, 'The tide is stronger than the wind yet, the tide has her every time.'

Some of the men were struggling now with the boats moored beneath the quay, she could hear them swear as they fumbled with a frape, and Rashleigh and Godolphin, peering down from the side of the quay, cursed them for the delay. 'Someone's monkey'd here with the frape,' shouted one of the men, 'the rope is parting, someone must have cut it with a knife,' and suddenly Dona had a vision of little Pierre Blanc, grinning to himself in the darkness, while the great bell clanged and jangled on the quay.

'Swim, one of you,' yelled Rashleigh, 'swim and bring me a boat. By God, I'll thrash the fellow who played the trick, I'll have him hanged.'

Now the ship was coming closer, Dona could see the men on the yards, and the great topsail shaking out, and someone was at the wheel there giving orders, someone with head thrown back, watching the sail draw taut.

'Ahoy, there! Ahoy!' yelled Rashleigh, and Godolphin too added his cry, 'Wear ship, man, wear ship before you lose your chance.'

And still the *Merry Fortune* held to her course; straight down channel and across the harbour she came, the ebb-tide ripping under her keel. 'He's crazy,' screamed someone, 'he's making for the harbour mouth, look there, all of you, look there.' For now that the ship was within hail Dona could see that there were three boats out in a line abreast, with a warp from the ship to each of them, and every man in them bent double to his oars, and still the topsail filled and pulled, and the courses too, and the ship heeled to a great puff of wind that came from the hills behind the town.

'He is going to sea,' shouted Rashleigh, 'by God, he is taking her to sea,' and suddenly Godolphin turned, and his great bulbous eyes fell upon Dona, who in her excitement had crept close to the edge of the quay. 'There's that boy,' he called, 'he is to blame for this, catch him, one of you, catch that boy there.' Dona turned, ducking swiftly under the arm of an old man who stared at her blankly, and she began to run, blindly, away from the quay and straight up the lane past Rashleigh's house, away from the church, and the town, towards the cover of the hills, while behind her she could hear a man shouting, and the sound of running feet, and a voice calling 'Come back, will you, come back, I say.'

There was a path to her left, winding amongst the gorse and the young bracken, and she took it, stumbling on the rough ground in her clumsy shoes, the rain streaming in her face, and down below her she caught a gleam of the harbour water and could hear the wash of the tide against the cliff wall.

Her only thought was to escape, to hide herself from those questing, bulbous eyes of Godolphin, for Pierre Blanc was lost to her now, and the *Merry Fortune* fighting her own battle in mid-harbour.

She ran on in the wind and the darkness, the path taking her along the side of the hill to the harbour mouth, and even now it seemed to her that she could hear the hideous clanging of the ship's bell on that quay, rousing the people of the town, and she could see the angry figure of Philip Rashleigh hurling curses upon the men who struggled with the frape. The path began to descend at last, and pausing in her headlong flight, and wiping the rain from her face, she saw that it led down to a cove by the harbour mouth, and then wound upwards again to the fort on the headland. She stared in front of her, listening to the sound of the breakers below, and straining her eyes for a glimpse of the *Merry Fortune*, and then, glancing back over her shoulder, she saw a pin-prick of light advancing towards her down the path, and she heard the crunch of footsteps.

She flung herself down among the bracken, and the footsteps drew nearer, and she saw it was a man bearing a lantern in his hand. He walked swiftly, looking neither to the right nor left of him, and he went straight past her, down to the cove, and then up again towards the headland; she could see the glimmer of his lantern as he climbed the hill. She knew then that he was going to the fort, Rashleigh had sent him to warn the soldiers on duty at the fort. Whether suspicion had crossed his mind at last, or whether he still thought that the master of the *Merry Fortune* had lost his wits and was taking his ship to disaster, she could not tell, nor did it matter very much. The result would be the same. The men who guarded the entrance to the harbour would fire on the *Merry Fortune*.

And now she ran down the path to the cove, but instead of climbing to the headland as the man with the lantern was doing, she turned left along the beach, scrambling over the wet rocks and the sea-weed to the harbour mouth itself. It seemed to her that she was looking once again at the plan of Fowey Haven. She saw the narrow entrance, and the fort, and the ridge of rocks jutting out from the cove where she now found herself, and in her mind was the one thought that she must reach those rocks before the ship came to the harbour mouth, and in some way warn the Frenchman that the alarm had been sent to the fort.

She was sheltering momentarily, under the lee of the head-land, and no longer had to fight her way against the wind and the rain, but her feet slipped and stumbled on the slippery rocks, still running wet where the tide had left them, and there were cuts on her hands and her chin where she had fallen, while the hair that had come loose from the sash that bound it blew about her face.

Somewhere a gull was screaming. Its persistent cry echoed in the cliffs above her head, and she began to curse it, savagely and uselessly, for it seemed to her that every gull now was a sentinel, hostile to herself and to her companions, and this bird who wailed in the darkness was mocking her, crying that all her attempts to reach the ship were useless.

In a moment or two the ridges of rocks would be within reach, she could hear the breakers, and then, raising herself on her hands and looking forward, she saw the *Merry Fortune* bearing down towards the harbour mouth, the short seas breaking over her bows. The boats that had towed her were hoisted now on deck, and the men that had manned them were thronging the ship's side, for suddenly and miraculously the wind had shifted a point or two to the west, and with the strong ebb under her the *Merry Fortune* was sailing her way seaward. There were other boats upon the water now, little craft coming in pursuit, and men who shouted and men who swore, and surely that was Godolphin himself in one of them, with Rashleigh by his side. Dona laughed, wiping her hair out of her eyes, for nothing mattered now, neither Rashleigh's anger nor Godolphin's recognition of her should it come, for the *Merry Fortune* was sailing away from them, recklessly and joyfully, into the summer gale. Once again the gull screamed, and this time he was close to her; she looked about for a stone to throw at him, and instead she saw a small boat shoot past the ridge of rocks ahead of her, and there was Pierre Blanc, his small face upturned towards the cliffs, and once again he gave his sea-gull's cry.

Dona stood then, laughing still, and raised her arms above her head, and shouted to him, and he saw her and brought his boat in to the rocks beside her, and she scrambled down into the boat beside him, asking no question, nor he either, for he was pulling now into the short breaking seas towards the ship. The blood was running from the cut on her chin, and she was soaked to the waist, but she did not care. The little boat leapt into the steep seas, and the salt spray blew in her face with the wind and the rain. There was a flash of light, and the crash of a cannon, and something splashed into the water ten yards ahead of them, but Pierre Blanc, grinning like a monkey, pulled on into mid-channel, and here was the *Merry Fortune* herself, thrashing through the sea towards them, the wind thundering in her crowded sails.

Another flash, another deafening report, and this time there was a tearing sound of splintering wood, but Dona could see nothing, she only knew that someone had thrown a rope down into the boat, and someone was pulling them close to the side of the ship, and there were faces laughing down at her, and hands that lifted her, and away beneath her was the black swirl of water and the little boat upside down, disappearing in the darkness.

The Frenchman was standing at the wheel of the *Merry Fortune*, and he too had a cut on his chin, and his hair was blowing about his face, and the water streamed from his shirt, but for one moment his eyes held hers and they smiled at each other, and then 'Throw yourself on your face, Dona,' he said, 'they'll be firing again,' and she lay beside him on the deck, exhausted, aching, shivering with the rain and the spray, but nothing mattered, and she did not mind.

This time the shot fell short. 'Save your powder, boys,' he laughed, 'you'll not catch us this time,' while little Pierre Blanc, streaming wet and shaking himself like a dog, leant over the ship's side, his finger to his nose. And now the *Merry Fortune* reared and fell into the trough of the seas, and the sails thundered and shook, while someone shouted from the pursuing boats behind, and someone with a musket in his hand let fly at the rigging.

'There is your friend, Dona,' called the Frenchman, 'do you know if he shoots straight?' She crawled aft, looking over the stern rail, and there was the leading boat almost beneath them, with Rashleigh's face glaring up at them, and Godolphin raising a musket to his shoulder.

'There's a woman aboard,' shouted Rashleigh, 'look there!' But as he spoke Godolphin fired again, the ball whistling harmlessly over her head, and as the *Merry Fortune* heeled over in a sudden gust of wind Dona saw the Frenchman leave the wheel a moment to Pierre Blanc at his side. Laughing, he swung himself over the lee rail of the ship as it dipped in the sea, and Dona saw that he had a sword in his hand.

'Greetings to you, gentlemen,' he called, 'and a safe passage back to Fowey quay, but first of all we would like something to remember you by,' and reaching out with his sword he knocked Godolphin's hat off into the water, and pricking the great curled periwig with the point of his sword, he bore it aloft triumphantly, waving it in the air. Godolphin, bald as a naked baby, his bulbous eyes starting out of his scarlet face, fell backwards into the stern of the boat, his musket clattering beside him.

Then a squall of rain came, blotting them from sight, and the sea broke over the rail of the ship, knocking Dona down into the scuppers. When she could stand again and get her breath, wiping the hair from her face, there was the fort on the headland away astern of them, and the boats were out of sight, and the Frenchman was standing with his hand on the wheel of the *Merry Fortune*, laughing at her, with Godolphin's wig dangling from the spokes.

Chapter 14

THERE were two ships in mid-channel, sailing in company about three miles distant from each other, and the leading ship had a curious rakish air about her, with her slanting masts and her coloured paintwork, as though she were leading the sober merchantman that followed her to uncharted waters beyond the far horizon.

The summer gale that had thrashed the sea for twenty-four hours without ceasing had now blown itself out, and the sky was hard and blue without a single cloud. The swell too had died away, leaving the sea quiet and curiously still, so that the two ships, with only the breath of a northerly breeze to drive them, stayed almost motionless in the channel, their sails hanging uselessly upon the yards. A smell of cooking came from the galley of the *Merry Fortune*, the warm brown smell of roasting chicken, and the fragrance of it crept into the open port-hole of the cabin, mingling with the fresh salt air and the warm sun. Dona opened her eyes, and she became aware for the first time that the ship was no longer pitching and tossing in the trough of the Atlantic swell, the sickness that had overtaken her was gone, and above all she was hungry, hungrier than she had been in her life. She yawned, stretching her arms above her head, smiling to herself because she was no longer sea-sick, and then she swore softly, using one of Harry's more stable-sounding oaths, for she remembered that by being sea-sick she had forfeited her wager. She put her hands up to her ears, fingering her ruby ear-rings reluctantly, and as she did so she realized with full consciousness that she was stark naked under the blanket, and there was no trace of her clothes upon the cabin floor.

It seemed eternity since she had stumbled down the companion-way in the dark, drenched, and exhausted, and sick, and flinging off her shirt and her breeches, and those lumping blistering shoes, had crept into the warmth of those comforting blankets, longing only for stillness and for sleep.

Someone must have come into the cabin while she was sleeping, for the port-hole was wide open that had been closed before against the weather, her clothes had been taken away, and in their place was a ewer of boiling water and a towel.

She climbed from the spacious bunk where she had lain for a day and a night, thinking, as she stood naked upon the floor of the cabin and washed, that whoever had been master of the *Merry Fortune* believed in comfort before vigilance. Glancing out of the port-hole as she parted her hair she saw away on the starboard bow the spars of *La Mouette*, gleaming scarlet in the sun. Once more the smell of chicken came to her nostrils, and then, hearing the sound of footsteps on the deck outside, she climbed back into her berth, dragging the blanket to her chin.

'Are you awake yet?' called the Frenchman. She bade him come in, leaning back against the pillow, her heart beating foolishly, and he stood there in the doorway smiling down at her, and he had a tray in his hands. 'I have lost my ear-rings after all,' she said.

'Yes, I know,' he said.

'How do you know?'

'Because I came below once to see how you were, and you threw a pillow at my head and damned me to hell,' he answered.

She laughed, shaking her head. 'You are lying,' she said, 'you never came, I never saw a soul.'

'You were too far gone to remember anything about it,' he said, 'but we will not argue. Are you hungry?'

'Yes.'

'So am I. I thought we might have dinner together.'

He began to lay the table, and she watched him from under cover of her blanket.

'What is the time?' she asked.

'About three o'clock in the afternoon,' he told her.

'And what day would it be?'

'Sunday. Your friend Godolphin will have missed his morning in church, unless there is a good barber in Fowey.'

He glanced up at the bulkhead, and following his eyes she saw the curled periwig hanging upon a nail above her head.

'When did you put it there?' she laughed.

'When you were sick.' he said.

And now she was silent, hating the thought that he had seen her at such a moment, so shaming, so grossly undignified, and she pulled the blanket yet more closely round her, watching his hands busy with the chicken.

'Can you eat a wing?' he asked.

'Yes,' she nodded, wondering how she could sit up without a stitch upon her body, and when he had turned his back to uncork the wine she sat up swiftly, and draped the blanket about her shoulders.

He brought her a plate of chicken, looking her up and down as he did so. 'We can do better for you than that,' he said, 'you forget the *Merry Fortune* had been to the Indies,' and going outside for a moment he stooped to a large wooden box that stood beside the companion-way, and lifting the top he brought out a gaily-coloured shawl, all scarlet and gold, with a silken fringe. 'Perhaps Godolphin had this in mind for his wife,' he said. 'There are plenty more down in the hold if you want them.'

He sat down at the table, tearing off a drumstick from the chicken, and eating it in his hand. She drank her wine, watching him over the rim of the glass.

'We might have been hanging from that tree in Godolphin's park,' she said.

'We would have been, but for that slant of wind from the west,' he answered.

'And what are we going to do now?'

'I never make plans on a Sunday,' he told her.

She went on eating her chicken, seizing the wing in her hands as he was doing, and from the bows of the ship came the sound of Pierre Blanc's lute, and the men's voices singing softly.

'Do you always have the devil's own luck, Frenchman?' she said.

'Always,' he answered, throwing his drumstick out of the port-hole, and taking the fellow.

The sun streamed in upon the table, while the lazy sea lapped against the side of the ship, and they went on eating, each aware of the other, and the hours that stretched before them.

'Rashleigh makes his seamen comfortable,' said the Frenchman presently, looking about him, 'perhaps that was why they were all asleep when we climbed on board.'

'How many were there then?'

'Half-a-dozen, that is all.'

'And what did you do with them?'

'Oh, we bound them back to back and gagged them, and cast them adrift in a boat. They were picked up by Rashleigh himself I dare say.'

'Will the sea be rough again?'

'No, that is all finished.'

She leant back on her pillow, watching the pattern that the sun made on the bulkhead.

'I am glad I had it, the danger and the excitement,' she said, 'but I am glad it is over too. I do not want to do it again, not that waiting outside Rashleigh's house, and hiding on the quay, and running across the hills to the cove until I thought my heart would burst.'

'You did not do too badly, for a cabin-boy,' he said.

He looked across at her, and then away again, and she began to plait the silk fringe of the shawl he had given her. Pierre Blanc was still playing his lute, playing the little rippling song she had heard when she saw *La Mouette* for the first time anchored in the creek below Navron.

'How long shall we stay in the *Merry Fortune*?' she said.

'Why, do you want to go home?' he asked.

'No – No, I just wondered,' she said.

He got up from the table, and crossing to the port-hole looked out at *La Mouette* where she lay almost becalmed some two miles distant.

'That's the way of it at sea,' he said, 'always too much wind or too little. We'd be at the French coast by now with a capful of breeze. Perhaps we shall get it, tonight.'

He stood there with his hands deep in his breeches pockets, his lips framing the song that Pierre Blanc was playing on the lute.

'What will you do when the wind does come?' she asked.

'Sail within sight of land, and then leave a handful of men to take the *Merry Fortune* into port. As for ourselves, we shall return on board *La Mouette*.'

She went on playing with the tassel of the shawl.

'And then where do we go?' she said.

'Back to Helford of course. Do you not want to see your children?'

She did not answer. She was watching the back of his head, and the set of his shoulders.

'Perhaps the night-jar is still calling in the creek at midnight,' he said. 'We could go and find him, and the heron too. I never finished the drawing of the heron, did I?'

'I do not know.'

'There are many fish too in the river waiting to be caught,' he said.

Pierre Blanc's song dwindled and died, and there was no sound but the lapping of water against the side of the ship. The *Merry Fortune*'s bell struck the half-hour, and this was echoed by *La Mouette*, away in the distance. The sun blazed down upon the placid sea. Everything was peaceful. Everything was still.

He turned away then from the port-hole, and came and sat down on the bunk beside her, still whistling the song under his breath.

'This is the best moment for a pirate,' he said. 'The planning is over and done with, and the game a success. Looking back on it one can remember only the good moments, and the bad are put aside until next time. And so, as the wind will not blow before night-fall, we may do as we please.'

Dona listened to the lapping of the sea against the hull.

'We might swim,' she said, 'in the cool of the evening, before the sun goes down.'

'We might,' he said.

There was silence between them, and she went on watching the reflection of the sun above her head.

'I cannot get up until my clothes are dry,' she said.

'No, I know.'

'Will they be very long, out there, in the sun?'

'At least three hours more, I should say.'

Dona sighed, and settled herself down against her pillow.

'Perhaps you could lower a boat,' she said, 'and send Pierre Blanc off to *La Mouette* for my gown.'

'He is asleep by now,' said the captain of the ship, 'they are all asleep. Didn't you know that Frenchmen like to be idle between one and five in the afternoon?'

'No,' she said, 'I did not.'

She put her arms behind her head, and closed her eyes.

'In England,' she said, 'people never sleep in the afternoon. It must be a custom peculiar to your countrymen. But in the meanwhile, what are we going to do until my clothes are dry?'

He watched her, the ghost of a smile on his lips.

'In France,' he said, 'they would tell you there is only one thing we could do. But perhaps that also is a custom peculiar to my countrymen.'

She did not answer. Then leaning forward he stretched out his hand, and very gently he began to unscrew the ruby from her left ear.

Chapter 15

DONA stood at the wheel of *La Mouette*, and the ship plunged into the long green seas, tossing the spray back upon the deck towards her. The white sails stretched and sang above her head, and all the sounds that she had grown to love came to her ears now in beauty and in strength. The creaking of the great blocks, the straining of ropes, the thud of the wind in the rigging, and down in the waist of the ship the voices of the men, laughing and chafing one another, now and again looking up to see if she observed them, showing off like children to win a glance from her. The hot sun shone upon her bare head, and when the spray blew back upon the deck the taste came to her lips, and even the deck itself had a warm pungent smell, an odour of tar, and rope, and blue salt water.

And all this, she thought, is only momentary, is only a fragment in time that will never come again, for yesterday already belongs to the past and is ours no longer, and tomorrow is an unknown thing that may be hostile. This is our day, our moment, the sun belongs to us, and the wind, and the sea, and the men for'ard there singing on the deck. This day is forever a day to be held and cherished, because in it we shall have lived, and loved, and nothing else matters but that, in this world of our own making to which we have escaped. She looked down at him, as he lay on the deck against the bulwark, his hands behind his head, and his pipe in his mouth. Now and again he smiled to himself as he slept there in the sun, and she remembered the feel of his back that had lain against hers all the night, and she thought with pity of all the men and women who were not light-hearted when they loved, who were cold, who were reluctant, who were shy, who imagined that passion and tenderness were two things separate from one another, and not the one, gloriously intermingled, so that to be fierce was also to be gentle, so that silence was a speaking without words. For love, as she knew it now, was something without shame and without reserve, the possession of two people who had no barrier between them, and no pride; whatever happened to him would happen to her too, all feeling, all movement, all sensation of body and of mind.

The wheel of *La Mouette* lifted under her hands, and the ship heeled over in the freshening breeze, and all this, she thought, is part of what we feel for each other, and part of the loveliness of living, the strength that lies in the hull of a ship, the beauty of sails, the surge of water, the taste of the sea, the touch of the wind on our faces, and even the little simple pleasures of eating, and drinking, and sleeping, all these we share with delight and understanding, because of the happiness we have in one another.

He opened his eyes and looked at her, and taking the pipe out of his mouth he shook the ashes on the deck, and they blew away, scattering in the wind, and then he rose and stretched himself, yawning in idleness and peace and contentment, and he came and stood beside her at the wheel, putting his hands on the spokes above her hands, and they stood there, watching the sky and the sea and the sails, and never speaking.

The coast of Cornwall was a thin line on the far horizon, and the first gulls came to greet them, wheeling and crying above the masts, and they knew that presently the land smell would drift towards them from the distant hills, and the sun would lose its strength, and later the wide estuary of Helford would open to them with the setting sun shining red and gold upon the water.

The beaches would be warm where the sun had shone all day, and the river itself full and limpid with the tide. There would be sanderling skimming the rocks, and oyster-catchers brooding on one leg by the little pools, while higher up the river, near the creek, the heron would stand motionless, like a sleeping thing, only to rise at their approach and glide away over the trees with his great soundless wings.

The creek itself would seem still and silent after the boisterous sun and the lifting sea, and the trees, crowding by the water's edge, would be kindly and gentle. The night-jar would call as he had said, and the fishes plop suddenly in the water, and all the scents and sounds of midsummer would come to them, as they walked in the twilight under the trees, amongst the young green bracken and the moss.

'Shall we build a fire again, and cook supper, in the creek?' he said to her, reading her thoughts. 'Yes,' she said, 'on the quay there, like we did before,' and leaning against him, watching the thin line of the coast becoming harder and more distinct, she thought of the other supper they had cooked together, and of the little shyness and restraint between them then that could never come again, for love was a thing of such simplicity once it was shared, and admitted, and done, with all the joy intensified and all the fever gone.

So *La Mouette* stole in once more towards the land, as she had done that first evening that seemed so long ago now, when Dona had stood on the cliffs and watched her, premonition already in her heart. The sun went down, and the gulls came out to greet them, and the rising tide and the little evening wind brought the ship gently and in silence up the channel of the estuary. Even in the few days they had been absent a depth of colour had come to the trees that had not been before, and there was a richness in the green of the hills, and the still warm fragrance of midsummer hovered in the air like the touch of a hand. As *La Mouette* drifted with the tide a curlew rose with a whistle and sped away up the river, and then, the ship losing way with the lack of wind as they came to the creek, the boats were lowered, and the warps made fast, and the ship was brought to her secret anchorage as the first shadows fell upon the water.

The cable rattled with a hollow sound in the deep pool beneath the trees, and the ship swung round to meet the last of the flood tide, and suddenly from nowhere came a swan and his mate, like two white barges sailing in company, and following them three cygnets, soft and brown. They went away down the creek, leaving a wake behind them as a vessel would, and presently when all was snugged down for the night and the decks deserted, the smell of cooking came from the galley forward, and the low murmur of voices as the men talked in the fo'c'sle.

The captain's boat waited beneath the ladder, and coming up from the cabin he called to Dona, who was leaning against the rail on the poop deck watching the first star above a dark tree, and they pulled away down the creek where the swans had gone, the little boat lapping against the water.

141

Soon the fire glowed in the clearing, the dried sticks snapping and breaking, and this night they cooked bacon, curling and streaky and crisp, with bread that was burnt also by the fire and was toasted and black. They broke the bacon in their hands, and then brewed coffee, strong and bitter, in a saucepan with a bent handle, and afterwards he reached for his pipe and his tobacco, and Dona leant against his knee, her hands behind her head.

'And this', she said, watching the fire, 'could be forever, if we wished. Could be tomorrow, and the next day, and a year ahead. And not only here, but in other countries, on other rivers, in lands of our own choosing.'

'Yes,' he said, 'if we so wished. But Dona St Columb is not Dona the cabin-boy. She is someone who has a life in another world, and even at this moment she is waking in the bedroom at Navron, with her fever gone, remembering only very faintly the dream she had. And she rises, and dresses, and sees to her household and her children.'

'No,' she said, 'she has not woken yet, and the fever is still heavy upon her, and her dreams are of a loveliness that she never knew in her life before.'

'For all that,' he told her, 'they are still dreams. And in the morning she will wake.'

'No,' she said. 'No, no. Always this. Always the fire, and the dark night, and the supper we have cooked, and your hand here against my heart.'

'You forget', he said, 'that women are more primitive than men. For a time they will wander, yes, and play at love, and play at adventure. And then, like the birds do, they must make their nest. Instinct is too strong for them. Birds build the home they crave, and settle down into it, warm and safe, and have their babies.'

'But the babies grow up,' she said, 'and fly away, and then the parent birds fly away too, and are free once more.'

He laughed at her, staring into the fire, watching the flames.

'There is no answer, Dona,' he said, 'for I could sail away now in *La Mouette* and come back to you in twenty years' time, and what should I find but a placid, comfortable woman in place of my cabin-boy, with her dreams long forgotten, and I myself a weather-beaten mariner, stiff in the joints, with bearded face, and my taste for piracy gone with the spent years.'

'My Frenchman paints a dismal picture of the future,' she said.

'Your Frenchman is a realist,' he answered.

'And if I sailed with you now, and never returned to Navron?' she asked.

'Who can tell? Regret perhaps, and disillusion, and a looking back over your shoulder.'

'Not with you,' she said, 'never with you.'

'Well then, perhaps no regrets. But more building of nests, and more rearing of broods, and I having to sail alone again, and so a losing once more of adventure. So you see, my Dona, there is no escape for a woman, only for a night and for a day.'

'No, you are right,' she said, 'there is no escape for a woman. Therefore if I sail with you again I shall be a cabin-boy, and borrow Pierre Blanc's breeches once and for always, and there will be no complications of a primitive nature, so that our hearts and our minds can be easy, and you can seize ships and make your landings on the coast, and I, the humble cabin-boy, will brew your supper for you in the cabin, and ask no questions, and hold no conversation with you.'

'And how long would we endure that, you and I?'

'For as long as we pleased.'

'You mean, for as long as I pleased. Which would be neither for a night nor an hour, and anyway, not this night and not this hour, my Dona.'

The fire burnt low, and sank away to nothing, and later she said to him, 'Do you know what day this is?'

'Yes,' he said, 'midsummer day. The longest in the year.'

'Therefore,' she said, 'tonight we should sleep here, instead of in the ship. Because it will never happen again. Not for us. Not in this way, in the creek here.'

'I know,' he said, 'that is why I brought the blankets in the boat. And the pillow for your head. Did you not see them?'

She looked up at him, but she could not see his face any longer, for it was in shadow, the fire-light being gone, and then without a word he got up and went down to the boat, and then came back to her with the bedding and pillow in his arms, and he spread them out in the clearing under the trees close to the water's edge. The tide was ebbing now, and the mud flats showing. The trees shivered in a little wind, and then were still again. The night-jars were silent and the sea-birds slept. There was no moon, only the dark sky above their heads, and beside them the black waters of the creek.

'Tomorrow, very early, I shall go to Navron,' she told him, 'at sunrise, before you are awake.'

'Yes,' he said.

'I will call William before the household is astir, and then if all is well with the children, and there is no need for me to stay, I will return to the creek.'

'And then?'

'Well, I do not know. That is for you to say. It is unwise to plan. Planning so often goes astray.'

'We will make a pretence of planning,' he said, 'we will make a pretence that you come back to breakfast with me, and afterwards we take the boat and go down the river, and you shall fish again, but this time perhaps more successfully than the last.'

'We will catch many fish?'

'That we will not decide tonight. We will leave that until the moment comes.'

'And when we have done with fishing,' she went on, 'we will swim. At noon, when the sun is hottest upon the water. And afterwards, we will eat, and then sleep on our backs on a little beach. And the heron will come down to feed with the turn of the tide, so that you can draw him again.'

'No, I shall not draw the heron,' he said, 'it is time I made another drawing of the cabin-boy of *La Mouette*.'

'And so another day,' she said, 'and another, and another. And no past and no future, only the present.'

'But today,' he said, 'is the longest day. Today is midsummer. Have you forgotten that?'

'No,' she said. 'No, I have not forgotten.'

And, somewhere, she thought, before she slept, somewhere there is another Dona, lying in that great canopied bed in London, restless and lonely and knowing nothing of this night beside the creek, or of *La Mouette* at anchor there in the pool, or of his back against mine here in the darkness. She belongs to yesterday. She has no part in this. And somewhere too there is a Dona of to-morrow, a Dona of the future, of ten years away, to whom all this will be a thing to cherish, a thing to remember. Much will be for-gotten then, perhaps, the sound of the tide on the mud flats, the dark sky, the dark water, the shiver of the trees behind us and the shadows they cast before them, and the smell of the young bracken and the moss. Even the things we said will be forgotten, the touch of hands, the warmth, the loveliness, but never the peace that we have given to each other, never the stillness and the silence.

When she woke there was a grey light upon the trees, and a mist upon the water, and the two swans were coming back up the creek like ghosts of the morning. The ashes of the fire were white as dust. She looked at him beside her, as he lay sleeping, and she wondered why it was that men seemed children when they slept. All lines were smoothed away, all knowledge too, they became again the small boys they had been long ago. She shivered a little in the first chill of the day, and then, throwing aside the blanket, she stood with bare feet upon the ashes of the fire, and watched the swans disappear into the mist.

Then she leaned down for her cloak, and wrapped it about her, and turned away from the quay towards the trees, and the narrow twisting path that would bring her to Navron.

She tried to pick up the threads of her normal life. The children in their beds. James in his cot, with face flushed and fists clenched; Henrietta lying upon her face as she always did, her fair curls tumbled on the pillow; Prue, with open mouth, sleeping beside them. While William, faithful William, kept watch upon the house, and lied for her sake and his master's.

Soon the mist would clear, and the sun would come up over the trees beyond the river, and even now, as she came out of the woods and stood upon the lawn, the morning light laid a finger upon Navron, as it slept, still and shuttered, while she stood there watching it. She crept across the lawn, silver with dew, and tried the door. It was locked, of course. She waited a moment, and then went round to the courtyard behind the house, for William's window looked upon it, and it might be that she could make him hear, if she called softly. She listened beneath his window. It was open, and the curtain was not drawn.

'William?' she said softly. 'William, are you there?'

There was no answer, and stooping, she picked up a little pebble and threw it against the pane. In a moment his face appeared, and he stared at her as though she were a phantom, and then he put his finger to his lips and disappeared. She waited, anxiety in her heart, for his face was white and haggard, the face of a man who had not slept. James is ill, she thought, James is dead. He is going to tell me that James is dead. Then she heard him draw the bolts gently in the great door, and the door itself open a small space to admit her. 'The children?' she said, laying her hand on his sleeve, 'the children, are they ill?' He shook his head, still motioning her to silence, glancing over his shoulder to the stairway in the hall.

She entered the house, looking about her as she did so, and then, her heart leaping in sudden understanding, she saw the great-coat on the chair, the riding-whip, the usual disorder of arrival, and there was a hat flung carelessly upon the stone floor, and a second riding-whip, and a thick plaided rug.

'Sir Harry has come, my lady,' said William. 'He came just before sundown, he had ridden from London. And Lord Rockingham is with him.' She said nothing. She went on staring at the great-coat on the chair. And suddenly, from above, she heard the shrill yapping of a little spaniel dog.

Chapter 16

ONCE again William glanced up the stairway, his small eyes gleaming in his pale face, but Dona shook her head silently, and crossing the hall on tip-toe she led the way into the salon. William lit two candles, and then stood before her, waiting for her to speak.

'What reason did he give?' she said. 'Why have they come?'

'I gather that Sir Harry was becoming restless in London without you, my lady,' said William, 'and a word from Lord Rockingham decided him. It seems that his lordship met a relative of Lord Godolphin's at Whitehall, who told him that Sir Harry's presence in Cornwall was urgently needed at the present time. That is all I could discover from their conversation at supper, my lady.'

'Yes,' said Dona, as though she had not heard him. 'Yes, it would be Rockingham. Harry is too lazy to come without persuasion.'

William stood motionless before her, the candle in his hand.

'What did you tell Sir Harry?' she asked. 'How did you keep him from my room?'

For the first time a trace of a smile appeared on William's face, and he looked at his mistress with understanding.

'Sir Harry would not have passed into your room, my lady,' he said, 'he must have slain me first. I explained to the gentlemen, as soon as they had dismounted, that you had been in bed for several days with a high fever, that at last you were obtaining some measure of sleep, and that it would be extremely prejudicial to your health if Sir Harry as much as ventured into the room. Absolute quiet was essential.'

'And he accepted your story?'

'Like a lamb, my lady. He swore a trifle at first, and cursed me for not having sent for him, but I explained that it was your ladyship's strict orders that he was not to be told. And then Miss Henrietta and Master James came running to meet Sir Harry, telling the same tale, that your ladyship was poorly and confined to your bed, and Prue of course came too, with a woebegone face, saying that your ladyship would not even admit her to tend upon you. So after having played with the children and supped, and taken a turn round the gardens, my lady, Sir Harry and Lord Rockingham retired. Sir Harry is in the blue room, my lady.'

Dona smiled at him, and put her hand on his arm.

'Faithful one,' she said, 'and then you did not sleep yourself for thinking of the morning that was to come. And supposing I had not returned?'

'No doubt I would have arrived at some decision, my lady, although the problem was a little hard.'

'And my lord Rockingham? What did he say to all this?'

'His lordship appeared disappointed, my lady, that you were not down to receive them, but he said very little. It seemed to interest him when Prue told Sir Harry that no one was looking after you but myself. I observed that his lordship looked upon me with curiosity, my lady, and if I might venture to say so, with new eyes.'

'He would, William, Lord Rockingham has that sort of mind. He is a person to watch, for he has a long nose like a terrier dog.'

'Yes, my lady.'

'It is strange, William, what fatality lies in the making of plans. I thought to breakfast with your master in the creek, and to fish with him, and to swim, and to cook our supper under the stars again as we did last night, and now all that is finished and done with.'

'But not for long, my lady.'

'That we cannot tell. At all costs word must be sent to *La Mouette*, and she must leave the creek with the next tide.'

'It would be more prudent to wait until night-fall my lady.'

'Your master will decide of course. Ah, William.'

'My lady?'

But she shook her head, shrugging her shoulders, telling him with her eyes the things that she could never say in speech, and suddenly he bent down, patting her shoulder as though she were Henrietta, his funny button mouth twisted.

'I know, my lady,' he said, 'but it will come all right. You will be together again,' and then because of the anti-climax of homecoming, because she was tired, because he patted her shoulder in his kind ridiculous way, she felt the tears running down her cheeks, and she could not stop them. 'Forgive me, William,' she said.

'My lady.'

'So foolish, so unutterably foolish and weak. It is something to do with having been so happy.'

'I know, my lady.'

'Because we were happy, William. And there was the sun, and the wind, and the sea, and – loveliness such as has never been.'

'I can imagine it, my lady.'

'It does not happen often, does it?'

'Once in a million years, my lady.'

'Therefore I will shed no more tears, like a spoilt child. For whatever happens we have had what we have had. No one can take that from us. And I have been alive, who was never alive before. Now, William, I shall go to my room, and undress, and get into bed. And later in the morning you shall call me, with my breakfast, and when I am sufficiently prepared for the ordeal, I will see Sir Harry, and find out how long he intends to stay.'

'Very good, my lady.'

'And somehow, in some way, word must be sent to your master in the creek.'

'Yes, my lady.'

And so, with the daylight coming through the chinks in the shutters, they left the room, and Dona, her shoes in her hands and her cloak about her shoulders, crept up the stairway she had descended some five days earlier, and it seemed to her that a year and a life-time had passed since then. She listened for a moment outside Harry's room, and yes, there were the familiar snuffling snores of Duke and Duchess, the spaniels, and the heavy slow breathing of Harry himself. Those things, she thought, were part of the pattern that irritated me once, that drove me to absurdities, and now they no longer have any power to touch me, for they are not of my world now, I have escaped.

She went to her own room, and closed the door. It smelt cool and sweet, for the window was open on to the garden, and William had put lilies-of-the-valley beside her bed. She pulled aside the curtains and undressed, and lay down with her hands over her eyes, and now, she thought, now he is waking beside the creek, putting out his hand for me beside him and finding me gone, and then he remembers and smiles, and stretches, and yawns, and watches the sun come up over the trees. And later he will get up and sniff the day, like I have seen him do, whistling under his breath, scratching his left ear, and then walk down to the creek and swim. He will call up to the men on *La Mouette*, as they scrub the decks, and one of them will lower the rope ladder for him to climb, and another launch a boat to bring back the little boat and the supper things and the blankets. Then he will go to the cabin, and rub himself dry with a towel, glancing out of the port-hole on to the water as he does so, and presently, when he has dressed, Pierre Blanc will bring breakfast, and he will wait a little, but then because he will be hungry he will eat it without me. Later he will come up on deck and watch the path through the trees. She could see him fill his pipe, and lean against the poop rail, looking down into the water, and perhaps the swans would come back, and he would throw bread to them, idle, contented, filled with a warm laziness after his morning swim, thinking perhaps of the day's fishing to come, and the hot sun, and the sea. She knew how he would glance up towards her, if she came through the trees down to the creek, and how he would smile, saying nothing, never moving from the rail on the deck, throwing the bread down to the swans as though he did not see her. And what is the use, thought Dona, of going over this in my mind, for all that is finished, and done with, and will not happen again, for the ship must sail before she is discovered. And here am I, lying on my bed at Navron, and there is he, down in the creek, and we are not together any more, and this then, that I am feeling now, is the hell that comes with love, the hell and the damnation and the agony beyond all enduring, because after the beauty and the loveliness come the sorrow and the pain. So she lay on her back, her arms across her eyes, never sleeping, and the sun came up and streamed into the room.

It was after nine o'clock that William came in with her breakfast, and he put the tray down on the table beside her bed, and 'Are you rested, my lady?' he asked. 'Yes, William,' she lied, breaking off a grape from the bunch he had brought her.

'The gentlemen are below breakfasting, my lady,' he told her. 'Sir Harry bade me inquire whether you were sufficiently recovered for him to see you.'

'Yes, I shall have to see him, William.'

'If I might suggest it, my lady, it would be prudent to draw the curtains a trifle, so that your face is in shadow. Sir Harry might think it peculiar that you look so well.'

'Do I look well, William?'

'Suspiciously well, my lady.'

'And yet my head is aching intolerably.'

'From other causes, my lady.'

'And I have shadows beneath my eyes, and I am exceedingly weary.'

'Quite, my lady.'

'I think you had better leave the room, William, before I throw something at you.'

'Very good, my lady.'

He went away, closing the door softly behind him, and Dona, rising, washed and then arranged her hair, and after drawing the curtains as he had suggested, she went back to her bed, and presently she heard the shrill yapping of the spaniels, and their scratching against the door, followed by a heavy footstep, and in a moment Harry was in the room, and the dogs with delighted barking hurled themselves upon her bed.

'Get down, now, will you, you little devils,' he shouted. 'Hi, Duke, Hi, Duchess, can't you see your mistress is ill, come here, will you, you rascals,' making, as was his wont, more ado than the dogs themselves, and then, sitting heavily upon the bed in place of them, he brushed away the marks of their feet with his scented handkerchief, puffing and blowing as he did so.

'God dammit, it's warm this morning,' he said, 'here I am sweating through my shirt already, and it's not ten o'clock. How are you, are you better, where did you get this confounded fever? Have you a kiss for me?' He bent over her, the smell of scent strong upon him, and his curled wig scratched her chin, while his clumsy fingers prodded her cheek. 'You do not look very ill, my beautiful, even in this light, and here was I expecting to find you at death's door itself, from what the fellow told me. What sort of a servant, is he, anyway? I'll dismiss him if you don't like him, you know.'

'William is a treasure,' she said, 'the best servant I have ever had.'

'Ah, well, as long as he pleases you, that's all that matters. So you've been ill, have you? You should never have left London. London always suits you. Although I admit it's been damned dull without you. Not a play worth seeing, and I nearly lost a fortune at piquet the other night. The King has a new mistress, they tell me, but I haven't seen her yet. Some actress or other. Rockingham's here, you know, and all agog to see you. God dammit, he said to me, in town, let's go down to Navron and see what Dona is up to, and here we are, and you a confounded invalid in bed.'

'I am much better, Harry. It was only a passing thing.'

'Well, I'm glad to hear that. As I say, you look well enough. You have a tan on you, haven't you? You're as dark as a gypsy.'

'The illness must have made me yellow.'

'And your eyes are larger than ever they were, dammit.'

'The result of the fever, Harry.'

'Queer sort of fever. Must be something to do with the climate down here. Would you like the dogs up on your bed?'

'No, I think not.'

'Hi, Duke, give your mistress a kiss, and then get down. Here Duchess, here's your mistress. Duchess has a sore patch on her back, and she's nearly scratched herself raw, look at that now, what would you do to her? I've rubbed in some pomade, but it does her no good. I've bought a new horse, by-the-way, she's down there in the stable. A chestnut, with a deuce of a temper, but she covers the ground quick enough. "I'll give you a thousand for her," says Rockingham, and "Make it five thousand," I tell him, "and I might bite," but he won't play. So the county's infested with pirates, is it, and robbery, rape, and violence causing havoc amongst people?'

'Where did you hear that?'

'Well, Rockingham brought back a story in town one day. Met a cousin of George Godolphin's. How is Godolphin?'

'A little out of temper when I last saw him.'

'So I should think. He sent me a letter a while back, which I forgot to answer. And now his brother-in-law has lost a ship, it seems. Do you know Philip Rashleigh?'

'Not to speak to, Harry.'

'Well, you'll meet him soon. I invited him over here. We met him in Helston yesterday. He was in a devil of a temper, and so was Eustick, who was with him. It seems this infernal Frenchman sailed the vessel straight out of Fowey harbour, right under the nose of Rashleigh and Godolphin. What infernal impudence, eh? And then off to the French coast, of course, with not a damned ship in pursuit. God knows what the vessel was worth, she was just home from the Indies.'

'Why did you invite Philip Rashleigh here?'

'Well, it was Rockingham's idea really. "Let's take a hand in the game," he said to me, "you're an authority, you know, in this part of the world. And we might have some sport out of it." "Sport?" says Rashleigh, "you'd think it sport no doubt if you'd lost a fortune like I've done." "Ah," says Rockingham, "you're all asleep down here. We'll catch the fellow for you, and then you'll have sport enough." So we'll hold a meeting, I thought, and collect Godolphin and one or two others, and set a trap for the Frenchman, and when we've caught him we'll string him up somewhere, and give you a laugh.'

'So you think you'll succeed, Harry, where others have failed?'

'Oh, Rockingham will think of something. He's the fellow to tackle the job. I know I'm no damn use, I haven't got a brain in my head, thank God. Here, Dona, when are you going to get up?'

'When you have left the room.'

'Still aloof, eh, and keeping yourself to yourself? I don't get much fun out of my wife, do I, Duke? Hi, then, fetch a slipper, where is it, boy, go seek, go find,' and throwing Dona's shoe across the room he sent the dogs after it, and they fought for it, yapping and scratching, and returning, hurled themselves upon the bed.

'All right then, we'll go, we're not wanted, dogs, we're in the way. I'll go and tell Rockingham you're getting up, he'll be as pleased as a cat with two tails. I'll send the children to you, shall I?'

And he stamped out of the room, singing loudly, the dogs barking at his heels.

So Philip Rashleigh had been in Helston yesterday, and Eustick with him. And Godolphin too must have returned by now. She thought of Rashleigh's face as she had seen it last, scarlet with rage and helplessness, and his cry, 'There's a woman aboard, look there,' as he stared up at her from the boat in Fowey Haven, and she, with the sash gone from her head, and her curls blowing loose, had laughed down at him, waving her hand.

He would not recognize her. It would be impossible. For then she was in shirt and breeches, her face and hair streaming with the rain. She got up, and began to dress, her mind still busy with the news that Harry had given her. The thought of Rockingham here at Navron, bent on mischief, was a continual pin-prick of irritation, for Rockingham was no fool. Besides, he belonged to London, to the cobbled streets, and the playhouses, to the over-heated, over-scented atmosphere that was St James's, and at Navron, her Navron, he was an interloper, a breaker of the peace. The serenity of the place was gone already, she could hear his voice in the garden beneath her window, and Harry's too, they were laughing together, throwing stones for the dogs. No, it was done with and finished. Escape was a thing of yesterday. And *La Mouette* might never have returned after all. The ship might still have lain becalmed and quiet off the coast of France, while her crew took the *Merry Fortune* into port. The breakers on the white still beach, the green sea golden under the sun, the water cold and clean on her naked body, and after swimming, the warmth of the dry deck under her back, as she looked up at the tall, raffish spars of *La Mouette* stabbing the sky.

Then there were knockings on the door, and the children came in, Henrietta with a new doll that Harry had brought her, and James stuffing a rabbit into his mouth, and they flung themselves upon her with small hot hands and generous kisses, Prue curtsy-ing in the background with anxious inquiries for her health, and somewhere, thought Dona, as she held them to her, somewhere there is a woman who cares for none of these things, but lies upon the deck of a ship and laughs with her lover, and the taste of salt is on their lips, and the warmth of the sun and the sea. 'My doll is nicer than James's rabbit,' said Henrietta, and James, jigging up and down on Dona's knee, his fat cheek pressed against hers, shouted 'No, no, mine, mine,' and taking his rabbit from his mouth hurled it in his sister's face. So then there were tears, and scoldings, and reconciliations, and more kisses, and a finding of chocolate, and much fuss and chatter, and the ship was no more, and the sea was no more, but Lady St Columb of Navron, with her hair dressed high off her forehead, and clad in a soft blue gown, descended the stairs to the garden below, a child in either hand.

'So you have had a fever, Dona?' said Rockingham, advancing towards her, and kissing the hand she gave him. 'At all events,' he added, drawing back to look at her, 'it was a most becoming fever.'

'That's what I say,' said Harry. 'I told her so upstairs, she's got a tan on her like a gypsy,' and bending down he seized the children, bearing them high on his shoulder, and they screamed delightedly, the dogs joining in the clamour.

Dona sat down on the seat on the terrace, and Rockingham, standing before her, played with the lace at his wrists.

'You don't appear very delighted to see me,' he said.

'Why should I?' she answered.

'It's some weeks since I saw you,' he said, 'and you went off in such an extraordinary way, after the escapade at Hampton Court. I suppose I did something to offend you.'

'You did nothing,' she said.

He looked at her out of the corners of his eyes, and shrugged his shoulders. 'What have you been doing with yourself down here?' he asked. Dona yawned, watching Harry and the children as they played on the lawn with the dogs. 'I have been very happy,' she said, 'alone here, with the children. I told Harry, when I left London, that I wanted to be alone. I am angry with both of you for breaking my peace.'

'We have not come entirely for pleasure,' said Rockingham 'we are here on business as well. We propose catching the pirate who seems to be giving you all so much trouble.'

'And how do you propose doing that?'

'Ah, well . . . we shall see. Harry is quite excited at the idea. He's been getting bored with nothing to do. And London in midsummer stinks too much, even for me. The country will do us both good.'

'How long do you propose to stay?'

'Until we have caught the Frenchman.'

Dona laughed, and picking a daisy from the grass, began tearing off the petals. 'He has gone back to France,' she said.

'I think not,' said Rockingham.

'Why so?'

'Because of something that fellow Eustick was saying yesterday.'

'The surly Thomas Eustick? What had he to say?' said Dona.

'Only that a fishing craft from St Michael's Mount had reported seeing a vessel in the early hours of yesterday morning, making towards the English coast.'

'Slender evidence. Some merchantman returning from abroad.'

'The fisherman thought not.'

'The coast of England goes a long way, my dear Rockingham. From the Land's End to the Wight is a precious stretch to watch.'

'Yes, but the Frenchman leaves the Wight alone. It seems he leaves everything alone, but for this narrow strip of Cornwall. Rashleigh will have it that he has even visited your Helford river here.'

'He must do it by night then, when I am in bed and asleep.'

'Possibly he does. At any rate, he will not dare to do it much longer. It will be vastly amusing to stop his little game. I suppose there are many creeks and inlets round your coast here?'

'No doubt. Harry could tell you better than I.'

'And the country hereabouts is sparsely inhabited. Navron is the only big house in the district I understand.'

'Yes, I suppose it is.'

'How ideal for a law-breaker. I almost wish I were a pirate myself. And if I knew the house was without masculine protection, and that the lady of the manor was as beautiful as you, Dona . . .'

'Yes, Rockingham?'

'If I were a pirate, I repeat, knowing all these things, I should be most tempted to return to the district again and again.'

Dona yawned once more, and threw away the mutilated daisy.

'But you are not a pirate, my dear Rockingham, you are only a grossly spoilt, over-dressed, exceedingly decadent member of the aristocracy, with too great a fondness for women and for alcohol. So shall we leave the subject alone? I am becoming rather bored.'

She got up from the seat, and began to wander towards the house.

'Time was', he said casually, 'when you were not bored either by me or by my conversation.'

'You flatter yourself.'

'Do you remember a certain evening at Vauxhall?'

'I remember many evenings at Vauxhall, and one in particular when, because I had drunk two glasses of wine and was feeling intolerably sleepy, you had the audacity to kiss me and I was too idle to protest. I disliked you ever afterwards, and myself more so.'

They stopped at the long window, and he gazed at her, a flush on his face. 'What a delightful speech,' he said. 'The Cornish air has made you almost venomous. Or possibly it is the result of the fever.'

'Possibly it is.'

'Were you as churlish as this to the curious-looking manservant who attended you?'

'You had better ask him.'

'I think I shall. If I were Harry I should ask him many questions, and all of an extremely personal nature.'

'Who's this, what's this all about?' and Harry himself joined them, flinging himself down in a chair in the salon, wiping his forehead with a lace handkerchief. 'What are you discussing, both of you?'

'We were discussing your manservant,' said Rockingham, with a brilliant smile, 'so strange that Dona would permit no one else to attend her while she was ill.'

'Yes, by heaven, he's a rum-looking devil, and no mistake. Wouldn't trust him too far, if I were you, Dona. What d'you see in the fellow?'

'He is quiet, he is discreet, he walks soundlessly, and nobody else in the house does those things. Therefore I determined I should be nursed by him and by no one else.'

'Extremely pleasant for the manservant,' said Rockingham, polishing his nails.

'Yes, hang it,' blustered Harry, 'Rock's quite right, you know, Dona. The fellow might have taken infernal liberties. It was a damned risky thing to do. You lying weak and helpless in bed, and the fellow creeping about round you. He's not like an old retainer either, I know very little about him.'

'Oh, so he has not been in your service long?' said Rockingham.

'No. Hang it, Rock, we never come to Navron, as you know. And I'm so confounded idle I never know half the time who my servants are. I've a mind to dismiss him.'

'You will do nothing of the kind,' said Dona; 'William shall remain in my service for as long as it pleases me.'

'All right, all right, no need to be tricky about it,' said Harry, picking up Duchess and fondling her, 'but it looks a trifle queer to have the fellow hanging about your bedroom. Here he is anyway, bringing a letter from someone. He looks as if he were sickening for some fever himself.' Dona glanced at the door, and there was William, with a note in his hand, and his face paler than usual, and there was something of strain in his eyes.

'What's this, eh?' said Harry.

'A letter from Lord Godolphin, Sir Harry,' answered William. 'His man has just brought it, and waits for an answer.'

Harry tore open the letter, and then threw it across to Rockingham with a laugh. 'The hounds are gathering, Rock,' he said, 'we shall have some fun out of this.'

Rockingham read the note with a smile, and then tore it into fragments.

'What answer will you give?' he said.

Harry examined the back of his spaniel, pulling aside the dog's coat. 'She has another patch of eczema here, confound it,' he said, 'that pomade I'm trying is no use at all. What d'you say? Oh, yes, an answer for Godolphin. Tell the man, will you, William, that her ladyship and I will be delighted to receive his lordship and the other gentlemen this evening for supper.'

'Very good, sir,' said William.

'And what invitation is this?' asked Dona, patting her curls in the mirror, 'and who shall I be delighted to receive?'

'George Godolphin, Tommy Eustick, Philip Rashleigh, and half-a-dozen others,' said Harry, flinging the dog off his knee, 'and they're going to catch the froggie at last, aren't they, Duchess, and we shall be in at the kill.'

Dona said nothing, and looking back into the room through the mirror she saw that Rockingham was watching her.

'It will be an amusing party, do you not think?' he said.

'I rather doubt it,' said Dona, 'knowing Harry as a host. You will all be under the table by midnight.'

She went out of the room and when she had closed the door she called to William softly, and he came to her at once, his eyes troubled.

'What is it?' she said, 'you are anxious. Lord Godolphin and his friends, they can't do anything, it will be too late, *La Mouette* will have sailed.'

'No, my lady,' said William, 'she will not have sailed. I have been down to the creek to warn my master. And I found the ship had grounded with the morning's tide, a rock piercing her planking under-water. They were working on her when I went to the creek. And she will not be fit to sail for twenty-four hours.'

His eyes wandered from her face, he moved away, and Dona, glancing over her shoulder saw that the door she had just closed had been opened again, and Rockingham was standing in the entrance, playing with the lace at his wrists.

Chapter 17

THE long day dragged to its close. The hands of the stable clock seemed reluctant to move, and the chimes every half-hour had a sombre tone. The afternoon was sultry and grey, with that heavy look about the sky that comes when thunder brews but does not break.

Harry had lain out upon the lawns with a handkerchief over his face, snoring loudly, with his two dogs snuffling by his side, and Rockingham sat with a book open in his hands, the pages of which he seldom turned and when Dona glanced across at him from time to time she would be aware of his gaze upon her, curious and hungry.

He knew nothing, of course, but some uncanny intuition, almost feminine in quality, had observed the change in her, and he was suspicious, suspicious of the weeks she had spent here at Navron, of her familiarity with the manservant William, and of this more than ordinary aloofness towards Harry and himself, which he could swear came not from boredom but from something more vital, more dangerous. She was more silent than of old, she did not chatter, tease, and gibe at Harry as she was wont to do, but sat plucking the stems of grass with her hands, her eyes half-closed, like one who dreams in secret. All this he observed, and she knew that he was watching her, and the tension between them became more marked as the hours passed. It seemed to her that he had the brooding watchfulness of a cat, crouching beneath a tree, and she was the bird, silent amongst the long grass, waiting her chance to escape.

And Harry, oblivious to all atmospheres, slumbered and sighed.

Dona knew that the men would be working on the planking of the ship. She pictured them at low tide, with bare feet, stripped to the waist, the sweat pouring off their backs, and *La Mouette*, with the wound in her hull exposed, heeling slightly, her planking grey with the mud.

He would be working with them, his forehead wrinkled, his lips compressed, with that look of concentration upon his face that she had grown to love and to respect, for the repairing of his ship would be a thing of life and of death even as the landing at Fowey had been, and there would be no time now for idleness, for dreams.

Somehow, before tonight, she must go to the creek, and beg him to sail with the next tide, although *La Mouette* might still be taking in water, for the net was drawing in upon him, and to linger even one night longer must be fatal for him and for his crew.

The ship had been seen drawing towards the coast, so Rockingham had told her, and now nearly twenty-four hours had come and gone, and much might have been achieved in that time by his enemies, much might have been foreseen and planned. There would be watchers perhaps upon the headlands, and spies on the hills and in the woods, and tonight Rashleigh, Godolphin, and Eustick would themselves be seated at Navron, with God knows what purpose in their minds.

'You are thoughtful, Dona,' said Rockingham, and she, looking across at him, saw that he had laid his book aside and was considering her, his head upon one side, his narrow eyes unsmiling. 'It must be the fever that has altered you so,' he continued, 'for in town you were never silent for five minutes at a time.'

'I am getting old,' she said lightly, chewing a stem of grass, 'in a few weeks I shall be thirty.'

'A curious fever', he said, ignoring her words, 'that leaves the patient with gipsy colouring and eyes so large. You did not see a physician, it seems?'

'I was my own physician.'

'With the advice of the excellent William. What an unusual accent he has, by-the-way. Quite a foreign intonation.'

'All Cornishmen speak likewise.'

'But I understand he is not a Cornishman at all, at least so the groom informed me in the stable this morning.'

'Perhaps he is from Devon then. I have never questioned William about his ancestry.'

'And it seems that the house was entirely empty until you came? The unusual William took the responsibility of Navron upon his shoulders with no other servants to help him.'

'I did not realize you engaged in stable gossip, Rockingham.'

'Did you not, Dona? But it is one of my favourite pastimes. I always learn the latest scandals in town from the servants of my friends. The chatter of back-stairs is invariably true, and so extremely entertaining.'

'And what have you learnt from the back-stairs at Navron?'

'Sufficient, dear Dona, to pique the curiosity.'

'Indeed?'

'Her ladyship, I understand, has a passion for long walks in the heat of the day. She takes a joy, it seems, in wearing the oldest clothes, and returning, sometimes, be-splashed with mud and river water.'

'Very true.'

'Her ladyship's appetite is fitful, it appears. Sometimes she will sleep until nearly midday, and then demand her breakfast. Or she will taste nothing from noon until ten o'clock at night, and then, when her servants are abed, the faithful William brings her supper.'

'True again.'

'And then, after having been in the rudest of health, she unaccountably takes to her bed, and shuts her doors upon her household, even upon her children, because it seems she suffers from a fever, although no physician is sent for, and once again the unusual William is the only person admitted within her door.'

'And what more, Rockingham?'

'Oh, nothing more, dear Dona. Only that you seem to have recovered very quickly from your fever, and show not the slightest pleasure in seeing your husband or his closest friend.'

There was a sigh, and a yawn, and a stretching of limbs, and Harry threw his handkerchief from his face and scratched his wig.

'God knows that last remark you made was true enough,' he said, 'but then Dona always was an iceberg, Rock, old fellow; I have not been married to her for close on six years without discovering that! Damn these flies! Hi, Duchess, catch a fly. Stop 'em from plaguing your master, can't you?' And sitting up he waved his handkerchief in the air, and the dogs woke up and jumped and yapped, and then the children appeared round the corner of the terrace for their half-hour's romp before bed-time.

It was just after six when a shower sent them indoors, and Harry, still yawning and grumbling about the heat, sat down with Rockingham to play piquet. Three hours and a half yet until supper, and *La Mouette* still at anchor in the creek.

Dona stood by the window, tapping her fingers on the pane, and the summer shower fell heavy and fast. The room was close, smelling already of the dogs, and the scent that Harry sprinkled on his clothes. Now and again he burst into a laugh, gibing at Rockingham for some mistake or other in the game. The hands of the clock crept faster than she wished, making up now for the slowness of the day, and she began to pace up and down the room, unable to control her growing premonition of defeat.

'Our Dona seems restless,' observed Rockingham, glancing up at her from his cards, 'perhaps the mysterious fever has not entirely left her?'

She gave him no answer, pausing once more by the long window.

'Can you beat the knave?' laughed Harry, throwing a card down upon the table, 'or have you lost again? Leave my wife alone, Rock, and attend to the game. Look you there, there's another sovereign gone into my pocket. Come and sit down, Dona, you are worrying the dogs with your infernal pacing up and down.'

'Look over Harry's shoulder, and see if he is cheating,' said Rockingham, 'time was when you could beat the pair of us at piquet.'

Dona glanced down at them, Harry loud and cheerful, already a little flushed with the drink he had taken, oblivious to everything but the game he was playing, and Rockingham humouring him as he was wont to do, but watchful still, like a sleek cat, his narrow eyes turned upon Dona in greed and curiosity.

They were set there though, for another hour at least, she knew Harry well enough for that, and so yawning, and turning from the window, she began to walk towards the door.

'I shall lie down until supper,' she said. 'I have a headache. There must be thunder in the air.'

'Go ahead, Rock, old boy,' said Harry, leaning back in his chair, 'I'll wager you don't hold a heart in your hand. Will you increase your bid? There's a sportsman for you. Fill up my glass, Dona, as you're up. I'm as thirsty as a crow.'

'Don't forget', said Rockingham smiling, 'that we may have work to do before midnight.'

'No, by the Lord, I have not forgotten. We're going to catch the froggie, aren't we? What are you staring at me for, my beautiful?'

He looked up at his wife, his wig a little askew, his blue eyes filmy in his handsome florid face.

'I was thinking, Harry, that you will probably look like Godolphin in about ten years' time.'

'Were you, damme? Well, and what of it? He's a stout fellow, is George Godolphin, one of my oldest friends. Is that the ace you're holding in front of my face? Now God damn you for a blasted cheat and a robber of innocent men.'

Dona slipped from the room, and going upstairs to her bedroom she shut the door, and then pulled the heavy bell-rope that hung beside the fireplace. A few minutes later someone knocked, and a little maidservant came into the room.

'Will you please send William to me,' said Dona.

'I am sorry, my lady,' said the girl, with a curtsy, 'but William is not in the house. He went out just after five o'clock and he has not returned.'

'Where has he gone?'

'I have no idea, my lady.'

'It does not matter then, thank you.'

The girl left the room, and Dona threw herself down on her bed, her hands behind her head. William must have had the same idea as herself. He had gone to see what progress had been made upon the ship, and to warn his master that his enemies would be supping at Navron this very night. Why did he delay though? He had left the house at five and it was now nearly seven.

She closed her eyes, aware in the stillness of her quiet room that her heart was thumping now as it had done once before, when, standing on the deck of *La Mouette*, she had waited to go ashore in Lantic bay. She remembered the chilled cold feeling she had had, and how, when she had gone below to the cabin, and eaten and drunk a little, the fear and the anxiety left her, and she had been filled with the glow of adventure. Tonight though it was different. Tonight she was alone, and his hand was not in hers, and his eyes had not spoken to her. She was alone, and must play hostess to his enemies.

She went on lying there on her bed, and outside the rain fell away to a drizzle and ceased, and the birds began to sing, but still William did not come. She got up and went to the door and listened. She could hear the low murmur of the men's voices from the salon, and once Harry laughed and Rockingham too, and then they must have continued with their playing of piquet, for there came only the murmur again, and Harry swearing at one of the dogs for scratching. Dona could wait no longer. She wrapped a cloak around her, and stole downstairs into the great hall on tiptoe, and went out by the side-door into the garden.

The grass was wet after the rain, there was a silver sheen upon it, and there was a warm damp smell in the air like an autumn mist.

The trees dripped in the wood, and the little straggling path that led to the creek was muddied and churned. It was dark in the wood too, for the sun would not return now after the rain, and the heavy green foliage of midsummer made a pall over her head. She came to the point where the path broke off and descended rapidly, and she was about to turn leftwards as usual down the creek when some sound made her pause suddenly, and hesitate, and she waited a moment, her hand touching the low branch of a tree. The sound was that of a twig snapping under a foot, and of someone moving through the bracken. She stood still, never moving, and presently, when all was silent again, she looked over the branch that concealed her, and there, some twenty yards away, a man was standing, with his back to a tree, and a musket in his hands.

She could see the profile under the three-cornered hat, and the face was one she did not recognize, and did not know, but he stood there, waiting, peering down towards the creek.

A heavy rain-drop fell upon him from the tree above, and taking off his hat he wiped his face with his handkerchief, turning his back to her as he did so, and at once she moved away from the place where she had stood, and ran homewards along the path by which she had come. Her hands were chilled, and she drew her cloak more closely about her shoulders, and that, she thought, that is the reason why William has not returned, for either he has been caught and held, or he is hiding in the woods, even as I hid just now. For where there is one man there will be others, and the man I have just seen is not a native of Helford, but belongs to Godolphin, to Rashleigh, or to Eustick. And so there is nothing I can do, she thought, nothing but return to the house, and go up to my room, and dress myself, and put on my ear-rings and my pendants and my bracelets, and descend to the dining-hall with a smile on my lips, and sit at the head of the table with Godolphin on my right and Rashleigh on my left, while their men keep a watch here in the woods.

She sped back along the path to the house, the rain-drops falling from the clustered trees, and the blackbirds were silent now, and the evening curiously still.

When she came to the clearing in the trees in front of the green lawns, and looked towards the house, she saw that the long window of the salon was open on to the terrace, and Rockingham was standing there, gazing up into the sky, while the dogs, Duke and Duchess, pattered at his heels. Dona drew back under cover, and then one of the dogs, snuffling at the lawn, came upon her footprints in the wet grass, and followed them, wagging her tail. She saw Rockingham watch the dog, and then he glanced up at the window above his head, and after a moment or two he advanced cautiously, stepping to the edge of the lawn and looking down upon the tell-tale footprints where they crossed the grass and disappeared amongst the trees.

Dona slipped back into the woods, and she heard Rockingham call the dog softly by her name, 'Duchess ... Duchess,' and a little to the left of her she could hear the dog nosing amongst the bracken. She turned now amongst the trees, making her way towards the drive which would bring her back to the front of the house, and to the courtyard, and Duchess must have followed her track through the wood towards the creek, for Dona could hear her no longer, and she came to the courtyard without discovery.

She let herself into the house through the great door, and luckily the dining-hall was still in shadow, the candles not being lit, for at the farther side a maid-servant was carrying plates and piling them on a side-table, while Harry's man from London assisted her. And still no sign of William.

Dona waited in the shadows, and after a moment the servants withdrew through the opposite door to the kitchens at the back, and swiftly she climbed the stairs and so along the passage to her bedroom.

'Who's that?' called Harry from his room. She did not answer, but slipped into her room, shutting the door, and in a few moments she heard his footsteps outside her door, and only just in time she flung her cloak aside and lay down on her bed, throwing her coverlet over her knees, for he burst in without knocking, as was his custom, clad only in his shirt and his breeches.

'Where the devil has that fellow William gone to?' he said. 'He has the key of the cellar hidden somewhere, and Thomas came to me about the wine. He tells me William is nowhere to be found.'

Dona lay still, her eyes shut, and then she turned on her side and looked up at Harry yawning, as though he had woken her from sleep.

'How should I know where William is?' she said, 'perhaps he is chatting with the grooms in the stables. Why don't they search for him?'

'They have searched,' fumed Harry; 'the fellow has simply disappeared, and here we are with George Godolphin and the rest coming to supper and no wine. I tell you, Dona, I won't stand for it. I shall sack him, you know.'

'He will come back directly,' said Dona wearily, 'there is plenty of time.'

'Confounded impudence,' said Harry, 'that's what happens to a servant when there's no man about the place. You have let him do exactly as he pleases.'

'On the contrary, he does exactly what pleases me.'

'Well, I don't like it, I tell you. Rock's quite right. The fellow has a familiar impudent manner about him. Rock's always right about these things.' He stood in the middle of the room, looking moodily down at Dona, his face flushed, his blue eyes choleric, and she recognized at once his usual manner when a little drunk, and that in a moment or two he would become abusive.

'Did you win at piquet?' asked Dona, seeking to distract him, and he shrugged his shoulders, and walked over to the mirror and stared at himself, smoothing the pouches under his eyes with his fingers. 'Do I ever win for ten minutes at a time playing with Rock?' he grumbled. 'No, it always ends with my losing twenty or thirty sovereigns, which I can ill afford. Look here, Dona, am I going to be allowed in here tonight?'

'I thought you were to be employed in catching pirates.'

'Oh, that will be over by midnight, or soon afterwards. If the fellow's in hiding on the river somewhere, as Godolphin and Eustick seem to think, he won't stand a dog's chance. There are men to be posted everywhere from here to the headland, and on either side of the river to boot. He won't slip away from the net this time.'

'And what part do you propose to take yourself?'

'Oh, I shall be a looker-on, and come in at the kill. And we'll all have a drink, and have no end of fun. But you haven't answered my question, Dona.'

'Shall we leave it until the time comes? Knowing what you are usually like after midnight you won't be caring very much if you lie down in my room or under the dining-table.'

'That's only because you're always so damned hard on me, Dona. I tell you it's a bit thick, this business of you running off here to Navron and leaving me to kick my heels in town, and then catching some Tom-fool fever when I do come after you.'

'Shut the door, Harry. I want to sleep.'

'Sleep my foot. You're always wanting to sleep. It's been your answer to me under every circumstance now for God knows how long,' and he stamped out of the room, banging the door, and she heard him stand a moment on the staircase and bawl out to the servant below whether that scoundrel William had returned.

And Dona, getting up from her bed and looking out of the window, saw Rockingham come back across the lawn, with the little dog Duchess pattering at his heels.

She began to dress, slowly and with great care, curling her dark ringlets round her fingers and placing them behind her ears, and into the ears themselves she screwed the rubies, and round her neck she clasped the ruby pendant. For Dona St Columb in her cream satin gown, with her ringlets and her jewels, must bear no resemblance to that bedraggled cabin-boy of *La Mouette*, who with the rain streaming down his thin shirt, had stood beneath Philip Rashleigh's window only five days ago. She looked at herself in the mirror, and then up at the portrait on the wall, and she saw how she had changed, even in the short while she had been at Navron, for her face had filled out, and the sulky look had gone from her mouth, and there was something different about her eyes, as Rockingham had said. As for her gypsy tan, there was no concealing it, and her hands and throat were burnt too by the sun. Who in the world will believe, she thought to herself, that this is the result of a fever, that the sunburn is a jaundice – Harry perhaps, he has so little imagination, but Rockingham, never.

Presently she heard the jangle of the stable bell in the courtyard, and this was the first of the guests arriving, his carriage driving to the steps. Then, after a few minutes' grace, the clatter of horses' hoofs, and once again the jangle of the bell, and now she could hear the sound of voices come from the dining-hall below, and Harry's voice booming out above the others, and the barking of Duke and Duchess. It was nearly dark, the garden was in shadow outside her window, and the trees were still. Down there in the woods, she thought, that sentinel is standing, peering down towards the creek, and perhaps he has been joined now by others, and they are all waiting there, with their backs to the trees, in silence, until we have finished our supper here in the house, and Eustick looks across at Godolphin, and Godolphin at Harry, and Harry at Rockingham, and then they will push back their chairs and smile at one another and, fingering their swords, go down into the woods. And if this were a hundred years ago, she thought, I would be prepared for this, and there would be sleeping draughts to put in their wine, or I would have sold myself to the devil and placed them under a spell, but it is not a hundred years ago, it is my own time, and such things do not happen any more, and all I can do is to sit at the table and smile upon them, and encourage them to drink.

She opened the door, and the sound of voices rose from the dining-hall. There were the pompous tones of Godolphin, and that scratchy querulous cough of Philip Rashleigh, and a question from Rockingham, silken and smooth. She turned along the corridor to the children's room before descending and kissed them as they slept, pulling aside the curtain so that the cool night air should come to them from the open casement, and then, as she walked once more to the head of the stairs, she heard a sound behind her, slow and dragging, as though someone, uncertain of his way in the darkness, shuffled in the passage.

'Who is there?' she whispered, and there was no answer. She waited a moment, a chill of fear upon her, while the loud voices of the guests came from below, and then once again there was the dragging shuffling sound in the dark passage, and a faint whisper, and a sigh.

She brought a candle from the children's room, and holding it high above her head, looked down into the long corridor whence the sound had come, and there, half-crouching, half-lying against the wall, was William, his face ashen pale, his left arm hanging useless at his side. She knelt down beside him, but he pushed her back, his small button mouth twisted with pain. 'Don't touch me, my lady,' he whispered, 'you will soil your gown, there is blood on my sleeve.'

'William, dear William, are you badly hurt?' she said, and he shook his head, his right hand clasping his shoulder.

'It is nothing, my lady,' he said, 'only somewhat unfortunate ... tonight of all nights.' And he closed his eyes, weak with pain, and she knew he was lying to her.

'How did it happen?' she asked.

'Coming back through the woods, my lady,' he said, 'I saw one of Lord Godolphin's men, and he challenged me. I managed to evade him, but received this scratch.'

'You shall come to my room, and I will bathe your wound, and bind it for you,' she whispered, and because he was barely conscious now, he protested no longer, but suffered her to lead him along the passage to her room, and once there she closed the door and bolted it, and helped him to her bed. Then she brought water and a towel, and in some fashion cleansed the cut in his shoulder, and bound it for him, and he turned his eyes up to her and said, 'My lady, you should not do this for me,' and 'Lie still,' she whispered, 'lie still and rest.'

His face was deadly white still, and she, knowing little of the depth of the wound or what she could do to ease his pain, felt helpless suddenly, and despairing, and he must have sensed it for he said 'Do not worry, my lady, I shall be all right. And at least my mission was successful, I went to *La Mouette* and saw my master.'

'You told him?' she asked. 'You told him that Godolphin, and Eustick, and the others were supping here tonight?'

'Yes, my lady, and he smiled in that way of his, my lady, and he said to me, "Tell your mistress I am in no way disturbed, and that *La Mouette* has need of a cabin-boy."' As William spoke there was a footstep outside, and someone knocked at the door. 'Who is there?' called Dona, and the voice of the little maid-servant answered, 'Sir Harry sends word to your ladyship, that he and the gentlemen are awaiting supper.'

'Tell Sir Harry to start, I will be with them directly,' said Dona, and bending down again to William she whispered, 'And the ship herself, is all well with the ship, and will she sail tonight?' But he stared back at her now without recognition, and then closed his eyes, and she saw that he had fainted.

She covered him with her blankets, scarcely knowing what she did, and washed the blood from her hands in the water, and then, glancing in the mirror and seeing that the colour had drained away from her face too, she dabbed rouge high on her cheek-bones with unsteady fingers. Then she left her room, leaving William unconscious on her bed, and walking down the stairs into the dining-hall she heard the scraping of the chairs on the stone floor as the guests rose to their feet and waited for her. She held her head high in the air, and there was a smile on her lips, but she saw nothing, not the blaze of the candles, nor the long table piled with dishes, nor Godolphin in his plum-coloured coat, nor Rashleigh with his grey wig, nor Eustick fingering his sword, nor all the eyes of the men who stared at her and bowed low as she passed to her seat at the head of the table, but only one man, who stood on the deck of his ship in the silent creek, saying farewell to her in thought as he waited for the tide.

Chapter 18

So, for the first time for many years, there was a banquet in the great dining-hall of Navron House. The candles shone down upon the guests as they sat shoulder to shoulder, six a side, at the long table, and the table itself was splendid with silver and rose-bordered plate and large bowls piled high with fruit. At one end the host, blue-eyed and flushed, his blond wig a little askew, laughed a shade too loudly and too long at every jest that passed. At the other end the hostess toyed with the dishes set before her, cool, unperturbed, throwing glances now and again at the guests beside her as though he on her right hand and he on her left were the only men who mattered in the world, she was theirs for this evening, or longer if they so desired. Never before, thought Harry St Columb, kicking at one of the dogs under the table, never before had Dona flirted so blatantly, made eyes so outrageously. If this was the result of that confounded fever, God help all the fellows present. Never before, thought Rockingham, watching her across the table, never before had Dona looked so provocative; what was passing through her head that moment, and why had she walked through the woods towards the river at seven o'clock that evening, when he thought her asleep in her bed?

And this, thought every guest who sat at her table, this is the famous Lady St Columb, of whom, from time to time, we hear so much gossip, so much scandal; who sups in London taverns with the ladies of the town, who rides bare-back in the streets at midnight in her husband's breeches, who has given something of herself, no doubt, to every philanderer at St James's, not to mention His Majesty himself.

So at first the guests were suspicious, inarticulate, and shy, but when she talked, and looked across at them with a word and a smile, and asked them about their homes, their hobbies and pursuits, and who was married and who was not, and gave them, in turn, to understand that every word they uttered had importance to her, had charm, and that given the opportunity she would understand them as they had never been understood before, then they relaxed, then they melted, and to hell, thought young Penrose, with all the people who have maligned her, the jealous chit-chat of plain women of course, and God's truth, what a wife to have and to keep, thought Eustick, under lock and key, and never let out of your sight. There was Tremayne from beyond Probus, and red-wigged Carnethick who owned all the land on the west coast, and the first had no wife and no mistress and so watched her dumbly, in sulky adoration, and the second had a wife ten years older than himself, and wondered, when Dona flashed him a glance across the table, whether there was any possibility of seeing her alone, later, when supper was over. Even Godolphin the pompous, Godolphin with his protruding eyes and his bulbous nose, admitted to himself, somewhat grudgingly, that Harry's wife had charm, although of course he did not approve of her and never would, and somehow he could not see Lucy taking to her as a companion, there was something bold about her eyes that made him feel uncomfortable. Philip Rashleigh, always taciturn with women, always gruff and silent, suddenly began to tell her about his boyhood, and how fond he had been of his mother, who had died when he was ten.

'And it's now nearly eleven o'clock,' thought Dona, 'and we are still eating, and drinking, and talking, and if I can go on like this, even for a little longer, it will give him time down there in the creek, for the tide must be making all the while, and no matter whether *La Mouette* has a gap in her hull or not, what repairs they have done to her must hold, and the ship must sail.'

She signalled with her eyes to the servants waiting, the glasses were filled once more, and while the hum and chatter of voices rang in her ear, and she glanced at her left-hand neighbour with a smile, she wondered if William had woken from his faint, or if he still lay upon her bed, ashen pale, with his eyes closed and that dark red stain on his shoulder. 'We should have music,' said Harry, his eyes half-closed, 'we should have music like my grandfather used to, up there in the gallery you know, when the old Queen was still alive, damn it, why does nobody have minstrels nowadays? I suppose the confounded Puritans killed 'em all.' He is well away, thought Dona, watching him, knowing the signs, he will give little trouble this evening. 'I consider that sort of foolery better dead,' said Eustick frowning, the gibe at the Puritans pricking him, for his father had fought for Parliament.

'Is there much dancing then at Court?' questioned young Tremayne, flushing all over his face, looking up at her eagerly. 'Why yes,' she answered him, 'you should come to town you know, when Harry and I return, I will find a wife for you.' But he shook his head, stammering a refusal, a dog-like appeal in his eyes. 'James will be his age in twenty years' time,' she thought, 'creeping into my room at three in the morning to tell me of his latest scrape, and all this will be forgotten, and put aside, and perhaps I shall remember it suddenly, seeing James's eyes and his eager face, and I shall tell him how I kept twelve men at supper until nearly midnight, so that the only man I have ever loved should escape to France and out of my life for ever.'

What was Rockingham saying, out of the corner of his mouth, to Harry? 'Yes, by thunder,' called Harry down the table, 'that rascal of a servant of yours has never come back, do you know that, Dona?' And he thumped the table with his fist, the glasses shaking, and Godolphin frowned, for he had spilt his wine down his lace cravat. 'I know,' smiled Dona, 'but it has made no difference, we have done very well without him.'

'What would you do, George,' shouted Harry, determined to air his grievances, 'with a servant who takes the night off when his master has guests for supper?'

'Dismiss him, naturally, my dear Harry,' said Godolphin.

'Thrash him into the bargain,' added Eustick.

'Yes, but that's all very well,' said Harry, hiccoughing, 'the blasted fellow is a pet of Dona's. When she was ill he was in and out of her bedroom all hours of the day and night. Would you put up with that, George? Does your wife have a man-servant hanging about her bedroom, eh?'

'Certainly not,' replied Godolphin. 'Lady Godolphin is in a very delicate state of health at the moment, and can't abide any-one but her old nurse with her, excepting of course myself.'

'How charming,' said Rockingham, 'how rural and touching. Lady St Columb, on the contrary, seems to have no women servants about her at all,' and he smiled across at Dona, raising his glass, and 'How did you enjoy your walk, Dona?' he said, 'did you find it wet there in the woods?'

Dona did not answer. Godolphin looked upon her with suspicion, for really if Harry permitted his wife to dally with servants he would soon be the talk of the countryside, and now he came to think of it he remembered an impertinent scrap of a groom driving the carriage the day Harry's wife had taken tea with them. 'How is your wife bearing with the heat?' Dona inquired. 'I think of her so often,' but she did not hear his reply, for Philip Rashleigh was talking in her left ear. 'I swear I have seen you before, dear lady,' he was saying, 'but I cannot for the life of me recollect the time or the place.'

And he stared at his plate, wrinkling his brows, as though by force of concentration he would bring back the scene.

'Some more wine for Mr Rashleigh,' said Dona, smiling graciously, pushing his glass towards him. 'Yes, I also feel that we have met, but it must have been six years ago, when I came here as a bride.'

'No, I'll take my oath on that,' said Rashleigh, shaking his head. 'It is an inflection in your voice I believe, and I have heard it not so long ago either.'

'But Dona has that effect on every man,' said Rockingham; 'they always feel, after seeing her, that they have known her before. You will find, my dear Rashleigh, that it will keep you awake at night.'

'I gather you speak from experience?' said Carnethick, and they exchanged glances, and Rockingham smiled, adjusting the lace at his wrists.

'How I detest him,' thought Dona; 'those narrow cat-like eyes, that meaning smile. He would like every man at this table to believe he makes love to me.'

'Were you ever in Fowey?' asked Philip Rashleigh.

'Never, to my certain knowledge,' she answered, and he drank down his wine, still shaking his head doubtfully.

'You have heard how I was robbed?' he said.

'Yes, indeed,' she answered, 'so very distressing for you. And you have never had news of your ship since?'

'Never a word,' he said bitterly. 'Ah, she's snug in a French port by now, with no legal means of extracting her. That's what comes of having a Court packed with foreigners, and a King who speaks better French, by all accounts, than he does English. However, I hope to settle accounts tonight, once and for all.'

Dona glanced up at the clock above the stairs. It wanted twenty minutes to midnight. 'And you, my lord?' she said, smiling upon Godolphin, 'were you also involved in the loss of Mr Rashleigh's ship?'

'I was, madam,' he replied stiffly.

'But I trust you received no hurt?'

'Luckily none. The rascals were too glad to show us their heels. Like every Frenchman, they preferred to run for it rather than face up to an honest fight.'

'And was their leader really the desperate man you have led me to believe?'

'Twenty times worse, madam. The most impudent, blood-thirsty, evil-looking rogue I've ever clapped eyes upon. We have heard since that his own ship carried a full complement of women, on every voyage, and most of them, poor wretches, kidnapped from our villages. Needless to say, I have told nothing of this to my wife.'

'Naturally not, it might precipitate matters unduly,' murmured Dona.

'He had a woman aboard the *Merry Fortune*,' said Philip Rashleigh. 'I could see her there on the deck above me, as plain as I see you now. A bold-faced baggage if ever there was one, with a cut on her chin, and her hair all over her eyes. Some harlot from the French docks, no doubt.'

'And there was a boy,' added Godolphin, 'a wretched scrap of a boy who came knocking on Philip's door; I'll take my oath he had a hand in it. He had a whining way of speaking, and a womanish cut about him that was most unpleasing.'

'These Frenchmen are so decadent,' said Dona.

'They'd never have slipped away from us, but for that wind,' snorted Rashleigh; 'down came a puff from Readymoney Cove, and her sails filled. You'd say it was the work of the devil himself. George here had the villain covered with his musket, but he missed him.'

'And how was that, my lord?'

'I was temporarily at a disadvantage, madam,' began Godolphin, the colour mounting to his face, and Harry, looking down from the opposite end of the table, slapped his hand on his knee and shouted, 'We've heard all about it, never fear, George. You lost your wig, didn't you? The rascal of a froggie pinched your wig?' and immediately all eyes turned on Godolphin, who sat stiff as a ramrod, staring at the glass in front of him.

'Take no notice of them, dear Lord Godolphin,' smiled Dona, 'only have a little more to drink. For what, after all, is the loss of a wig? It might have been something so much more precious, and what would Lady Godolphin do then?' And Rashleigh's neighbour Carnethick, on her left, choked suddenly over his wine.

A quarter to midnight, ten minutes, five minutes to midnight, and there was young Tremayne discussing cock-fighting with Penrose of Tregony, and a man from Bodmin whose name she had not heard was digging Rockingham in the ribs, whispering some bawdy story behind his hand, and Carnethick was leering at her across the table, and Philip Rashleigh was picking off grapes with a wrinkled hairy hand, and Harry, half lolling in his chair, was singing a song to himself that had no tune, one hand caressing his glass, and the other fondling the spaniel on his lap. But suddenly, Eustick, glancing at the clock, leapt to his feet and called in a voice of thunder, 'Gentlemen, we have wasted time enough. Have you all forgotten we have met tonight on very desperate business?'

There was silence at once. Tremayne looked down at his plate, blushing, and Carnethick wiped his mouth with a lace handkerchief, gazing straight in front of him. Someone coughed awkwardly, someone shuffled with his feet under the table, and only Harry continued smiling, humming his tuneless drunken song, and out in the courtyard the stable clock struck midnight. Eustick looked meaningly at his hostess. Dona rose to her feet at once, and 'You wish me to go?' she said.

'Nonsense,' called Harry, opening one eye, 'let my wife stay at her own table, damme. The party will fall flat without her, parties always do. Here's your health, my beautiful, even if you do permit servants in and out of your bedroom.'

'Harry, the time for jesting is over,' said Godolphin, and turning to Dona, 'We could talk more freely if you were not here. As Eustick has just observed, we have all become a little forgetful of our purpose.'

'But of course I understand,' said Dona, 'I would not dream of hindering in any way,' and as they all stood to let her pass, the great bell jangled in the court outside.

'Who the devil's that?' yawned Harry. 'Someone two-and-a-half hours late for supper? Let's open another bottle of wine.'

'We are all here,' said Eustick, 'we expect none other. What about you, Godolphin?'

'No, I have warned no one else,' frowned Godolphin. 'The meeting was a secret one in any case.'

Once again the bell jangled. 'Go and open the door, some-one,' shouted Harry. 'Where the deuce are all the servants?'

The dog jumped from his knees, and ran barking to the door.

'Thomas, one of you, what are you doing?' called Harry, over his shoulder, and Rockingham, rising, went to the door at the back of the hall that led to the kitchen, and flung it open. 'Hullo, there,' he cried, 'are you all asleep?' but no answer came to him, and the passage was dark and silent.

'Someone has blown the candles,' he said. 'It's as black as pitch here in the passage. Hullo, there, Thomas.'

'What orders did you give your servants, Harry?' said Godolphin, pushing back his chair. 'Did you tell them to go to bed?'

'To bed, no,' said Harry, rising unsteadily, 'the fellows are waiting in the kitchen somewhere. Give 'em another call, Rock, can't you?'

'I tell you there's no answer,' said Rockingham, 'and there's not a light anywhere. The kitchen itself yonder is as black as a pit.'

The bell jangled for the third time, and Eustick, with an oath strode towards the door, and began to draw back the bolts.

'It must be one of our people come to report,' said Rashleigh, 'one of the men we have posted in the woods. Someone has given us away, and the fight's begun.'

The door swung open, and Eustick stood on the threshold, calling into the darkness, 'Who asks for Navron House?'

179

'Jean-Benoit Aubéry, at the service of all you gentlemen,' came the answer, and into the hall walked the Frenchman, a sword in his hand, and a smile on his lips. 'Don't move, Eustick,' he said, 'and the rest of you, stay where you are. I have you covered, all of you. The first man who moves will have a bullet through his brains.'

And Dona, looking up the staircase to the gallery above, saw Pierre Blanc with a pistol in his hands, and Edmund Vacquier beside him, while at the door leading to the kitchen stood William, white and inscrutable, one arm hanging useless by his side, the other with a naked cutlass pointing at Rockingham's throat.

'I pray you be seated, gentlemen,' said the Frenchman, 'and I will not keep you long. As for her ladyship, she may please herself, but first she must give me the rubies she wears in her ears, for I have had a wager about them with my cabin-boy.'

And he stood before her, bowing, playing with his sword, while twelve men stared at him in hatred and in fear.

Chapter 19

THEY might have all been dead men, frozen in their seats at the table. No one spoke a word, but every man watched the Frenchman as he stood there smiling, his hand outstretched for the jewels.

Five against twelve, but the five were armed, and the twelve had supped unwisely and too well, and the swords by their sides were sheathed. Eustick still had his hand upon the door, but Luc Dumont from *La Mouette* stood beside him, pointing a pistol to his ribs, and slowly Eustick closed the door, and drew the bolts into their sockets. Down the staircase from the gallery above came Pierre Blanc and his companion, and they took up positions at either end of the long hall, so that if any man's hand strayed to his sword that man would have fallen, even as their master said. Rockingham leant against the wall, watching the point of William's cutlass, and he passed his tongue over his lips and did not speak. Only the host, who had sunk once again into his chair, surveyed the scene with bland bewilderment, a glass, half-filled with wine, raised to his lips.

Dona unscrewed the rubies from her ears, and laid them in the outstretched hand before her.

'Is that all?' she said.

He pointed with his sword to the pendant around her throat.

'Won't you spare me that as well?' he said, one eyebrow raised, 'my cabin-boy will curse me otherwise. And the bracelet on your arm, I must ask you for that too.'

She unfastened the bracelet and the pendant, and without a word and without a smile she placed them in his hand.

'Thank you,' he said, 'I trust you are recovered from your fever?'

'I thought so,' she answered, 'but your presence here will doubtless bring it back again.'

'That would be a pity,' he said gravely. 'My conscience would be uneasy. My cabin-boy suffers from fever from time to time, but the sea air does wonders for him. You ought to try it.' And bowing he placed the jewels in his pocket, and turned away from her.

'Lord Godolphin I believe,' he said, standing before his lordship. 'Last time we met I relieved you of your wig. That also was the fault of a wager. This time, perhaps, I might take something a little more substantial.' He reached for the decoration on Godolphin's breast, a ribbon and a star, and cut it away with his sword.

'Your weapon also, I regret to say, is something I cannot leave upon your person,' and Godolphin's sheath clattered upon the ground. The Frenchman bowed again, and passed on to Philip Rashleigh. 'Good evening, sir,' he said, 'you are looking a trifle less warm than when I saw you last. I must thank you for the gift of the *Merry Fortune*. She is a splendid vessel. You would not recognize her now, I swear. They have given her a new rig on my side of the channel, and a coat of paint into the bargain. Your sword, sir, if you please. And what have you in your pockets?'

The veins stood out in Rashleigh's forehead, and his breath came quick and fast. 'You'll pay for this, God damn you,' he said.

'Possibly,' said the Frenchman, 'but in the meanwhile, it is you who are paying,' and he emptied Rashleigh's sovereigns into a bag tied at his waist.

Slowly he made the circuit of the table, and each guest in turn lost the weapon at his side, and the money from his pockets, with the rings from his fingers, and the pin from his cravat. And as the Frenchman strolled round the table, whistling a tune under his breath, he would lean, now and again, to the bowl of fruit, and pluck a grape, and once, while waiting for the stout guest from Bodmin to divest himself of the many rings on his fingers, swollen with gout, he sat on the edge of the table, amongst the silver and the dishes, and poured himself a glass of wine from a carafe.

'You have a good cellar, Sir Harry,' he said. 'I should advise you to keep this a year or so longer; it is a wine that will improve. I had some half-dozen bottles of the same vintage in my own house in Brittany, and like a fool I drank it all too soon.'

182

'Death and damnation,' spluttered Harry, 'of all the confounded . . .'

'Don't worry,' smiled the Frenchman, 'I could have the key of
the cellar from William if I wanted it, but I would not deprive
you of the fun of drinking this in four or five years' time.' He
scratched his ear, and glanced down at the ring on Harry's finger.

'That is a very fine emerald,' he said.

For answer Harry tore it from his finger and threw it at the
Frenchman's face, but he caught it in his hands, and held it to
the light.

'Not a single flaw,' he said, 'which is rare in an emerald.
However, I will not take it. On second thoughts, Sir Harry, I have
robbed you enough.' and bowing, he handed the ring back to
Dona's husband. 'And now, gentlemen,' he said, 'I have a last
request to make. It is, perhaps, a little crude, but under the circumstances, very necessary. You see, I wish to return to my ship,
and to have you join your fellows in the woods and give chase to
me would, I fear, somewhat prejudice my plans. In short, I must
ask you to take off your breeches and hand them over to my men
here. Likewise your stockings, and your shoes.' One and all they
stared at him in rage, and 'By heaven, no,' shouted Eustick, 'have
you not made game of us enough?'

'I am sorry,' smiled the Frenchman, 'but really I must insist.
The night is warm, you know, and yesterday was midsummer.
Lady St Columb, perhaps you would be good enough to go into
the salon? These gentlemen will not care to undress themselves
before you in public, however much they may desire to do so in
private.'

And he held open the door for her to pass, and looking over
his shoulder to the guests he called, 'I will give you five minutes,
but no more. Pierre Blanc, Jules, Luc, William – keep a close
watch upon the gentlemen, and while they are disrobing, her
ladyship and I will discuss the affairs of the day.'

He followed her into the salon and shut the door.

'And you,' he said, 'with your proud smile, standing at the
head of the table, shall I make you do the same, my cabin-boy?'
and he threw his sword on the chair, and laughed, and held out
his arms. She went to him, and put her hands on his shoulders.

'Why are you so reckless?' she asked, 'so shameless, and so wicked? Do you know that the woods and the hills are black with men?'

'Yes,' he said.

'Why did you come here then?'

'Because, as in all my undertakings, the most hazardous performance is usually the most successful. Besides, I had not kissed you for nearly twenty-four hours.' And he bent his head, and took her face in his hands.

'What did you think,' she said, 'when I did not come for breakfast?'

'There was little time to think,' he answered, 'because I was woken just after sunrise by Pierre Blanc, to tell me *La Mouette* was aground, and taking in water. We have had the devil's own time with her, as you can imagine. And then, later on, when we were all stripped to the waist and working on her, William came down with your news.'

'But you did not know then, what was being planned for – tonight?'

'No, but I soon had a shrewd suspicion. One of my men saw a figure on the beach, up the river, and another in the hills opposite. And we knew then, that we were working against time. Even so, they had not found *La Mouette*. They were guarding the river and the woods, but they had not come down to the creek.'

'And then William came the second time?'

'Yes, between five and six this evening. He warned me of your party here at Navron, and I decided then what I should do. I told him of course, but that cut he received from the fellow in the woods on his way back to you did not help much.'

'I kept thinking of him, during supper, lying wounded and fainting on my bed.'

'Yes, but he dragged himself to the window, all the same, to admit us, just as we had planned. Your servants, by-the-way, are all shut up in your game larder, tied back-to-back, like the fellows we found on the *Merry Fortune*. Do you want your trinkets back again?' He felt in his pocket for her jewels, but she shook her head.

'You had better keep them,' she said, 'to remember me by.'

He said nothing, but looked over her head, stroking her curls.

'*La Mouette* will sail within two hours, if all goes well,' he said. 'The patch in her side is rough, but it must hold until she reaches the French coast.'

'What of the weather?' she asked.

'The wind is fair, and steady enough. We should reach Brittany in eighteen hours or less.'

Dona was silent, and he went on touching her hair.

'I have no cabin-boy,' he said. 'Do you know of a likely lad who would sail with me?' She looked at him then, but he was not smiling any more, and he moved away from her, and picked up his sword.

'I shall have to take William, I'm afraid,' he said. 'He has played his part at Navron, and your household will know him no longer. He has served you well, has he not?'

'Very well,' she answered.

'If it were not for the scrap he had tonight with Eustick's man, I would have left him,' he said, 'but recognition would come swift and fast, and Eustick would have hanged him without scruple. Besides, I hardly think he would have stayed to serve your husband.'

He glanced about the room, his eyes alighting for a moment on Harry's portrait, and then he walked to the long window, and flung it open, drawing back the curtains. 'Do you remember the first night I supped with you?' he said, 'and afterwards you stared into the fire, and I drew your picture. You were angry with me, were you not?'

'No,' she said, 'not angry. Only ashamed, because you guessed too much.'

'I will tell you one thing,' he said, 'you will never make a fisherman. You are too impatient. You will keep getting tangled up in your line.'

Someone knocked at the door, and 'Yes?' he called in French, 'have the gentlemen done what I commanded them?'

'They have, Monsieur,' answered William, through the door.

'Very well then. Tell Pierre Blanc to tie their hands behind their backs, and escort them to the bedrooms above. Close the doors upon them and turn the keys. They will not trouble us for two hours, which will give me the time we need.'

'Very good, Monsieur.'

'And William?'

'Monsieur?'

'How is your arm?'

'A trifle painful, Monsieur, but not seriously so.'

'That is good. Because I want you to take her ladyship by carriage to that spit of sand three miles this side of Coverack.'

'Yes, Monsieur.'

'And there await my further orders.'

'I understand, Monsieur.'

She stared at him, puzzled, and he came and stood before her, his sword in his hand. 'What are you going to do?' she said.

He waited a moment before he answered, and he was not smiling any more, and his eyes were dark.

'You remember how we talked together last night by the creek?'

'Yes,' she said.

'And we arranged that it was impossible for a woman to escape, except for an hour and a day?'

'Yes.'

'This morning,' he said, 'when I was working on the ship, and William brought me the news that you were alone no longer, I realized that our make-believe was over, and the creek was our sanctuary no more. From this time forward *La Mouette* must sail other waters, and find different hiding-places. And although she will be free, and the men on board her free, her master will remain captive.'

'What do you mean?' said Dona.

'I mean that I am bound to you, even as you are bound to me. From the very first, I knew that it would be so. When I came here, in the winter, and lay upstairs in your room, my hands behind my head, and looked at your sullen portrait on the wall, I smiled to myself, and said, "That – and none other." And I waited, and I did nothing, for I knew that our time would come.'

'What else?' she said.

'You, too,' he said, 'my careless indifferent Dona, so hard, so

186

disillusioned, playing the boy in London with your husband and his friends, you guessed that somewhere, in heaven knew what country and what guise, there was someone who was part of your body and your brain, and that without him you were lost, a straw blown by the wind.'

She went to him, and put her hand over his eyes.

'All that,' she said, 'all that you feel, I feel. Every thought, every wish, every changing mood. But it's too late, there is nothing we can do. You have told me so already.'

'I told you so last night,' he said, 'when we had no cares, and we were together, and the morning was many hours away. At those times a man can afford to shrug his shoulders at the future, because he holds the present in his arms, and the very cruelty of the thought adds, in some desperate fashion, to the delight of the moment. And when a man makes love, my Dona, he escapes from the burden of that love, and from himself as well.'

'Yes,' she said, 'I know that. I have always known it. But not every woman.'

'No,' he said, 'not every woman.' He took the bracelet from his pocket and clasped it on her wrist. 'And so,' he went on, 'when the morning came and I saw the mist on the creek, and you were gone from my side, there came also, not disillusion, but realization. I knew that escape, for me too, was impossible. I had become like a prisoner in chains, and the dungeon was deep.'

She took his hand, and laid it against her cheek.

'And all day long you worked upon your ship,' she said, 'and you sweated, and toiled, and said nothing, and frowned that frown of concentration I have come to understand, and then – when you had finished – what was your answer?'

He looked away from her, towards the open window.

'My answer', he said slowly, 'was still the same. That you were Dona St Columb, wife of an English baronet, and mother of two children, and I was a Frenchman, and an outlaw, a robber of your country, an enemy to your friends. If there is an answer, Dona, you must make it and not me.'

He crossed to the window once more, and looked back at her over his shoulder.

'That is why I have asked William to take you to the cove near

187

Coverack,' he said, 'so that you can decide what you wish to do. If I, and Pierre Blanc and the rest of us, return safely to the ship through this cordon in the wood, and hoist sail without delay, and leave with the tide, we shall be abreast of Coverack by sunrise. I will put off in a boat to have your answer. Should there be no sign of *La Mouette* by daylight, you will know that something has gone amiss with my plan. And Godolphin perhaps will have at last the satisfaction of hanging that hated Frenchman from the tallest tree in his park.'

He smiled, and stepped out on to the terrace. 'I have loved you, Dona,' he said, 'in almost every mood. But mostly, I think, when you threw yourself down on the deck of the *Merry Fortune*, in Pierre Blanc's breeches, with blood on your face, and the rain streaming down your torn shirt, and I looked at you and laughed, and a bullet whistled over your head.'

Then he turned, and vanished in the darkness.

She stood still, without moving, her hands clasped in front of her, while the minutes sped. Then at last she realized, like someone who has woken from a dream, that she was alone, and the house was silent, and that she held her ruby ear-rings and her pendant in her hands. A draught came from the open window, blowing the candles on the wall, and hardly aware of what she did she went to it, and closed and bolted it, and then went to the door leading to the dining-hall, and opened it wide.

There were the plates and the dishes on the table, and the bowls piled high with fruit, and the silver goblets and the glasses. The chairs were pushed back, as though the guests had risen from their supper, and withdrawn, and there was a strange forlorn air about the table, like a still-life picture drawn by an amateur brush, in which the food, and the fruit, and the spilt wine lack life and reality. The two spaniels crouched on the floor, and Duchess, lifting her nose from between her paws, looked up at Dona, and whined uncertainly. One of the men from *La Mouette* must have snuffed the candles, and then left, in haste, before extinguishing them all; for there were three that remained burning, the grease dripping on the floor, and the light they gave was sinister and queer.

One of them went out, and only two stayed now to flicker and dance upon the wall. The men of *La Mouette* had done their work and departed. They were creeping through the woods now to the ship in the creek, and their master was with them, his sword in his hand. The clock in the stable yard struck one; a high thin note, like the echo of a bell. Upstairs, unclothed and with their wrists tied, the guests of Navron House would be lying helpless and enraged upon the floor. All except Harry, and he would be asleep, on his back, and snoring, his wig askew and his mouth wide open, for not all the ill-treatment in the world would keep a St Columb from his bed, when he had supped too well. William must be attending to his own hurt, in his own room, and her conscience reproached her, for she had been forgetting him. So she turned then, to the great staircase, and placed her hand on the rail, when a sound from above made her look upwards to the gallery. And there, staring down at her with narrow, unsmiling eyes, stood Rockingham with a gash across his face, and a knife in his hand.

Chapter 20

FOR eternity it seemed he stood there staring down at her, and then slowly he descended, never taking his eyes from her face, and she backed away from him, feeling for the table, and sat down in her chair, and watched him. He was clad only in his shirt and breeches, and she saw now that there was blood upon the shirt, and on the knife that he held in his hand. She knew then what had happened. Somewhere, in one of the dark passages above, a man lay mortally wounded, or even dead, and it might be one of the crew from *La Mouette*, or it might be William. This struggle had taken place in silence and in darkness, while she had sat in the salon alone and dreaming, her rubies in her hands. Now he stood at the bottom of the stairs, and still he said nothing, but he went on watching her with his narrow cat-like eyes, and then he sat himself in Harry's chair at the far end of the table, and put the knife down on the plate before him.

When at last he spoke the familiarity of his voice sounded odd in contrast to his altered looks, for the man who faced her was not the Rockingham she had jested with in London, ridden beside at Hampton Court, and despised as a degenerate and a rake. This man had something cold about him, something evil, and from henceforward he was her enemy, wishing her suffering and pain.

'I see', he said, 'that your jewels have been returned to you.'

She shrugged her shoulders without answering, for how much he had guessed was of little consequence. The only thing that mattered was to know the plan in his head, and what movement he would make.

'And what', he said, 'did you give in place of your jewels?'

She began to replace the rubies in her ears, watching him over her arm as she did so. And then, because his gaze was something that she hated now, and could even grow to fear, she said to him, 'We have become very serious, Rockingham, all of a sudden. I should have thought this evening's jest would have amused you well.'

'You are right,' he answered, 'it has amused me much. That twelve men could be disarmed and unbreeched in so short a time by so few jesters bears a curious likeness to the pranks we used to play at Hampton Court. But that Dona St Columb should look upon the leader of the jesters in the way she did – in a way that could mean one thing only – no, that I did not find amusing.'

She leant her elbows on the table, and cupped her chin in her hands.

'And so?' she asked.

'And so in a flash I understood much that had puzzled me since my arrival here last night. That servant of yours, a spy of course of the Frenchman's. The friendliness between you, that you knew he was a spy. And those walks of yours, those wanderings in the woods, that elusive look in your eye that I had never seen before, yes, indeed, elusive to me, to Harry, to all men but one man, and I have seen that man tonight.' His voice was low now, scarcely above a whisper, and all the time he looked at her with hatred.

'Well?' he said, 'do you deny it?'

'I deny nothing,' she answered.

He picked up the knife from his plate, and began tracing lines with it upon the table, as though abstracted.

'You know', he said, 'that you could be imprisoned for this, and possibly hanged, should the truth come out?'

Once again she shrugged her shoulders, and did not answer.

'Not a very pleasant ending, for Dona St Columb,' he said. 'You have never been inside a jail, have you? You have never smelt the heat and the filth, you have never tasted the black broken bread, or drunk the water, thick with scum. And the feeling of a rope about your neck, as it tightens, and chokes you. How would you like that, Dona?'

'My poor Rockingham,' she said slowly, 'I can imagine all these things far better than you can describe them. What is your object? Do you wish to frighten me? Because you are not succeeding.'

'I thought it only wise', he said, 'to remind you of what may happen.'

'And all this?' she said, 'because my lord Rockingham fancies I smiled upon a pirate when he asked me for my jewels. Tell your

story to Godolphin, to Rashleigh and to Eustick, to Harry even –
they will say that you are mad.'

'Possibly,' he said, 'with your Frenchman on the high seas, and
yourself sitting at your ease in Navron House. But supposing
your Frenchman was not on the high seas, supposing he was
caught, and bound and brought before you, and we played with
him a little, as they played with prisoners some hundred years
ago, Dona, with you for audience. I rather believe you would give
yourself away.'

Once again she saw him as she had seen him earlier in the day,
a sleek cat crouching in the long grass, a bird between his claws,
so padded, so soft, and she realized, her memory streaking back
to the past, how she had always suspected in him some quality of
deliberate and cruel depravity which, because of the foolhardy
lightness of the age in which they lived, was well concealed.

'It pleases you to be dramatic,' she said, 'but the days of the
thumb-screw and the rack are over. We no longer burn our heretics at the stake.'

'Not our heretics perhaps,' he said, 'but our pirates are hanged,
and drawn, and quartered, and their accomplices suffer the same
fate.'

'Very well,' she said, 'since you believe me an accomplice,
do what you wish. Go upstairs, and unbind the guests who
supped here tonight. Wake Harry from his drunken slumbers.
Call the servants. Fetch horses, fetch soldiers and weapons. And
then when you have caught your pirate, you may hang us both
side by side from the same tree.'

He did not answer. He stared at her across the table, balancing
the knife in his hand.

'Yes,' he said, 'you would suffer that, would you not, and be
proud and glad. You would not mind dying now, because you
have had, at last, the thing you wanted all your life. Is not that
true?'

She looked back at him, and then she laughed.

'Yes,' she said, 'it is true.'

He turned very white, and the gash on his face showed vivid
red in contrast, altering the shape of his mouth, like a strange
grimace.

'And it might have been me,' he said, 'it might have been me.'

'Never,' she said, 'that I swear. Never in this world.'

'If you had not left London, if you had not come down here to Navron, it would have been me. Yes, though it were from boredom, from idleness, from indifference, even from disgust, it would have been me.'

'No, Rockingham . . . never. . . .'

He got up slowly from his chair, still balancing the knife in his hands, and he kicked the spaniel away from under his feet, and he rolled his sleeves above his elbows.

She rose too, gripping the sides of her chair, and the murky light from the two candles on the wall flickered down upon his face.

'What is it, Rockingham?' she asked.

Then for the first time he smiled, and he pushed back his chair, and laid one hand on the corner of the table.

'I believe', he whispered, 'that I am going to kill you.'

In a moment she had flung a glass of wine, close to her hand, straight in his face, and for half a second it blinded him, while the glass shivered to fragments on the floor. Then he made a lunge towards her across the table, but she eluded him, reaching for one of the heavy chairs beside her, and she lifted it, and sent it crashing amongst the silver and the fruit on the table, the leg of it striking his shoulder. He breathed quickly, with the pain of it, and hurling the chair from the table to the ground, he held his knife poised an instant, high above his shoulder, and threw it from him, straight at her throat. It struck the ruby pendant around her neck, cracking it in two, and she felt the cold steel slip away from her, pricking her skin, catching itself in the folds of her gown. She fumbled for it, sick with horror and with pain, but before she could seize it he was upon her, one hand doubling her wrist behind her back, and the other pressing her mouth in suffocation. She felt herself falling back against the table, the glasses and the plates crashing to the ground, and somewhere beneath her was the knife which he wished to find. The dogs were barking now, furiously excited, imagining this was some new sport designed for their amusement, and they leapt up at him, scratching with their paws, so that he was forced to turn a moment, and kick them from under him, releasing the pressure of his hand upon her mouth.

She bit through the palm of his hand, and drove her left fist into his eyes, and now he released her wrist, doubled up beneath her back, so that he could have two hands on her throat, and she felt the pressure of his thumbs on her wind-pipe, choking her. Her right hand struggled for the knife, and suddenly her fingers closed upon it, and gripping the cold hasp she drove it upwards, under his arm-pit, and she felt the horrid yielding of his soft flesh to the blade, surprisingly easy, surprisingly warm, with the blood running thick and fast on her hand. He sighed, long-drawn and strange, his hand no longer pressing upon her throat, and fell sideways on the table amongst the glass, and she pushed him from her and stood once more on her feet, her knees trembling, with the dogs barking madly about her legs. And now he was dragging himself from the table, too, his glazed eyes turned upon her, one hand pressed to the wound under his arm, and with the other he reached for a great silver carafe that still stood upon the table, and with this he would have smashed her face and trodden her to the ground, but even as he moved towards her the last candle flickered on the wall and was gutted, and they were in darkness.

She felt the edge of the table with her hands, and worked her way round it, out of his reach, and she heard him groping for her in the black hall, stumbling over a chair that stood in his way. Now she was making for the staircase, she could see a glimmer of pale light from the window in the gallery, and here were the stairs themselves, and the rail, and she was climbing the stairs, with the two dogs barking at her heels. Somewhere from above she could hear shouts and cries, and the thumping of fists upon a door, but all this was confusion, was a dream having no connexion with the battle that was hers alone. Looking back over her shoulder, sobbing, she saw Rockingham at the foot of the stairs, and he was not standing upright as he had before, but was climbing towards her on all fours like the dogs at her heels. She reached the top of the stairs, and the shouts and thumps were louder now. There was Godolphin's voice amongst them, and Harry's too, while the barking of the dogs joined the clamour, and from the direction of the nurseries came the high-pitched frightened scream of a child, woken from his sleep. Then she knew anger at last, and not fear. Then she was resolute, and calm, and cold.

The grey light from the window, where the moon struggled through the clouds, shone feebly upon a shield hanging on the wall, some trophy of a dead St Columb, and she tore it from its place on the wall, heavy and dusty with age, and the weight of it dragged her to her knees. Still Rockingham came. She could see his back, humped against the rail, as he paused for breath, and she could hear the scratching of his hands upon the stairs and the quick sound of his breathing. When he turned the corner of the stair and stood a moment, turning his head, looking for her in the darkness, she hurled the shield at him, driving it full in his face, and he staggered and fell, turning over and over on the stairs, crashing with the shield on top of him to the stone floor below. And the dogs went down after him, excited and barking, scampering in play, nosing his body as it lay there on the floor. Dona stood motionless, all feeling spent, a great ache behind her eyes, the sound of James's cry still ringing in her ears, and somewhere now there were footsteps, and a voice calling in anxiety and fear, and the splintering tearing noise of breaking wood. It would be Harry perhaps, or Eustick, or Godolphin, beating down the locked door of the bedroom where they were imprisoned, and it seemed to her that these things mattered little, for she was too weary now to care. She wanted to lie down in the darkness, and to sleep with her face between her hands, and she remembered that somewhere along this passage was her room, and her own bed, where she could hide and be forgotten. Somewhere, in the river, there was a ship called *La Mouette*, and the man she loved stood at the wheel now, taking his ship to the sea. She had promised to give him her answer at day-break, and to wait for him on the little spit of sand that jutted out into the sea. William would take her to him, William the faithful, somehow they would find their way across the country in the darkness, and when they reached the cove the boat would put off from the ship towards them, even as he had said. She thought of the coast of Brittany as she had seen it once before, golden at sunrise, with the rocks about it jagged and crimson, like the coast of Devon. The white breakers hurled themselves upon the sand, and the spray threw a fine mist on to the cliffs, the smell of it mingling with the warm earth and the grass.

Somewhere there was a house which she had never seen, but he would take her to it, and she would feel the grey walls with her hands. She wanted to sleep now, and dream of these things, and remember no more the guttering candles in the dining-hall below, with the smashed glass and the broken chairs, and Rockingham's face when the knife touched his flesh. She wanted to sleep, and it seemed to her suddenly that she stood no longer, that she was falling too, as Rockingham had done, and the blackness came about her and covered her, and there was a rushing of wind in her ears. . . .

Surely it was long afterwards that people came and bent over her, and hands lifted her and carried her. And someone bathed her face, and her throat, and laid pillows under her head. There were many voices in the distance, men's voices, and the coming and going of heavy footsteps, and there must have been horses in the courtyard outside the house; she could hear their hoofs on the cobbles. Once too she heard the stable clock strike three.

And dimly, in the back of her mind, something whispered, 'He will be waiting for me on the spit of sand, and I am lying here, and I cannot move, and I cannot go to him,' and she tried to raise herself from her bed, but she had no strength. It was still dark, while outside her window she could hear a little thin trickle of rain. Then she must have slept, the heavy dull sleep of exhaustion, for when she opened her eyes it was daylight, and the curtains had been drawn, and there was Harry kneeling by her side, fondling her hair with his great clumsy hands. He was peering into her face, his blue eyes troubled, and he was blubbing like a child.

'Are you all right, Dona?' he said, 'are you better, are you well?'

She stared at him without understanding, the dull ache still behind her eyes, and she thought how ridiculous it was that he should kneel there, in so foolish a manner, and she felt a sort of shame upon her that he should do so.

'Rock's dead,' he said. 'We found him dead there, on the floor, with his poor neck broken. Rock, the best friend I have ever had.' And the tears rolled down his cheeks, and she went on staring at him. 'He saved your life, you know,' said Harry; 'he must have fought that devil single-handed, alone there in the darkness, while you fled up here to warn us. My poor beautiful, my poor sweet.'

She did not listen to him any more, she sat up, looking at the daylight as it streamed into her window. 'What is the time?' she said, 'how long has the sun been risen?'

'The sun?' he said blankly, 'why, it's nearly noon I believe. What of it? You are going to rest, are you not? You must, after all you have suffered last night.'

She put her hands over her eyes and tried to think. It was noon then, and the ship would have sailed, for he could not have waited for her after the day had broken. She had lain here sleeping on her bed, while the little boat put into the spit of sand and found it empty.

'Try and rest again, my lovely,' said Harry, 'try and forget the confounded God-damned night. I'll never drink again, I swear it. It's my fault, I ought to have stopped it all. But you shall have your revenge, I promise you that. We've caught him, you know, we've got the blasted fellow.'

'What do you mean?' she said slowly, 'what are you talking about?'

'Why, the Frenchman of course,' he said, 'the devil who killed Rock, and would have killed you too. The ship's gone, and the rest of his battered crew, but we've got him, the leader, the damned pirate.'

She went on staring at him without understanding, dazed, as though he had struck her, and he, seeing her eyes, was troubled, and began once more to fondle her hair and to kiss her fingers, murmuring, 'My poor girl, what a confounded to-do, eh, what a night, what a devilish thing.' And then, pausing a moment he looked at her, and flushed, a little confused, still holding her fingers, and because the despair in her eyes was something dark and new, was a thing he did not understand, he said to her awkwardly, like a shy and clumsy boy: 'That Frenchman, that pirate, he didn't molest you in any way, did he, Dona?'

Chapter 21

Two days came and went, things without hours or minutes in which she dressed herself, and ate, and went out into the garden, and all the while she was possessed by a strange sense of unreality as though it was not she who moved, but some other woman, whose very words she did not understand. No thoughts came to her mind: it was as though part of her slept still, and the numbness spread from her mind to her body, so that she felt nothing of the sun when it came from two clouds and shone a moment, and when a little chill wind blew she was not cold.

At one time the children ran out to greet her, and James climbed on her knee, and Henrietta, dancing before her, said 'A wicked pirate has been caught, and Prue says he will be hanged.' She was aware of Prue's face, pale, rather subdued, and with an effort she remembered that there had been death, of course, at Navron, that at this moment Rockingham would be lying in a darkened church awaiting burial. There was a dull greyness about these days, like the Sundays she remembered as a child, when the Puritans forbade dancing on the green. There was a moment when the rector of Helford Church appeared and spoke to her gravely, condoling with her on the loss of so great a friend. And afterwards he rode away, and Harry was beside her again, blowing his nose, and speaking in a hushed voice entirely unlike himself. He stayed by her continually, humble and anxious to please, and kept asking her whether she needed anything, a cloak, or a coverlet for her knees, and when she shook her head, wishing he would leave her quietly, so that she could sit, staring at nothing, he began protesting once more how much he loved her, and that he would never drink again: it was all because he had drunk too much that fatal night that they had let themselves be trapped in such a way, and but for his carelessness and sloth poor Rockingham would be alive.

'I'll cut out gambling too,' he said. 'I'll never touch another card, and I'll sell the town house, and we'll go and live in Hampshire, Dona, near your old home, where we first met. I'll live the life of a country gentleman at last, with you and the children, and I'll teach young James to ride and to hawk. How would you like that, eh?'

Still she did not answer, but went on staring in front of her.

'There's always been something baleful about Navron,' he said, 'I remember thinking so as a boy. I never felt well here: the air is so soft. It doesn't suit me. It doesn't suit you, either. We'll go away as soon as this business is over and done with. If only we could lay our hands on that damned spy of a servant, and hang 'em both at the same time. God, when I think of the danger you were in, you know, trusting that fellow.' And he began to blow his nose again, shaking his head. One of the spaniels came fawning up to her, licking her hands, and suddenly she remembered the furious barking of the night, the yapping, the excitement, and in a flash her darkened mind became alive again, awake and horribly aware. Her heart beat loudly, for no reason, and the house, and the trees, and the figure of Harry sitting beside her took shape and form. He was talking and she knew now that every word he uttered might be of importance, and that she must miss nothing, for there were plans to make, and time itself was now of desperate value.

'Poor Rock must have outwitted the servant from the first,' he was saying. 'There were signs of the struggle in his room, you know, and a trail of blood leading along the passage, and then it stopped suddenly, and we found no trace of the fellow. Somehow he must have got away, and perhaps have joined those other rascals on the ship, though I think it doubtful. They must have used some part of the river time and again as a sneak-hole. By thunder, Dona, if we'd only known.'

He smote his fist in the palm of his hand, and then, remembering that Navron had been a house of death and that to talk loudly, or to swear, was to show irreverence towards the dead, he lowered his voice, and sighed, and said 'Poor Rock. I hardly know how we shall do without him, you know.'

She spoke at last, her voice sounding strange to her own ears, because her words were careful, like a lesson learnt by heart.

'How was he caught?' she said, and the dog was licking her hand again, but she did not feel it.

'You mean that damned Frenchman?' said Harry, 'well, we – we rather hoped you could tell us a bit about it, the first part, because you were with him, weren't you, in the salon there. But I don't know, Dona, you seemed so stunned and strange when I asked you. I said to Eustick and the others, "Hell, no, she's been through too much," and if you'd rather not tell me about it, well, that's all there is to it, you know.'

She folded her hands on her lap and said, 'He gave me back my ear-rings and then he went.'

'Oh, well,' said Harry, 'if that was all. But then he must have come back, you know, and tried to follow you upstairs. Perhaps you don't remember fainting there, in the passage by your room. Anyway, Rock must have been there by then, and guessing what the scoundrel was after, threw himself on the fellow, and in the fight that followed – for your safety, Dona, you must always remember that – he lost his life, dear staunch friend that he was.'

Dona waited a moment, watching Harry's hand as he stroked the dog.

'And then?' she said, looking away from him, across the lawn.

'Ah, the rest we owe to Rock too. It was his plan, from the first. He suggested it to Eustick and George Godolphin when we met them at Helston. "Have your men posted on the beaches," he said, "and boats in readiness, and if there is a vessel hiding up the river, you'll get her as she comes down by night, on the top of the tide." But instead of getting the ship, we got the leader instead.'

And he laughed, pulling at the dog's ears, and tickling her back.

'Yes, Duchess, we got the leader, and he'll hang for piracy and murder, won't he? And the people will sleep easy in their beds once more.'

Dona heard herself saying sharply in a clear cold voice, 'Was he wounded at all? I don't understand.'

'Wounded? God bless me, no. He'll hang without a scratch on him, and he'll know what it feels like. The devilry up here had delayed him, you see, and those three other scoundrels, and they were making for a point below Helford to join their vessel in mid-

200

river. He must have told the rest of his crew to get the ship under way when he was up at the house. God knows how they managed it, but they did. When Eustick and the others got down to the point agreed upon, there was the ship in midstream, and the fellows swimming out to her, all but their leader, and he was standing on the beach, as cool as a blade of steel, fighting two of our people at once, while his men got away. He kept shouting over his shoulder to them in his damned lingo as they swam to the ship, and though the boats were launched from the beaches, as we arranged, they were too late to catch the scoundrels or the ship. She sailed out of Helford with a roaring tide under her, and a fair wind on her quarter, and the Frenchman watched her go, and God damn it, he was laughing, Eustick said.'

As Harry spoke it seemed to Dona that she could see the river where it broadened, and met the sea, and she could hear the wind in the rigging of *La Mouette* as she had heard it once, and the escape would be a repetition of all the escapes that had gone before, but this time they sailed without their captain, this time they went alone. Pierre Blanc, Edmond Vacquier, and the rest, they had left him there on the beach because he had bid them do so, and she guessed what his words must have been, as he stood there, facing his enemies, while they swam to the ship. He had saved his crew, and he had saved his ship, and even now, in whatever prison he found himself, that calm unfettered brain of his would be working and planning some new method of escape, and she realized now that she was stunned and afraid no longer, for the manner of his capture had killed all fear within her.

'Where have they taken him then?' she asked, rising now, throwing on the ground the wrap that Harry had put round her shoulders. He told her 'George Godolphin has him, in the keep, strongly guarded, and they're for moving him up to Exeter or Bristol when an escort comes down for him in forty-eight hours.'

'And what then?'

'Why, they'll hang him, Dona, unless George and Eustick and the rest of us save His Majesty's servants the trouble of doing so, and hang him on Saturday midday, as a treat to the people.'

They entered the house, and she stood now on the spot where he had bidden her farewell, and she said, 'Would that be within the law?' 'No, perhaps not,' said Harry, 'but I don't think His Majesty would trouble us for a reason.'

So there was little time to lose, she thought, and much to be done. She remembered the words he had spoken: how the most hazardous performance was often the most successful. That was a piece of advice she would repeat to herself continually during the next hours, for if any situation appeared beyond all saving and all hope, the saving of him did so at this moment.

'You are all right again, are you not?' said Harry anxiously, putting an arm about her. 'It was the shock of poor Rock's death I believe that made you so strange these two days. That was it, wasn't it?'

'Perhaps,' she said. 'I don't know. It does not matter. But I am well again now. There is no need for you to be anxious.'

'I want to see you well,' he repeated. 'That's all I care about, damn it, to see you well and happy.' And he stared down at her, his blue eyes humble with adoration, and he reached clumsily for her hand.

'We'll go to Hampshire then, shall we?' he said.

'Yes,' she answered, 'yes, Harry, we'll go to Hampshire.' And she sat down on the low seat before the fireplace where no fire burnt because it was midsummer, and she stared at the place where the flames should have been while Harry, forgetting that Navron had been a house of death called, 'Hi, Duke ... Hi, Duchess, your mistress says she'll come with us to Hampshire. Find it, then, go seek.'

It was imperative of course that she should see Godolphin, and talk to him, and persuade him into granting her an interview alone with his prisoner. That part of it should be easy, because Godolphin was a fool. She would flatter him, and during the interview she could pass weapons, a knife or a pistol if she could procure one, and so far, so good, because the actual method of escape could not be of her choosing. They supped quietly, she and Harry, in the salon before the open window, and soon afterwards Dona went up to her room, pleading weariness, and he had the intuition to say nothing, and to let her go alone.

When she was undressed, and lying in her bed, her mind full of her visit to Godolphin, and how she should achieve it, she heard a

202

gentle tapping at her door. 'Surely,' she thought, her heart sinking, 'it is not Harry, in this new wistful penitent mood, not to-night.' But when she did not answer, hoping he would think her asleep, the tapping came again. Then the latch lifted, and it was Prue standing there in her nightgown, a candle in her hand, and Dona saw that her eyes were red and swollen with crying.

'What is it?' said Dona, sitting up at once. 'Is it James?'

'No, my lady,' whispered Prue, 'the children are asleep. It's only – it's only that I have something to tell you, my lady.' And she began weeping again, rubbing her eyes with her hand.

'Come in, and shut the door,' said Dona. 'What is the matter, then, why are you crying? have you broken something? I shall not scold you.'

The girl continued to weep, and glancing about her, as though afraid that Harry himself might be there, and would hear her, she whispered between her tears, 'It's about William, my lady, I have done something very wicked.'

'Oh heaven,' thought Dona, 'she has been seduced by William while I was away in *La Mouette*, and now because he has gone, she is afraid and ashamed, and thinks she will have a baby, and that I will send her away,' and 'Don't be afraid, Prue,' she said softly, 'I won't be angry. What is it about William? You can tell me, you know. I shall understand.'

'He was always very good to me,' said Prue, 'and most attentive to me and the children, when you were ill, my lady. He could not do too much for us. And after the children were asleep, he used to come and sit with me, while I did my sewing, and he used to tell me about the countries he had visited, and I found it very pleasant.'

'I expect you did,' said Dona, 'I should have found it pleasant too.'

'I never thought', said the girl, sobbing afresh, 'that he had anything to do with foreigners, or with these terrible pirates we had heard about. He was not rough in his ways at all, with me.'

'No,' said Dona, 'I hardly suppose he was.'

'And I know it was very wrong of me, my lady, not to have told Sir Harry and the other gentlemen that night, when there was all that terrible to-do, and they came bursting out of their rooms, and poor Lord Rockingham was killed, but I had not the heart to give him up, my lady. So faint he was with loss of blood, and as white as a ghost, I just could not do it. If it's found out I shall be beaten and sent to prison, but he said I must tell you whatever happened.'

And she stood there, twisting her hands, with tears running down her cheeks.

'Prue,' said Dona, swiftly, 'what are you trying to tell me?'

'Only that I hid William in the nursery that night, my lady, when I found him lying in the passage, with a cut on his arm, and another on the back of his head. And he told me then that Sir Harry and the other gentlemen would kill him if he was found, that the French pirate was his master, and there had been fighting at Navron that night. So, instead of giving him up, my lady, I bathed and dressed his wounds, and I made him up a bed on the floor beside the children, and after breakfast, when the gentlemen were all away searching for him and the other pirates, I let him out, my lady, by the side door, and no one knows anything about it but you and me.'

She blew her nose noisily on her handkerchief, and would have cried again. But Dona smiled at her, and leaning forward patted her shoulder, and said, 'It's all right, Prue. You are a good faithful girl to tell me this, and I shall keep it to myself. I am fond of William, too, and should be greatly distressed if any harm came to him. But I want you to tell me something. Where is William now?'

'He said something about Coverack when he woke, my lady, and asked for you, and I told him you were in bed, very shocked and exhausted, as Lord Rockingham had been killed in the night. At that he seemed to think a while, my lady, and then when I had bathed and dressed his wounds afresh he said he had friends at Gweek who would shelter him, and would not betray him, and that he would be there if you wished to send word to him, my lady.'

'At Gweek?' said Dona. 'Very well then, Prue. I want you to go back to bed, and think no more of this, and say nothing of it ever again, to anyone, not even to me. Go on as you have always done, won't you Prue, and look after the children, and love them well.'

'Yes, my lady,' said Prue, and she curtsied, her tears still near the surface, and left the room, and went back to the nursery. And Dona smiled to herself in the darkness, for William the faithful was still at hand, her ally and her friend, and his master's escape from the keep had become a thing of possibility.

So she slept, her mind easier than it had been, and when she woke she saw that the listless sky had become blue again, and the clouds were gone, and there was something in the air of that midsummer that would not come again, a warmth and a brilliance belonging to the days when, careless and enraptured, she had gone fishing in the creek.

While she dressed she made her plans, and when she had breakfasted she sent word for Harry to come to her. Already he had recovered something of his former spirits, and as he came into the room he called to his dogs in his usual voice, hearty and well content with himself, and he kissed her on the back of her neck as she sat before her mirror.

'Harry,' she said, 'I want you to do something for me.'

'Anything in the world,' he promised eagerly, 'what is it?'

'I want you to leave Navron today,' she said, 'and take Prue and the children with you.'

His face fell, and he stared at her in dismay.

'But you?' he said, 'why will you not come with us?'

'I shall follow you,' she said, 'tomorrow.'

He began to pace up and down the room.

'I imagined we could all travel together, when this business is over,' he protested. 'They'll be hanging that fellow tomorrow in all probability. I thought of going over to see Godolphin and Eustick about it today. You'd like to see him hanged, would you not? We could fix it for nine in the morning, perhaps, and then start our journey afterwards.'

'Have you ever seen a man hanged?' she said.

'Why, yes, there's little to it, I admit. But this is rather different. Damn it, Dona, the fellow murdered poor Rock, and would have killed you too. Do you mean to say you have no wish for revenge?'

She did not answer, and he could not see her face, for her back was turned to him.

'George Godolphin would think it very cool of me', he said, 'to slip away without a word of explanation.'

'I would do the explaining,' she said. 'I propose calling on him myself this afternoon, after you have gone.'

'Do you mean that I should deliberately set off on the journey, without you, taking the children and the nurse, and leaving you here, all alone, with a handful of half-witted servants?'

'Exactly that, Harry.'

'And if I take the carriage for the children, and ride myself, how would you travel tomorrow?'

'I should hire a post-chaise from Helston.'

'And join with us at Okehampton you mean, in the evening?'

'And join with you at Okehampton, in the evening.'

He stood by the window, staring moodily out on to the garden.

'Oh, God damn it, Dona, shall I ever understand you?'

'No, Harry,' she said, 'but it does not matter very much.'

'It does matter,' he said, 'it makes life most confounded hell for both of us.'

She glanced up at him standing there with his hands behind his back.

'Do you really think that?' she said.

He shrugged his shoulders. 'Oh, damme,' he said, 'I don't know what I think. I only know I'd give everything in the world to make you happy, but the cursed trouble is I don't know how to, and you are fonder of James's finger-nail than you are of me. What's a fellow to do when his wife doesn't love him but drink and play cards? Will you tell me that?'

She stood beside him a moment, and put her hand on his shoulder. 'I shall be thirty in three weeks' time,' she said. 'Perhaps as I grow older, Harry, I shall grow wiser.'

'I don't want you any wiser,' he said sullenly, 'I want you as you are.'

She did not answer, and playing with her sleeve he said to her, 'Do you remember, before you came to Navron, you said some nonsense or other about feeling like that bird in your father's aviary. I couldn't make head or tail of it, and I still can't. It sounded such gibberish, you know. I wish I knew what you were driving at.'

'Don't think about it,' she said, patting his cheek, 'because the linnet found its way to the sky. And now, Harry, are you going to do what I asked you?'

'Yes, I suppose so,' he said, 'but I warn you, I don't like it, and I shall put up at Okehampton and wait for you. You won't delay your journey for any reason, will you?'

'No,' she said. 'No, I won't delay.'

And he went downstairs to make the necessary arrangements for departure, while she summoned Prue and told her of the sudden change of plans. At once all was bustle and confusion, the strapping up of bedding and boxes, the packing of food and clothing for the journey, while the children ran about like puppies, delighted in all movement, any sort of change for the variety it gave, and 'They don't mind leaving Navron,' thought Dona; 'in a month's time they will be playing in Hampshire fields, and Cornwall will be forgotten. Children forget places so easily, and faces even faster.'

They had cold meat at one o'clock, the children eating with herself and Harry for a treat. Henrietta danced about the table like a fairy, white with excitement because he was to ride beside their carriage. James sat on Dona's lap, endeavouring to put his feet up on the table, and when Dona permitted him, he looked about him with an air of triumph, and she kissed his fat cheek and held him to her. Harry caught something of his children's excitement, and he began to tell them about Hampshire, and how they would go there in all probability, for the rest of the summer. 'You shall have a pony, Henrietta,' he said, 'and James too, later on,' and he began to throw pieces of meat across the floor to the dogs, and the children clapped their hands and shouted.

The carriage came to the door, and they were bundled inside with packages, rugs, pillows, and the baskets for the two dogs, while Harry's horse champed at his bit, and pawed the ground.

'You must make my peace with George Godolphin,' said Harry, bending down to Dona, flicking his boots with his whip. 'He won't understand it, you know, my tearing off in this way.'

'Leave everything to me,' she answered, 'I shall know what to say.'

'I still don't know why you won't come with us,' he said, staring at her, 'but we'll be waiting for you, tomorrow evening, at Okehampton. When we pass through Helston today I will order your chaise for the morning.'

'Thank you, Harry.'

He went on flicking the toe of his boot. 'Stand still, will you, you brute?' he said to his horse; and then to Dona, 'I believe you've still got that damned fever on you, and you won't admit it.'

'No,' she said, 'I have no fever.'

'Your eyes are strange,' he said; 'they looked different to me the first moment I saw you, lying in bed there, up in your room. The expression has changed. God damn it, I don't know what it is.'

'I told you this morning,' she said, 'I'm getting older, and shall be thirty in three weeks' time. It's my age you can see in my eyes.'

'Damn it, it's not,' he said. 'Ah, well, I suppose I'm a fool and a blockhead, and will have to spend the rest of my days wondering what the hell has happened to you.'

'I rather think you will, Harry,' she said.

Then he waved his whip, and wheeled his horse about, and cantered away down the drive, while the carriage followed soberly, the two children smiling from the window and blowing kisses, until they turned the corner of the avenue and could see her no more.

Dona went through the empty dining-hall and into the garden. It seemed to her that the house already had a strange, deserted appearance, as though it knew in its old bones that soon the covers would be placed upon the chairs, and the shutters drawn, and the doors bolted, and nothing would be there any longer but its own secret darkness: no sunshine, no voices, no laughter, only the quiet memories of the things that had been.

Here, beneath this tree, she had lain on her back in the sun and watched the butterflies, and Godolphin had called upon her for the first time, surprising her with ringlets in disorder and the flowers behind her ears. And in the woods there had been bluebells, where there were bluebells no more, and the bracken had been young which was now waist-high and darkly green. So much loveliness, swiftly come and swiftly gone, and she knew in her heart that this was the last time of looking upon it all, and that she would never come to Navron again. Part of her would linger there for ever: a footstep running tip-toe to the creek, the touch of her hand on a tree, the imprint of her body in the long grass. And perhaps one day, in after years, someone would wander there and listen to the silence, as she had done, and catch the whisper of the dreams that she had dreamt there, in midsummer, under the hot sun and the white sky.

Then she turned her back on the garden, and calling to the stable-boy in the courtyard she bade him catch the cob who was in the meadow, and put a saddle on him, for she was going riding.

Chapter 22

WHEN Dona came to Gweek she made straight for a little cottage almost buried in the woods, a hundred yards or so from the road, and which she knew instinctively to be the place she sought. Passing there once before she had seen a woman at the doorway, young and pretty, and William, driving the carriage, had saluted her with his whip.

'There have been ugly rumours', Godolphin had said, 'of young women in distress,' and Dona smiled to herself, thinking of the girl's blush as she remembered it, and William's expression, his gallant bow, little guessing that his mistress had observed him.

The cottage appeared deserted, and Dona, dismounting, and knocking on the door, wondered for one moment if she had been mistaken after all. Then she heard a movement from the scrap of garden at the back, and she caught the glimpse of a petticoat disappearing into a door, and that door suddenly shutting, and the bolt being drawn. She knocked gently, and getting no answer called, 'Don't be afraid. It is Lady St Columb from Navron.'

In a minute or two the bolt was pulled back, and the door was opened, and on the threshold stood William himself, with the flushed face of the young woman peering behind his shoulder.

'My lady,' he said, staring at her, with his button mouth twisted. She feared for one moment he was going to break down and cry. Then he stiffened, and held the door open wide. 'Run upstairs, Grace,' he said to the girl, 'her ladyship wishes to speak to me alone.'

The girl obeyed him, and Dona preceded William into the little kitchen, and sat down by the low hearth, and looked at him.

He still wore his right arm in a sling, and his head was bandaged, but he was the same William, standing before her as though he awaited her instructions for the ordering of supper.

'Prue gave me your message, William,' she said, and because he stood there so stiffly, without expression, she smiled at him with understanding. He said humbly, his eyes downcast, 'My lady, what can I say to you? I would have died for you that night, and instead I proved false, and lay like a sick child on the floor of the nursery.'

'You could not help it,' she said. 'You were weak and faint from loss of blood, and your prisoner proved too swift and cunning for you. But I have not come to talk about that, William.'

For a moment his eyes entreated her, but she shook her head. 'No questions,' she said, 'for I know what you would ask me. I am well, and strong, and quite unhurt, and what happened that night does not concern you. It is all over and put aside. Do you understand?'

'Yes, my lady, since you insist.'

'Sir Harry and Prue and the children left Navron just after noon today. The only thing that matters now is that we help your master. You know what happened?'

'I know, my lady, that the ship was lucky enough to escape with the crew safe aboard, but that my master lies a prisoner in the care of Lord Godolphin.'

'And time is short, William, for his lordship and the others may take the law into their own hands, and do what they would do to him – before the escort comes from Bristol. We may have a few hours only, and therefore we must work tonight.'

She made him sit down on the stool beside the hearth, and she showed the pistol she had secreted in her habit, and the knife as well. 'The pistol is loaded,' she said, 'and when I leave you now, I shall proceed to his lordship's, and somehow gain admittance to the keep. It should not prove difficult, for his lordship is a fool.'

'And then, my lady?' he asked.

'And then I shall assume that your master already has a plan prepared, and we will act upon it. He will realize the desperate importance of time, and may wish us to have horses waiting, at an hour to be decided upon.'

'That should not prove impossible, my lady. There are ways and means of procuring horses.'

'I can believe it, William.'

'The young woman who is giving me hospitality ...'

'A very charming young woman, William.'

'Your ladyship is gracious. The young woman who is giving me hospitality may prove helpful over the matter of horses. You can safely leave the matter in my hands.'

'And the young woman also, as I did Prue, when I went away with your master.'

'My lady, I declare to you most solemnly that I never touched a hair of Prue's head.'

'Probably not, William, we will not discuss it. Very well, then. The first move in the game is understood. I shall return here, after my visit to Lord Godolphin, and tell you what has been arranged.'

'Very good, my lady.'

He opened the door for her, and she stood a moment, smiling at him, before she passed into the little overgrown garden.

'We are not going to fail, William,' she said. 'In three days' time, or less than that perhaps, you will see the cliffs of Brittany. It will please you, will it not, to smell France again?'

And he would have asked her a question, but she walked swiftly down the path, and to her horse, tethered to the bough of a tree. Now that she was employed, and action was demanded of her, she felt resolute and strong, and the strange wistfulness that had come upon her as she stood alone in the garden at Navron had gone with the moment that brought it. All that belonged to the past. She rode swiftly, the sturdy cob striding out well along the muddy lane, and soon she came to the park gates of Godolphin's estate, and in the distance she saw the grey outline of his house, and the squat tower and strong walls of the keep that formed part of the mansion. There was one narrow slit in the tower, midway between the battlement and the ground, and as she passed beneath it her heart beat strongly, with sudden excitement: that must be his prison, and he might have heard the sound of her horse and, climbing to the slit, be looking down upon her.

A servant ran forward to take her horse, glancing at her in surprise, and wondering, she thought, what the Lady St Columb of Navron could be doing in the heat of the afternoon upon a rough country cob, alone, and unattended by husband or by groom.

She passed into the long hall, inquiring whether his lordship would see her, and while she waited she looked out of the long windows on to the park, and she saw, roped apart from its fellows in the centre of the grass, a tall tree, far taller than its fellows, and there was a man upon one of the wide branches, working with a saw, calling down to a little group of men beneath.

She turned away, feeling cold suddenly, a little sick, and then she heard a footstep coming across the hall, and Lord Godolphin advanced towards her, his usual composure somewhat ruffled. 'My very humble apologies, madam,' he said, kissing her hand, 'I fear I kept you waiting, the truth is that your visit is somewhat inopportune – we are all rather concerned – the fact of the matter is that my wife is in labour, and we await the physician.'

'My dear Lord Godolphin, you must forgive me,' said Dona, 'and had I known I would never have disturbed you. But I bring messages from Harry, you see, and his apologies. Something in London necessitated his immediate return, he left at noon today with the children, and ...'

'Harry left for town?' he said, in astonishment, 'but it was all arranged that he should come tomorrow. Half the countryside will be gathered here for the occasion. The men are preparing the tree, as you can see. Harry was most insistent that he must see the Frenchman hang.'

'He asked most humbly for your forgiveness,' she said, 'but the matter was really pressing. His majesty himself, I believe, is concerned in it.'

'Oh, well, naturally madam, under such circumstances, I understand. But it is a pity, a very great pity. The occasion is so unusual, and such a triumph. And as things are turning out, it looks as though we may celebrate something else at the same time.' He coughed, bridling with self-esteem and importance, and then, as the sound of carriage wheels came to their ears, he looked away from her, towards the door. 'This will be the physician,' he said quickly, 'you will, I am sure, excuse me a moment.'

'But of course, Lord Godolphin,' she smiled, and turning away, wandered into the small salon and stood thinking rapidly, while from the hall she heard voices, and murmurs, and heavy footsteps, and 'He is so agitated', she thought, 'that if we seized his wig again, he could not notice it.'

The footsteps and the voices disappeared up the broad staircase, and Dona, looking from the window, saw that there were no guards outside the keep, or in the avenue; they must be within the keep itself. After five minutes Godolphin returned, looking if possible more flushed and concerned than before.

'The physician is with her ladyship now,' he said, 'but he seems to think nothing is likely to occur until late this evening. It seems rather remarkable, I had no idea, indeed I considered that any minute ...'

'Wait', she said, 'until you have been a father a dozen times, and then perhaps you will understand that babies are leisurely creatures, and like to linger over this business of entering the world. Dear Lord Godolphin, I wish I could distract you. I'm sure your wife is in no danger at all. Is that where the Frenchman is imprisoned?'

'Yes, madam, and spends his time, so his jailers tell me, in drawing birds upon a sheet of paper. The fellow is mad, of course.'

'Of course.'

'Congratulations are pouring in upon me from all over the county. I flatter myself that I have earned them. It was I, you know, who disarmed the scoundrel.'

'How courageous of you.'

'It is true he gave his sword into my hands, but nevertheless it was to me he gave it.'

'I shall make a great story of it at Court, Lord Godolphin, when I am next at St James's. His Majesty will be very impressed with your handling of the whole affair. You were the genius of it all.'

'Ah, you flatter me, madam.'

'No, indeed. Harry would agree with me I know. I wish I had some souvenir of the Frenchman to show His Majesty. Do you think, as he is a draughtsman, he would give me one of his drawings?'

'The easiest thing in the world. They are scattered all over his cell.'

'I have forgotten so much, heaven be praised, of that fearful night,' sighed Dona, 'that I cannot now recollect his appearance, except that he was extremely large and black and fierce, and appallingly ugly.'

'You are somewhat at fault, madam, I should not describe him so. He is not so large a man as myself, for instance, and like all Frenchmen, has a sly rather than an ugly face.'

'What a pity it is that I cannot see him, and so give a strictly accurate description of him to His Majesty.'

'You will not come then tomorrow?'

'Alas, no. I go to rejoin Harry and the children.'

'I suppose', said Lord Godolphin, 'that I could permit you a glimpse of the rascal in his cell. But I understood from Harry that after the tragedy the other night you could scarcely abide to speak of the fellow – that he had so terrified you in short, that . . .'

'Today, Lord Godolphin, is so different from the other night. I have you to protect me, and the Frenchman is unarmed. I would like to paint a picture to His Majesty of the notorious pirate, caught and put to death by the most faithful of his Cornish subjects.'

'Then you shall, madam, you shall. When I think what you might have endured at his hands, I would willingly hang him three times over. I believe it was the excitement and alarm of the whole affair that precipitated her ladyship's confinement.'

'Most probably,' said Dona gravely, and seeing that he still would talk of the matter, and might even yet plunge into domestic details which she understood more thoroughly than he did himself, she added, 'Let us go now, then, while the physician is with your wife.' Before he could protest, she walked out of the salon into the hall, and so to the steps before the house, and he was forced to accompany her, glancing up at the windows of the house as he did so.

'My poor Lucy,' he said, 'if only I could have spared her this ordeal.'

'You should have thought of that nine months ago, my lord,' she answered, and he stared at her, greatly embarrassed and shocked, and murmured something about having hoped for years for a son and heir.

'Which I am sure she will give you,' smiled Dona, 'even if you have ten daughters first.' And here they were at the keep, standing in the small stone entrance, where two men were standing, armed with muskets, and another was seated on a bench before a table. 'I have promised Lady St Columb a glance at our prisoner,' said Godolphin, and the man at the table looked up and grinned.

'He won't be fit for a lady to see this time tomorrow, my lord,' he said, and Godolphin laughed loudly. 'No, that is why her ladyship has come today.' The guard led the way up the narrow stone stairway, taking a key from his chain, and 'There is no other door,' thought Dona, 'no other stair. And the men below there, always on guard.' The key turned in the lock, and once again her heart began to beat, foolishly, ridiculously, as it always did whenever she was about to look on him. The jailer threw open the door, and she stepped inside, with Godolphin behind her, and then the jailer withdrew, locking the door upon them. He was sitting at a table, as he had done the first time she had seen him, and on his face was the same absorbed expression that he had worn then, intent upon his occupation, thinking of nothing else, so that Godolphin, put out of countenance by his prisoner's indifference, thumped his hand on the table and said sharply, 'Stand up, can't you, when I choose to visit you?'

The indifference was no play, as Dona knew, for so intent was the Frenchman upon his drawing, that he had not known the footstep of Godolphin from the jailor. He pushed the drawing aside – it was a curlew, Dona saw, flying across an estuary towards the open sea – and then for the first time he saw her, and making no sign of recognition, he stood up, and bowed, and said nothing.

'This is Lady St Columb,' said Godolphin stiffly, 'who, disappointed that she cannot see you hanged tomorrow, wishes to take one of your drawings back to town with her, so that His Majesty may have a souvenir of one of the biggest blackguards that ever troubled his faithful subjects.'

'Lady St Columb is very welcome,' said the prisoner. 'Having had little else to do during the last few days, I can offer her a fair selection. What is your favourite bird, madam?'

'That', answered Dona, 'is something I can never decide. Sometimes I think it is a night-jar.'

'I regret I cannot offer you a night-jar,' he said, rummaging amongst the papers on the table. 'You see, when I last heard one, I was so intent upon another occupation that I did not observe the night-jar as clearly as I might have done.'

'You mean', said Godolphin sternly, 'that you were so intent upon robbing one of my friends of his possessions for your personal gratification that you gave no thought to any other distraction.'

'My lord,' bowed the captain of *La Mouette*, 'I have never before heard the occupation in question so delicately described.'

Dona turned over the drawings on the table. 'Here is a herring-gull,' she said, 'but I think you have not given him his full plumage.'

'The drawing is unfinished, madam,' he replied, 'this particular sea-gull dropped one of its feathers in flight. If you know anything about the species you will remember, however, that they seldom venture far to sea. This particular gull, for instance, is probably only ten miles from the coast at the present moment.'

'No doubt,' said Dona, 'and then tonight he will return again to the shore, in search of the feather he has lost.'

'Your ladyship knows little of ornithology,' said Godolphin. 'For my part I have never heard of a sea-gull or any other bird picking up feathers.'

'I had a feather mattress as a child,' said Dona, talking rather quickly, and smiling at Godolphin, 'and I remember the feathers became loose after a while, and one of them fluttered from the window of my bedroom and fell into the garden below. Of course the window was a large one, not like the slit that gives light to this cell.'

'Oh, of course,' answered his lordship, a little puzzled, and he glanced at her doubtfully, wondering if she still had a touch of fever, for surely she sounded a little light in the head.

'Did they ever blow under the door?' inquired the prisoner.

'Ah, that I can't remember,' said Dona, 'I think that even a feather would have difficulty in passing beneath a door . . . unless

217

of course it was given assistance, like a strong breath of air, you know, say the draught from a barrel of a pistol. But I have not chosen my drawing. Here is a sanderling, I wonder if this would please His Majesty. My lord, do I hear wheels upon the drive? If so, it must be that the physician is departing.'

Lord Godolphin clicked his tongue in annoyance, and looked towards the door. 'He surely would not leave without consulting me first,' he said. 'Are you certain you hear wheels? I am a little deaf.'

'I could not be more certain in the world,' answered Dona.

His lordship strode to the door, and thumped upon it.

'Ho, there,' he called, 'unlock the door, will you, immediately?'

The jailer called in answer, and they could hear his footstep mount the narrow stair. In a moment Dona had passed the pistol and the knife from her riding-habit on to the table, and the prisoner had seized them from her, and covered them with a mass of his drawings. The jailer unlocked the door, and Godolphin turned, and looked at Dona.

'Well, madam?' he said, 'have you chosen your drawing?'

Dona fluttered the drawings in distraction, wrinkling her brow.

'It is really most monstrously difficult,' she said. 'I cannot decide between the sea-gull and the sanderling. Do not wait for me, my lord, you must know by this time that a woman can never make up her mind. I will follow you in a moment or two.'

'It is really imperative that I see the physician,' said Godolphin, 'so that if you will excuse me, madam. You remain here with her ladyship,' he added to the guard, as he left the cell.

Once again the guard closed the door, and this time stood against it, his arms folded, and he smiled across at Dona with understanding.

'We shall have two celebrations tomorrow, my lady,' he said.

'Yes,' she said, 'I hope for your sake that it proves to be a boy. There will be more ale for all of you.'

'Am I not the only cause for excitement?' asked the prisoner.

The guard laughed, and jerked his head towards the slit in the cell.

'You'll be forgotten by midday,' he said, 'you'll be dangling from the tree, while the rest of us drink to the future Lord Godolphin.'

'It seems rather hard that neither the prisoner nor myself will be here to drink the health of the son and heir,' smiled Dona, and she drew her purse from her pocket, and threw it to the jailer. 'I wager', she said, 'that you would rather do so now, than keeping watch below, hour after hour. Supposing we drink now, the three of us, while his lordship is with the physician?'

The jailer grinned and winked at his prisoner.

'If we do, it won't be the first time I've drunk ale before an execution,' he said. 'But I will say one thing, and that is that I've never seen a Frenchman hang yet. They tell me they die quicker than what we do. The bones in their neck are more brittle,' and winking again, he unlocked the door, and called down to his assistant.

'Bring three glasses, and a jug of ale.'

While his back was turned Dona questioned the prisoner with her eyes, and his lips moved soundlessly.

'Tonight at eleven.'

She nodded, and whispered 'William and I.'

The jailer looked over his shoulder. 'If his lordship catches us there'll be the devil to pay,' he said.

'I would absolve you,' said Dona, 'this is the sort of jest that will please His Majesty when I see him at Court. What is your name?'

'Zachariah Smith, my lady.'

'Very well, then, Zachariah, if trouble come of this, I will plead your case to the king himself.'

The jailer laughed, and his assistant coming this moment with the ale, he closed the door, and carried the tray to the table.

'Long life then to your ladyship,' he said, 'a full purse and a good appetite to myself, and to you, sir, a speedy death.'

He poured the ale into the glasses, and Dona, clicking hers against the jailer's, said, 'Long life, then, to the future Lord Godolphin.'

The jailer smacked his lips, and tilted his head.

The prisoner raised his glass and smiled at Dona.

'Should we not also drink to Lady Godolphin, at this moment, I imagine, suffering somewhat of discomfort?'

'And', replied Dona, 'to the physician also, who will be rather heated.' As she drank, an idea flashed suddenly to her mind, and glancing at the Frenchman, she knew instinctively that the same thought had come to him, for he was looking at her.

'Zachariah Smith, are you a married man?' she said.

The jailer laughed. 'Twice married,' he said, 'and the father of fourteen.'

'Then you know what his lordship is enduring at this moment,' she smiled, 'but with so able a physician as Doctor Williams there is little cause for anxiety. You know the doctor well, I suppose?'

'No, my lady. I come from the north coast. I am not a Helston man.'

'Doctor Williams', said Dona dreamily, 'is a funny little fellow, with a round solemn face, and a mouth like a button. I have heard it said that he is as good a judge of ale as any man living.'

'Then it's a great pity', said the prisoner, laying down his glass, 'that he does not drink with us now. Perhaps he will do so later, when his day's work is finished, and he has made a father of Lord Godolphin.'

'Which will not be much before midnight, what do you say, Zachariah Smith, and father of fourteen?' asked Dona.

'Midnight is generally the hour, your ladyship,' laughed the jailer, 'all nine of my boys were born as the clock struck twelve.'

'Very well, then,' said Dona, 'when I see Doctor Williams directly I will tell him that in honour of the occasion, Zachariah Smith, who can boast of more than a baker's dozen, will be pleased to drink a glass of ale with him before he goes on duty for the night.'

'Zachariah, you will remember this evening for the rest of your life,' said the prisoner.

The jailer replaced the glasses on the tray. 'If Lord Godolphin has a son,' he said, winking an eye, 'there'll be so much rejoicing on the estate that we'll be forgetting to hang you in the morning.'

Dona took up the drawing of the sea-gull from the table. 'Well,' she said, 'I have chosen my drawing. And rather than his

lordship should see you with the tray, Zachariah, I will descend
with you, and we will leave your prisoner with his pen and his
birds. Good-bye, Frenchman, and may you slip away tomorrow
as easily as the feather did from my mattress.'

The prisoner bowed. 'It will depend', he said, 'upon the
quantity of ale that my jailer consumes tonight with Doctor
Williams.'

'He'll have to boast a stout head if he can beat mine,' said
the jailer, and he unlocked the door, and held it open for her to
pass.

'Good-bye, Lady St Columb,' said the prisoner, and she stood
for a moment looking at him, realizing that the plan they had in
mind was more hazardous and more foolhardy than any that he
had yet attempted, and that if it should fail there would be no
further chance of escape, for tomorrow he would hang from the
tree there in the park. Then he smiled, as though in secret, and it
seemed to her that his smile was the personification of himself;
it was the thing in him that she had first loved, and would always
cherish, and it conjured the picture in her mind of *La Mouette*,
and the sun, and the wind upon the sea, and with it too the dark
shadows of the creek, the wood fire and the silence. She went out
of the cell without looking at him, her head in the air, and her
drawing in her hand, and 'He will never know', she thought, 'at
what moment I have loved him best.'

She followed the jailer down the narrow stair, her heart heavy,
her body suddenly tired with all the weariness of anti-climax. The
jailer, grinning at her, put the tray under the steps, and said,
'Cold-blooded, isn't he, for a man about to die? They say these
Frenchmen have no feelings.'

She summoned a smile, and held out her hand. 'You are a
good fellow, Zachariah,' she said, 'and may you drink many
glasses of ale in the future, and some of them tonight. I won't
forget to tell the physician to call upon you. A little man, remember, with a mouth like a button.'

'But a throat like a well,' laughed the jailer. 'Very good, your
ladyship, I will look out for him, and he shall quench his thirst.
Not a word to his lordship, though.'

'Not a word, Zachariah,' said Dona solemnly, and she went

221

out of the dark keep into the sunshine, and there was Godolphin himself coming down the drive to meet her.

'You were wrong, madam,' he said, wiping his forehead, 'the carriage has not moved, and the physician is still with my wife. He has decided after all that he will remain for the present, as poor Lucy is in some distress. Your ears must have played you false.'

'And I sent you back to the house, all to no purpose,' said Dona. 'So very stupid of me, dear Lord Godolphin, but then women, you know, are very stupid creatures. Here is the picture of a sea-gull. Do you think it will please His Majesty?'

'You are a better judge of his taste than I, madam,' said Godolphin, 'or so I presume. Well, did you find the pirate as ruthless as you expected?'

'Prison has softened him, my lord, or perhaps it is not prison, but the realization that in your keeping, escape is impossible. It seemed to me that when he looked at you he knew that he had at last met a better, and a more cunning brain than his own.'

'Ah, he gave you that impression, did he? Strange, I have sometimes thought the opposite. But these foreigners are half women, you know. You never know what they are thinking.'

'Very true, my lord.' They stood before the steps of the house, and there was the physician's carriage, and the servant still holding Dona's cob. 'You will take some refreshment, madam, before you go?' inquired Godolphin, and 'No,' she answered, 'no, I have stayed too long as it is, for I have much to do tonight before my journey in the morning. My respects to your wife, when she is in a state to receive them, and I hope that before the evening is out, she will have presented you with a replica of yourself, dear Lord Godolphin.'

'That, madam,' he said gravely, 'is in the hands of the Almighty.'

'But very soon,' she said, mounting her horse, 'in the equally capable hands of the physician. Good-bye.' She waved her hand to him, and was gone, striking the cob into a startled canter with her whip, and as she drew rein past the keep and looked up at the slit in the tower she whistled a bar of the song that Pierre Blanc played on his lute, and slowly, like a snow-flake, a feather

222

drifted down in the air towards her, a feather torn from the quill of a pen. She caught it, caring not a whit if Godolphin saw her from the steps of his house, and she waved her hand again, and rode out on to the high-road laughing, with the feather in her hat.

Chapter 23

DONA leaned from the casement of her bedroom at Navron, and as she looked up into the sky she saw, for the first time, the little gold crescent of the new moon high above the dark trees.

'That is for luck,' she thought, and she waited a moment, watching the shadows in the still garden, and breathing the heavy sweet scent of the magnolia tree that climbed the wall beneath her. These things must be stored and remembered in her heart with all the other beauty that had gone, for she would never look upon them again.

Already the room itself wore the appearance of desertion, like the rest of the house, and her boxes were strapped upon the floor, her clothes folded and packed by the maid-servant, according to instruction. When she had returned, late in the afternoon, hot and dusty from her ride, and the groom had taken the cob from her in the courtyard, the ostler from the inn at Helston was waiting to speak to her.

'Sir Harry left word with us, your ladyship,' he said, 'that you would be hiring a chaise tomorrow, to follow him to Okehampton.'

'Yes,' she said.

'And the landlord sent me to tell you, your ladyship, that the chaise will be available, and will be here for you at noon tomorrow.'

'Thank you,' she had said, staring away from him towards the trees in the avenue, and the woods that led to the creek, for everything he said to her lacked reality, the future was something with which she had no concern. As she left him and went into the house he looked after her, puzzled, scratching his head, for she seemed to him like a sleep-walker, and he did not believe she had fully understood what he had told her. She wandered then to the nursery, and stared down at the stripped beds, and the bare boards, for the carpets had been taken up. The curtains were drawn too, and the air was already hot and unused. Beneath one of the beds lay the arm of a stuffed rabbit that James had sucked, and then torn from the rabbit's body in a tantrum.

She picked it up and held it, turning it over in her hands. There was something forlorn about it, like a relic of bygone days. She could not leave it lying there on the floor, so she opened the great wardrobe in the corner, and threw it inside, and shut the door upon it, and then left the room and did not go into it again.

At seven her supper was brought to her on a tray, and she ate little of it, not being hungry. Then she gave orders to the servant not to disturb her again during the evening, for she was tired, and not to call her in the morning, for she would sleep late in all probability, before the tedium of the journey.

When she was alone, she undid the bundle that William had given her on her return from Lord Godolphin. Smiling to herself she drew out the rough stockings, the worn breeches, and the patched though gaily coloured shirt. She remembered his look of embarrassment as he had given them to her, and his words: 'These are the best Grace can do for you, my lady, they belong to her brother.' 'They are perfect, William,' she had replied, 'and Pierre Blanc himself could have done no better.' For she must play the boy again, for the last time, and escape from her woman's clothes for this night at least. 'I will be able to run better without petticoats,' she said to William, 'and I can ride astride my horse, like I used to as a child.' He had procured the horses, as he had promised, and was to meet her with them on the road from Navron to Gweek just after nine o'clock.

'You must not forget, my William,' she said, 'that you are a physician, and that I am your groom, and it were better that you should drop "my lady" and call me Tom.'

He had looked away from her in embarrassment. 'My lady,' he said, 'my lips could not frame the word, it would be too distressing.' She had laughed, and told him that physicians must never be embarrassed, especially when they had just brought sons and heirs into the world. And now she was dressing herself in the lad's clothes, and they fitted her well, even the shoes, unlike the clumsy clogs belonging to Pierre Blanc; there was a handkerchief too, which she wound about her head, and a leather strap for her waist. She looked at herself in the mirror, her dark curls concealed, her skin a gypsy brown, and 'I am a cabin-boy again,' she thought, 'and Dona St Columb is asleep and dreaming.'

She listened at her door, and all was still; the servants were safe in their own quarters. She braced herself for the ordeal of descending the stairway to the dining-hall, for this was what she dreaded most, in the darkness, with the candles unlit, and flooding her mind with sharp intensity was the memory of Rockingham crouching there, his knife in his hands. It was better, she thought, to shut her eyes, and feel her way along the landing to the stairs, for then she would not see the great shield on the wall, nor the outline of the stairs themselves. So she went down, her hands before her and her eyes tight shut, and all the while her heart was beating, and it seemed to her that Rockingham still waited for her in the darkest corner of the hall. With a sudden panic she flung herself upon the door, wrenching back the bolts, and ran out into the gathering dusk to the safety and stillness of the avenue. Once she was free of the house she was no longer afraid, the air was soft and warm, and the gravel crunched under her feet, while high in the pale sky the new moon gleamed like a sickle.

She walked swiftly, for there was freedom in her boy's clothes, and her spirits rose, and once again she fell to whistling Pierre Blanc's song, and she thought of him too, with his merry monkey face and his white teeth, waiting now on the deck of *La Mouette* somewhere in mid-channel, for the master he had left behind.

She saw a shadow move towards her, round the bend of the road, and there was William with the horses, and there was a lad with him, Grace's brother she presumed, and the owner of the clothes she wore.

William left the boy with the horses, and came towards her, and she saw, the laughter rising within her, that he had borrowed a black suit of clothes, and white stockings, and he wore a dark curled wig.

'Was it a son or a daughter, Doctor Williams?' she asked, and he looked at her with confusion, not entirely happy at the part he had to play: for that he should be the gentleman and she the groom seemed to him shocking, who was shocked at nothing else.

'How much does he know?' she whispered, pointing to the lad.

'Nothing, my lady,' he whispered, 'only that I am a friend of

Grace's, and am in hiding, and that you are a companion who would help me to escape.'

'Then Tom I will be,' she insisted, 'and Tom I will remain.' And she went on whistling Pierre Blanc's song, to discomfort William, and going to one of the horses she swung herself up into the saddle, and smiled at the lad, and digging her heels into the side of the horse, she clattered ahead of them along the road, laughing at them over her shoulder. When they came to the wall of Godolphin's estate they dismounted, and left the lad there with the horses, under cover of the trees. She and William went on foot the half-mile to the park-gates, for so they had arranged earlier in the evening.

It was dark now, with the first stars in the sky, and they said nothing to one another as they walked, for all had been planned and put in readiness. They felt like actors who must appear upon the boards for the first time, with an audience who might be hostile. The gates were shut, and they turned aside, and climbed the wall into the park, and crept towards the drive under shadow of the trees. In the distance they could see the outline of the house, and there was a light still in the line of windows above the door.

'The son and heir still tarries,' whispered Dona. She went on ahead of William to the house, and there, at the entrance to the stables, she could see the physician's carriage drawn up on the cobbled stones, and the coachman was seated with one of Godolphin's grooms on an upturned seat beneath a lantern, thumbing a pack of cards. She could hear the low murmur of the voices, and their laughter. She turned back again, and went to William. He was standing beside the drive, his small white face dwarfed by his borrowed wig and his hat. She could see the butt of his pistol beneath his coat, and his mouth was set in a firm thin line.

'Are you ready?' she said, and he nodded, his eyes fixed upon her, and he followed her along the drive to the keep. She had a moment of misgiving, for she realized suddenly that perhaps, like other actors, he lacked confidence in his part, and would stumble over his words, and the game would be lost because William, upon whom so much depended, had no skill. As they stood before the closed door of the keep she looked at him, and tapped him on the shoulder, and for the first time that evening he smiled, his small eyes twinkling in his round face, and her faith in him returned, for he would not fail.

He had become, in a moment, the physician, and as he knocked upon the door of the keep, he called, in full round tones surprisingly unlike the William she knew at Navron: 'Is there one Zachariah Smith within, and may Doctor Williams from Helston have a word with him?'

Dona could hear an answering shout from the keep, and in a moment the door swung open, and there was her friend the guard standing on the threshold, his jacket thrown aside because of the heat, his sleeves rolled high above his elbows, and a grin on his face from ear to ear.

'So her ladyship didn't forget her promise?' he said. 'Well, come inside, sir, you are very welcome, and we have enough ale here, I tell you, to christen the baby and yourself into the bargain. Was it a boy?'

'It was indeed, my friend,' said William, 'a fine boy, and the image of his lordship.' He rubbed his hands together, as though in satisfaction, and followed the jailer within, while the door was left ajar, so that Dona, crouching beside the wall of the keep, could hear them move about the entrance, and she could hear too the clink of glasses, and the laughter of the guard. 'Well, sir,' he was saying, 'I've fathered fourteen and I may say I know the business as well as you. What was the weight of the child?'

'Ah,' said William, 'the weight now ... let me see,' and Dona, choking back her laughter, could picture him standing there, his brows drawn together in perplexity, ignorant as a baby himself would be at such a question. 'Round about four pounds I should say, though I cannot recollect the exact figure ... ' he began, and there came a whistle of astonishment from the jailer, and a burst of laughter from his assistant.

'Do you call that a fine boy?' he said, 'why, curse me, sir, the child will never live. My youngest turned the scale at eleven pounds when he was born, and he looked a shrimp at that.'

'Did I say four?' broke in William hastily, 'a mistake of course.

228

I meant fourteen. Nay, now I come to remember, it was some-where around fifteen or sixteen pounds.'

The jailer whistled again.

'God save you, sir, but that's something over the odds. It's her ladyship you must look to, and not the child. Is she well?'

'Very well,' said William, 'and in excellent spirits. When I left she was discussing with his lordship what names she would bestow upon her son.'

'Then she's a pluckier woman than I'd ever give her credit for,' answered the jailer. 'Well, sir, it seems to me you deserve three glasses after that. To bring a child of sixteen pounds into the world is a hard evening's work. Here's luck, sir, to you, and the child, and to the lady who drank with us here this evening, for she's worth twenty Lady Godolphins if I'm not mistaken.'

There was silence a moment, and the clinking of glasses, and Dona heard a great sigh from the jailer, and a smacking of lips.

'I warrant they don't brew stuff like that in France,' he said, 'it's all grapes and frogs over there, isn't it, and snails, and such-like? I took a glass just now to my prisoner above, and you'll scarcely credit me, sir, but he's a cold-blooded fish for a dying man, as you might say. He quaffed his ale in one draught and he slapped me on the shoulder, laughing.'

'It's the foreign blood,' broke in the second guard. 'They're all alike, Frenchmen, Dutchmen, Spaniards, no matter what they are. Women and drink is all they think about, and when you're not looking it's a stab in the back.'

'And what does he do his last day,' continued Zachariah, 'but cover sheets of paper with birds, and sit there smoking and smiling to himself. You'd think he'd send for a priest, for they're all papists, these fellows; it's robbery and rape one minute and confession and crucifixes the next. But not our Frenchman. He's a law to himself, I reckon. Will you have another glass, doctor?'

'Thank you, my man,' said William. Dona could hear the sound of the ale as it was poured in to the tankard, and she wondered, for the first time, how strong a head William had, and whether it was altogether wise to accept the jailer's invitation with so good a grace.

William coughed, dry and hard, a little signal to herself.

'I should be interested to see the man,' he said, 'after what I have heard. A very desperate person, by all accounts. The country will be well rid of him. He's asleep now, I suppose, if a man can sleep on his last night?'

'Asleep? Bless you, no, sir. He's had two glasses of ale, and he said you'd pay me for them, and that if you did turn up at the keep here before midnight he'd join you in another glass, and drink to the son and heir.' The jailer laughed, and then lowering his voice he added, 'It's irregular, sir, of course, but then, when a man is going to be hanged in the morning, even if he is a pirate and a Frenchman, you can't exactly wish him ill, can you, sir?' Dona could not catch William's reply, but she heard the chink of coins, and the scrape of feet. The jailer laughed again and said, 'Thank you, sir, you're a true gentleman, and when my wife's expecting again, I shall think of you.'

Now she could hear their feet climbing the stair to the room above, and she swallowed, her nails digging into the palms of her hands. For this was the moment now she feared above all others, when a slip might cause disaster, when recognition might come and all be lost. She waited until she judged them outside his cell above, and going close to the door she listened, and heard the sound of voices and the turning of a key in the lock. Then, when she heard the heavy clanging of the door upon them, she ventured to the entrance of the keep and stepped inside, and saw the two remaining guards with their backs towards her. One was sitting on a bench against the wall, yawning and stretching himself, and the other stood looking up the stair.

The light was dim, for only one lantern swung from the beam. Keeping in the shadow of the door she knocked, and said, 'Is Doctor Williams within?' The men turned at the sound of her voice, and the one on the bench blinked at her and said, 'What do you want with him?'

'They've sent word from the house,' she answered. 'Her ladyship's been taken worse.'

'Small wonder,' said the man by the stair, 'after carrying sixteen pounds. All right, lad, I'll tell him.' He began to mount the stair, calling as he did so. 'Zachariah, they want the doctor up at the house yonder.' Dona watched him turn the corner of the stair, and beat upon the door, and as he did so she kicked the door of the entrance with her foot, and slammed it, and shot the bolt and closed the grill, before the guard on the bench could rise to his feet and shout, 'Hi, there, what the devil are you doing?'

The table was between them, and as he came towards her she leant against it, putting all her weight upon it, and the table crashed on the floor with him sprawling upon it, and as he fell she heard a stifled cry from the stair above, and the sound of a blow. Then, seizing the jug of ale beside her, she threw it at the lantern and the light was extinguished. The man on the floor scrambled from beneath the table, shouting for Zachariah, and as he raised his voice, cursing and stumbling in the darkness, Dona heard the Frenchman call to her from the stair, 'Are you there, Dona?' and 'Yes,' she panted, half dazed with laughter and excitement and fear, and he sprang over the rail of the stone stair to the ground beneath, and found the man in the darkness. She heard them fighting there, close to the steps. He was using the butt end of the pistol; she could hear the blow. The man fell against the table, groaning, and 'Give me your handkerchief, Dona, for a gag,' said the Frenchman, and she tore it from her head.

In a moment he had done what he wished. 'Watch him,' he said swiftly, 'he cannot move,' and Dona heard the Frenchman slip away from her in the darkness, and climb the stair again to the cell above. 'Have you got him, William?' he said, and there was a funny strangled sob from the room above, and the sound of something heavy being dragged along the floor. She could hear the gagged man gasping for breath beside her, and all the while the heavy dragging sound from above, and a sudden desire to laugh rose in her throat, a terrible strained feeling of hysteria, and she knew if she gave way to it she would never stop, it would swell up within her like a scream.

Then the Frenchman called to her from above, 'Open the door, Dona, and see if the road is clear,' and she felt her way to it in the darkness, her hands fumbling with the heavy bolts. She wrenched it open, and looked out, and from the direction of the house she heard the sound of wheels, and down the drive towards the keep came the physician's carriage; she could hear the driver crack his whip and call to his horse.

She turned back inside the keep to warn them, but already the Frenchman was at her side, and she looked up into his face, and in his eyes she saw the reckless laughter that she had seen before when he had pricked the curled wig from Godolphin's head, and 'By heaven,' he said softly, 'it's the physician going home at last.'

He stepped out bare-headed into the drive, holding up his hand. 'What are you doing?' she whispered, 'are you mad, are you crazy?' But he laughed, taking no notice. The driver pulled up his horse at the entrance to the keep, and the long thin face of the physician appeared at the carriage window.

'Who are you, what do you want?' he said in querulous tones, and the Frenchman put his hands on the window, and smiled, and 'Did you give his lordship an heir then, and is he pleased with his baby?' he said.

'Pleased my foot,' swore the physician. 'There are twin daughters up there at the hall, and I'll thank you to take your hands off my carriage window and to let me pass, for all I want is my supper and my bed.'

'Ah, but you'll give us a ride first, won't you?' said the Frenchman, and in a moment he had knocked the driver from his seat, tumbling him down into the drive below, and 'Climb beside me, Dona,' he said; 'we'll ride in style if we ride at all.' She did as he bade her, shaking with laughter. And there was William, in his strange black coat, without wig and without his hat, slamming the door of the keep behind him, a pistol in his hands pointing in the face of the startled physician. 'Get inside, William,' called the Frenchman, 'and give the doctor a glass of ale, if you have any left, for by the lord, he's had a harder time tonight than we have had these last few minutes.'

Down the drive sped the carriage, the physician's horse breaking into a gallop, who had never galloped before, and they came abreast the park gates, firmly shut. 'Open them wide!' called the Frenchman, as a sleepy head appeared at the window of the lodge. 'Your master has twin daughters, and the physician wants his supper, and as for me and my cabin-boy, we've had ale enough this night to last us for thirty years.'

The gates were flung back, the lodge-keeper staring at them in astonishment, his mouth wide open, while from within the carriage came the protesting cries of the physician.

'Where are we bound, William?' called the Frenchman, and William thrust his round face through the window of the carriage. 'There are horses a mile up the road, m'sieu,' he said, 'but we are bound for Porthleven on the coast.'

'We are bound for perdition, for all I care,' he answered, and he put his arm round Dona, and kissed her. 'Don't you know', he said, 'that this is my last night in the world, and I'm going to be hanged in the morning.'

And with the horse galloping like a mad thing, and the white dust flying from the wheels, the carriage swung out on to the hard high-road.

Chapter 24

THE adventure was over now, and the madness, and the laughter. Somewhere back on the road lay a carriage tumbled in a ditch, and a horse without bridle or rein grazed beside a hedge. There was a physician who walked along the high-road in search of his supper, and there were guards who lay bound and gagged upon a dungeon floor.

These things belonged to the evening, and had no place in the night that had come. For it was long past midnight now, and darker than it would ever be again. The stars were clustered thick like little pin-pricks of light, and the crescent moon had gone.

Dona stood beside her horse, looking down upon the lake, and she saw that it was separated from the sea by a bank of high shingle, and while the waves broke upon the shore the lake itself was still and undisturbed. There was no wind, and the sky for all its darkness had the strange clarity and radiance of midsummer. Now and again a wave a little larger than its fellows would spend itself upon the shingle beach, and murmur, and sigh, and the lake, catching a tremor from the sea would bear a ripple upon its surface of glass, and shiver an instant, while the ripple washed away into the bent reeds. Now and again there were bird noises from the pool, the startled cry of a moor-hen as it paddled amongst the reeds and hid itself, furtively rustling the tall stems, and there were whispers and stealthy movements from all the unknown nameless things that come out into the silent world at night, and live for a while, and breathe, and have their moment.

Beyond the woods and the hill lay the village of Porthleven where the fishing boats were moored against the quay, and William looked up into his master's face, and then over his shoulder again towards the hill.

'It would be wise, m'sieu,' he said, 'if I went now, before the day breaks, and found a boat. I will bring it round to the beach here, and we can leave as the sun rises.'

'Do you think you will find a boat?' said the Frenchman.

'Yes, m'sieu,' he answered, 'there will be a small boat at the harbour entrance. I made inquiries, m'sieu, before I left Gweek.'

'William is resourceful,' said Dona. 'He forgets nothing. And because of him there will be no hanging in the morning, but only a small boat putting out to sea.'

The Frenchman looked at his servant, and the servant looked at Dona, as she stood beside the lake, and suddenly he went from them, over the ridge of shingle to the hill beyond, a curious little figure in his long black coat and his large three-cornered hat. He disappeared into the darkness, and they were alone. The horses grazed on the grass beside the lake, and their soft mouths made a quiet crunching sound, and from the woods opposite the tall trees rustled and whispered and were still.

There was a hollow beside the lake, of smooth white sand, and there it was they built their fire, and presently a tongue of flame leapt upwards into the air, and the dry sticks crackled and broke.

He knelt close to the fire, the flame lighting his face and his throat and his hands, and 'Do you remember', said Dona, 'that once you told me you would cook chicken for me on a spit?'

'Yes,' he answered, 'but tonight I have no chicken, and I have no spit, and my cabin-boy must be content with burnt bread instead.'

He frowned, concentrating upon his task, and because the heat of the fire was great he shook his head, and wiped his forehead with the sleeve of his shirt, and she knew that this was a picture of him that could never be lost, the fire, the lake, the dark sky studded with stars, and the sea breaking upon the shingle behind them.

'And so,' he said later, as they ate their supper, with the fire smaller than before and the bitter smell of wood smoke lingering in the air, 'you fought a man, my Dona, and he died, on the floor of Navron House.'

She stared across at him, but he was not looking at her; he was crunching the bread between his teeth. 'How did you know?' she asked.

'Because I was accused of his murder,' he answered, 'and when I was accused I remembered the companion of Hampton Court, and the face of a man who looked on me with hatred as I robbed him of his rings, and I knew then what happened, Dona, when I left you that night.'

She clasped her hands round her knees, and looked out upon the lake. 'When we went fishing, you and I,' she said, 'I could not take the hook out of the fish, do you remember? But it was different, what I did that night. At first I was afraid, and then I was angry, and when I was angry I took the shield down from the wall, and afterwards – he died.'

'What made you angry?' he asked.

She thought a moment, trying to remember, and then, 'It was James,' she said, 'it was James who woke and cried.'

He said nothing, and glancing across at him she saw that he had finished his supper, and was sitting now as she did, with his hands around his knees, and he was staring at the lake.

'Ah,' he said, 'so it was James who woke and cried, and you and I, Dona, we meet at the Looe pool instead of Coverack, and your answer is the same as mine.'

He threw a pebble into the lake, and a ripple formed and spread across the surface of the water, and vanished as though it had never been, and then he lay on his back on the strip of sand, and put out his hand to her, and she went and lay beside him.

'I think', he said, 'that Lady St Columb will never more royster in the streets of London, for she has had her measure of adventure.'

'The Lady St Columb', she said, 'will become a gracious matron, and smile upon her servants, and her tenants, and the village folk, and one day she will have grandchildren about her knee, and will tell them the story of a pirate who escaped.'

'And what will happen to the cabin-boy?' he asked.

'The cabin-boy will vigil sometimes in the night, and tear his nails, and beat his pillow, and then he will fall asleep perhaps, and dream again.'

The pool lay dark and silent at their feet, and from behind them came the sound of the sea as it broke upon the shingle.

'There is a house in Brittany,' he said, 'where once a man lived called Jean-Benoit Aubéry. It may be that he will go back there again, and cover the bare walls from floor to ceiling with pictures of birds and portraits of his cabin-boy. But as the years go by the portraits of the cabin-boy will become blurred and indistinct.'

'In what part of Brittany does Jean-Benoit Aubréy have his house?' she asked.

'In Finistère,' he said, 'which means, my Dona, the land's end.'

It seemed to her that she could see the rugged cliffs and the scarred face of the headland, and she could hear the sea crash against the rocks, and the gulls cry, and she knew how sometimes the sun would beat upon the cliffs so that the grass became parched, and thirsty, and dry, and how sometimes a soft wind would blow from the west and there would be mist and rain.

'There is a jagged piece of rock,' he said, 'and it runs out into the Atlantic and we call it la Pointe du Raz. No tree can live upon it, and no blade of grass, for it is swept all day and all night by the west wind. And out in the sea, beyond the point, two tides meet, and surge together, and all the time forever there is a roughness and a boiling of surf and foam, and the spray rises fifty feet into the air.'

A little cold wind rose from the centre of the lake and blew upon them, and the stars went misty suddenly and dim, and it was that hour of night when all is silent and still: no movement of bird or beast, no whisper in the reeds, and nothing sounding but the breaking of the sea upon the shingle.

'Do you think', she said, 'that *La Mouette* is waiting for you, out there, on the sea, and that you will find her in the morning?'

'Yes,' he said.

'And you will climb aboard and be master of her again, and hold the wheel in your hand, and feel the deck under your feet?'

'Yes,' he said.

'And William,' she said, 'William who does not like the sea, he will be ill and wish himself back at Navron again.'

'No,' he said, 'William will feel the salt on his lips, and the wind in his hair, and before night-fall perhaps, if the breeze is steady, he will look upon the land again, and smell the warm grass on the headland, and it will mean Brittany and home.'

She lay on her back as he did, with her hands behind her head, and now there was a change in the sky, a pallor of false dawn, and the little wind blew stronger than before.

'I wonder', he said, 'when it was that the world first went amiss, and men forgot how to live and to love and to be happy. For once, my Dona, there was a lake like this one in the life of every man.'

'Perhaps there was a woman,' she said, 'and the woman told her man to build a house of reeds, and after that a house of wood, and after that a house of stone, and there came other men and other women, and soon there were no more hills and no more lakes, nothing but little round stone houses all alike.'

'And you and I,' he said, 'we have our lake and our hills, for this night only, and we have only three hours now to sunrise.'

It seemed to them, when the day came, that there was a whiteness and a cold clarity about it that they had never known before. The sky was hard and bright, and the lake lay at their feet like a sheet of silver. They got up from the spit of sand, and he bathed in the chill water, which was cold like the frozen water of the north. Presently the birds began to murmur and whisper in the woods, and he left the lake and dressed, and walked out on to the shingle beach where the tide was high, and a ridge of foam lapped against the stones. A hundred yards away from the beach a little fishing boat rocked at anchor, and when William saw the figures on the beach he drew out the long paddles and pulled towards them.

They stood there together on the beach, waiting for the boat, and suddenly on the far horizon Dona saw the white topsail of a ship, and the ship was drawing in towards the land. And the ship took shape and form, and she had raking crimson masts, and her sails were full.

La Mouette was returning for her master, and as he climbed into the waiting fishing boat, and hoisted the little sail on the single mast, it seemed to Dona that this moment was part of another moment, long ago, when she had stood upon a headland and looked out across the sea. The ship drifted on the horizon like a symbol of escape, and there was something strange about her in the morning light, as though she had no part in the breaking of the day, but belonged to another age and to another world.

She seemed a painted ship upon the still white sea, and Dona shivered suddenly, for the shingle felt cold and chill on her bare feet, while a little wave splashed upon them, and sighed, anc was no more. Then out of the sea, like a ball of fire, the sun came hard and red.

MORE ABOUT PENGUINS

Penguinews, which appears every month, contains details of all the new books issued by Penguins as they are published. From time to time it is supplemented by *Penguins in Print*, which is a complete list of all books published by Penguins which are still available. (There are well over three thousand of these.)

A specimen copy of *Penguinews* can be sent to you free on request, and you can become a subscriber for the price of the postage. For a year's issues (including the complete lists) please send 30p if you live in the United Kingdom, or 60p if you live elsewhere. Just write to Dept EP, Penguin Books Ltd, Harmondsworth, Middlesex, enclosing a cheque or postal order, and your name will be added to the mailing list.

Note: *Penguinews* and *Penguins in Print*
are not available in the U.S.A. or Canada

DAPHNE DU MAURIER

'Miss du Maurier's continued success leaves one gasping with admiration' – *The Times Literary Supplement*

Rebecca

Her triumphant novel that ranks with *Jane Eyre* and *Gone With the Wind*.

Jamaica Inn

The world of the Brontës transferred to the Cornwall of the early nineteenth century.

My Cousin Rachel

A superb study of that cancer of the human mind – suspicion.

The King's General

The Civil War story which immortalizes Menabilly, the author's Cornish home for over twenty years.

The Scapegoat

Alec Guinness starred in the film version of this modern story of an impersonation.

The Birds and Other Stories

'The Birds', now a Hitchcock horror film, gives the title to stories which 'continually provoke both pity and terror' – *Observer*

also available